LOSING GAME

THE WINNING ACE SERIES (BOOK 2)

TRACIE DELANEY

ALSO BY THE AUTHOR

For Annette

1

Rainwater trickled down Tally's neck as she ran home from the supermarket. Pete's flat was normally a ten-minute walk, but in this weather, it took her twice as long. As she moved away from the coast, the wind dropped, although the rain still soaked through her jeans. She dug the front-door key out of her pocket and inserted it into the lock. After kicking the door shut behind her, she shrugged off her wet coat and threw it over the banister.

Tally swapped her damp clothes for pyjamas even though it was still early. As she ate dinner at the small table squashed in the corner of a kitchen too cramped for furniture, loneliness engulfed her. Since breaking off her relationship with Cash, she had found it difficult to dredge up any emotion apart from an intense sadness that grew like a cancer until it was as much a part of her as blood and bones and sinew.

God, she missed him.

Cash Gallagher, tennis ace. Love of her life.

Cheating bastard.

Every time she closed her eyes, her mind was ransacked with images of Cash in the living room of her flat in London with those incriminating photographs fluttering from his hands. She pictured his earnest expression as he lied to her face about the woman he'd been kissing. He'd been so cruel to choose that moment to tell her, for the first time, he was in love with her.

Tally made herself a hot chocolate and wandered into the living room. She took a sip and picked up her phone, desperate to hear Em's voice.

"Hey, babes," Em said, answering so quickly Tally hadn't even heard a ringing tone. "How are you doing?"

Tally forced a smile, hoping it would filter into her voice. "Yeah, good, although the weather here is awful today."

"Tell me about it," Em said. "It's like a monsoon. Where the fuck is spring?"

"Hiding. I got drenched coming back from the supermarket today. I can hardly believe it's April next week."

"You're eating, then?"

Tally fidgeted in her seat. "A bit. I must admit the breakup diet does wonders for weight loss."

Em heaved a sigh. "That's not funny, Tal. You'd better be taking proper care of yourself because I swear to God, if you look scrawny when I get there this weekend, I'm going to cram sausage rolls down your throat."

Tally laughed. "I'm eating. Just not as much as I was. Let's face it, Em. I could afford to lose a few pounds—and now I have. I like the thinner me, although I still can't shift my fat arse."

"Hmm," Em replied, sounding not in the least bit convinced. "I'll make up my own mind on Friday. I should be down about seven."

"I can't wait," Tally said, and despite all the "no more crying" promises she'd made to herself, her voice broke on the last word.

"Come on, babes," Em said, her own voice quivering. "You're going to get through this."

"I miss him," she whispered as fat tears clung momentarily to her eyelashes before spilling down her cheeks. "It's not getting any easier."

"I know you do. But you have to stay strong, Tal. Otherwise, you'll end up crawling back to him and regretting it. You're better than that, and you deserve better than him."

"Doesn't help numb the pain, though."

Em caught her breath. "You're breaking my heart, Tal."

Tally dashed away her tears, making the back of her hand wet. She wiped it on her pyjama bottoms. "I'll be fine, especially when you get here. I'll spend this weekend planning next weekend."

"If this weather continues, we can stay in and watch trashy movies and eat takeaway pizza."

"Sounds perfect."

"Are you sleeping any better?"

"A little," Tally replied, yawning on cue.

"Get an early night. I'll call you tomorrow. Love you, babes."

"Love you too."

Tally hung up the phone as despair swamped her. Thoughts of Cash crept into her mind, but she shoved them away. She couldn't allow herself to think about him too much. Every time she dwelled on what could have been, even for a fraction of a second, the tears would come, and she'd cried too much already.

She grabbed her mug of hot chocolate and went to bed. She rubbed eyes that stung from lack of sleep. Her body might be exhausted, but her mind had other ideas.

Reluctantly, she took a sleeping pill. All she needed was a decent night's kip, then she'd be able to think more clearly. As the tablet took effect and her eyelids began to droop, her thoughts drifted to whether Cash was suffering too. The idea comforted her, but she couldn't carry on like this. Three weeks of wallowing in self-pity was long enough.

As the sleeping tablet dragged her under, she vowed that

tonight would be the last time she allowed Cash Gallagher to have a hold over her.

Tomorrow, she would take control.

TALLY AWOKE THE NEXT MORNING, groggy with sleep. The pill had done its job because she could barely crank open her eyes. She lay there for a few minutes, allowing her body to come around in its own time. Slowly, she swung her legs out of bed and padded over to the window.

The weather had improved from the day before. The sun hovered low in the sky, and wispy clouds bobbed along on a light breeze. She threw on her dressing gown and headed into the kitchen, full of determination to take control of her life. The first decision had been made. She was going to stick with her plans to freelance because it would give her freedom to travel. Her work would involve moving around, and moving around meant Cash would find it harder to track her down.

Not that he'd made any attempt to do that...

Ignoring the crushing weight on her chest, she made a cup of tea and stepped into the tiny courtyard. Outside space was at a premium this close to the coast in Brighton. Pete's backyard had barely enough space for a bistro-sized table, two chairs, and a few terracotta pots that were home to several neglected evergreen shrubs.

Feeling a distinct chill in the air, she warmed her hands around the mug as she sat on one of the iron chairs. In the last few weeks, she'd struggled to even motivate herself to get dressed, but that day felt like a new start. She'd never get over what Cash had done, but she had to find a way to come to terms with the fact they'd broken up. She had her whole life in front of her. She couldn't let a brief affair with her childhood idol define her entire future. She *wouldn't* allow that.

Unable to face breakfast, she threw on workout gear, tucked her iPod into the back pocket of her running pants, and headed down to the seafront. She'd always hated exercise, but these past few weeks she'd found solace in running. When she ran, she became so focused on controlling her breathing and the heavy ache in her legs that she momentarily forgot about Cash, which gave her a temporary reprieve from her constant companion —heartache.

Brighton seafront always had plenty of joggers running up and down, but because it was Saturday, Tally found herself having to dodge more people than usual. Despite the early-morning chill, it wasn't long before sweat dampened her T-shirt. She stopped to remove her jacket and tie it around her waist.

She ran towards Hove for about two miles before turning around. She was slowly building up endurance, although she hadn't quite cracked the five-mile mark yet. When she arrived back in Brighton, she headed for the pier, bought a bottle of water from one of the stand sellers, and mingled with the tourists while she caught her breath.

She finished drinking, tossed the bottle into a nearby recycling bin, and set off for home. The cool air chilled her skin as she walked. She couldn't wait to get into the warmth, take a hot shower, and drink an even hotter cup of tea.

She turned into her road and removed the front-door key from the back pocket of her running pants. The gate creaked as she opened it, and as it closed behind her, she promised to pop a bit of oil on it later. She inserted the key in the lock as the gate creaked again. She glanced over her shoulder. Her breath hitched, and all the blood drained from her head. She let go of the key and gripped the handle as she sagged against the front door.

"Hello, Natalia."

The sharp pain in her chest couldn't have been any worse if

someone had cracked open her ribcage, reached inside, and torn out her heart.

"Leave me alone, Cash," she croaked to the man she'd adored since she was fifteen.

"I can't do that."

She tightened her grip on the door handle, certain if she let go she'd crumple to the floor. "Don't you think I've been hurt enough?" she whispered.

Cash bowed his head, and his shoulders drooped. "I don't want to cause you any more pain."

"Then go away." She turned her back on him and opened the door.

"Please, Natalia. Can we go inside and talk?"

She rested her forehead against the doorframe. "No," she said in a wavering voice. Tears pricked behind her eyes. She dug her fingernails into her palm as she swallowed past an uncomfortable lump in her throat.

"I can explain," he said, his hand lightly touching her arm.

She spun out of his reach but kept her back to him. "I said no." Her chin trembled, and she clenched her jaw to stop the involuntary movement. "I'm not interested in anything you have to say."

"I know I've fucked up. Please, let me inside. I'll tell you everything. About Gracie, about my mother and father. Everything. It's what I should have done already."

"Cash, please." She faced him then, her voice cracking as the tears she'd desperately tried to hold back spilled down her cheeks. "Why are you doing this?"

"Oh, baby," he said, reaching for her again.

She staggered backwards and stumbled over the step. Her ankle twisted as she tried to save herself. Cash shot out an arm and pulled her against his chest. This time, she didn't have the energy to resist. She slumped against him as he dug around in his pocket.

He produced a crumpled tissue and wiped away her tears. "You're freezing. Let's go inside and get you warmed up."

Before she could protest, he ushered her through the door and into the tiny hallway. He walked straight ahead into the kitchen like he owned the damned place and then flicked the kettle on.

"Go and get a shower. I'll have the tea made by the time you get out."

She wanted to tell him no, that she could make her own bloody tea, but the words wouldn't come. She trudged into the bathroom and locked the door. She wouldn't put it past Cash to follow her, and she craved control even as she sensed it slipping out of reach.

She'd thought Brighton would be a refuge, a place to heal, but he'd found her so easily. Once she'd showered and dressed in clean clothes, she would be able to deal with Cash. She would listen to what he had to say and then politely ask him to leave.

And then she was going home to London.

2

Cash watched Natalia as she disappeared into the next room. He'd barely been able to contain his shock when he saw her. She'd lost so much weight. Her oval face had hollowed out, and her beautiful midnight-blue eyes had dulled—no doubt because of the pain he'd caused. She obviously hadn't been taking care of herself. His chest tightened uncomfortably. He closed his eyes and dragged in a shuddering breath as remorse gnawed at his insides. He'd fucked everything up, and now he had no choice but to share the very thing he'd kept hidden for so long. He was taking a monumental risk, but without it, he wouldn't have a chance of getting her back—and damn, he wanted her back.

Feeling an urge to take care of her, he opened her fridge. Inside, he found a couple of eggs, half a bag of spinach, and a small piece of cheese. He'd watched his housekeeper, Anna, make quite a few omelettes, so cooking one shouldn't be too difficult for his piss-poor culinary skills.

He beat the eggs in a bowl, grated the cheese, and tore up the spinach. The shower went silent. A couple of minutes later, the hairdryer started up. When it switched off, he poured a little oil into a frying pan and tipped in the eggy mixture.

Sensing rather than hearing Natalia behind him, he glanced over his shoulder. She was hovering in the doorway, nibbling on her fingernails.

"I made you an omelette," he said, pointing his chin at the small table in the corner, indicating for her to sit.

"Will it be edible?"

He gave her a crooked smile. "I hope so. It falls within my narrow repertoire, but then again, it's egg based."

Natalia didn't return his smile. Instead, she dug into the pocket of a coat hanging on the back of the kitchen door. She pulled out her phone and sank into a chair at the small table.

"Are you calling Pete, Emmalee, or the police?"

She met his gaze, but instead of the soft, loving expression she used to look at him with, her eyes held a hard edge. "I'm not calling anyone. I said I'd hear you out, and I will. But after that, I want you to respect my wishes and leave."

His insides tightened and fear congealed in his chest as he flipped the omelette over and slid it onto a plate. He put the food and a cup of tea in front of her and sat down opposite.

"I'm hoping when you've heard me out, you won't want me to leave."

She made a derisive sound as she sliced a piece of the omelette with her fork. "Sure of yourself as always, Cash?"

"No," he said quietly. "But sometimes things aren't as they seem."

She snorted. "Still sticking to the same story, I see."

Her harsh tone made his heart clench. "It's not a story. It happens to be the truth."

She laughed, the sound short and bitter. "If you say so."

Cash didn't bite. It wasn't worth it. He needed her full attention and to tell her everything from the beginning. Then she'd know he hadn't cheated.

She finished the omelette, put her knife and fork together on the plate, and picked up her tea. "That wasn't bad."

"I must be improving."

She sipped her drink, peering at him over the rim of the mug. "How did you find me?"

"Private detective. His name's Frank, and he's excellent."

She pressed her lips together in a tight line and glared at him. "Stalking women isn't something to be proud of."

She was being belligerent, but he could hardly blame her. He reached for her hand, but she snatched it away. "Don't."

He withdrew, ignoring the pang in his chest. She rose from her chair and, without saying a word, carried her tea into the next room. Cash took a deep breath and followed her. When he walked into the living room, Natalia was sitting on a chair, her feet tucked beneath her. She was nibbling at the inside of her cheek.

He sat on the sofa and leaned forward to warm his hands on the log fire. "This is a nice room."

Natalia let out a deep sigh. "Just say what you've come to say, Cash."

"Don't you love me anymore?" The words spilled out before he'd had the chance to filter them, and her eyes sparked in defiance as she gave a disbelieving shake of her head.

"Starting with the low blows, Cash? And if I remember rightly, I never said I loved you."

He exhaled on a gasp as though he'd been punched in the back, and his lungs burned in protest. "Wow." He looked away and stared out of the window, unwilling to let her see his pain.

"You destroyed any love I had for you with your secrets and lies and cheating."

Once again, he opened his mouth to deny he'd cheated on her, but it wouldn't do any good. "I'll tell you everything, and I ask only two things in return."

"What?" Natalia chewed on the skin around her thumb.

"Try not to judge me, at least until you've heard it all. Afterwards, if you choose to throw me out, well..." He shrugged. "There's not much more I can do."

"Okay. And the second?"

"Sit with me." He patted the spare seat next to his. "This is going to be the hardest thing I've ever done. I need you beside me."

Natalia hesitated, and for a minute, he thought she was going to refuse. But then she rose from her chair and sat alongside him.

He took a deep breath and wiped clammy hands on his jeans. This was going to be fucking painful.

3

Cash forced a swallow past his dry, sore throat. He took a sip of water, keeping the glass in his hand. If he didn't start talking soon, he'd lose his nerve. But where to begin? He wanted to reach for Natalia's hand, but her body language was stiff and awkward. The last thing he needed was to feel the bite of rejection if she snatched it away.

His eyes flickered towards hers, but he decided staring at the floor was preferable.

"My father was a clever man, even touted as a genius in his field. He set up his own software company before he was twenty. As the business began to take off, he met my mother. She was only seventeen, and they married as soon as she turned eighteen. Three years later, my father's company was already competing with the big boys.

"My mother had been an up-and-coming athlete. Track and field. She would have turned professional if she hadn't married my father, but he insisted he needed her full attention to support him and the growth of his business." He gave a wry smile. "So she gave up on her dreams and became the dutiful wife instead.

"I came along about eighteen months after they married, and

my mother put all of her energy into me. As soon as I could walk, she got me involved in all kinds of different sports: football, cricket, athletics. I guess because she hadn't been able to follow her own sporting dreams, she decided to live them vicariously through me. Then when I was five, she put a tennis racket in my hand for the first time, and that was it. Tennis became my one true love, and it wasn't long before experts in the sport began to sit up and take notice."

He paused again to sip his water. The cool liquid did nothing to soothe his burning throat. He risked a glance at Natalia. She was leaning forwards, her gaze locked on him, and as their eyes met, she nodded encouragingly for him to continue. He placed the glass on a small side table and returned to staring at the floor.

"Every night after school, and every weekend, my mother arranged for me to have professional coaching. However, my father wasn't quite as keen. He thought focusing on one thing only made my life too one dimensional, and he insisted I get involved in different pursuits outside of sport. He encouraged me to play guitar although I wasn't very good. When I turned eight, I joined the cubs, and later the scouts."

"I remember you telling me that on the way to Paris," Natalia said. "Your father used to take you every Wednesday."

"Yeah," he said, meeting her gaze. "And I was a complete bastard to you because you dared to ask about him."

She shrugged one shoulder. "Keep going."

He blew out a slow breath through his nose. "By the age of ten, I'd decided tennis was what I wanted to do with my life. Once I managed to convince my father, he finally gave up trying to push me into other things, although I still went to scouts for another year or so. Then when I was twelve, everything changed."

Cash leaned forward and rested his forearms on his knees, his fingers drumming against each other. "Sorry, give me a minute."

Natalia got to her feet. "Why don't I make a cup of tea?"

"Got any whiskey to top it up?" he said with a grimace.

For the first time, Natalia smiled, and hope surged within him.

"Pete may have a bottle tucked away at the back of a cupboard," she said, disappearing into the kitchen. Cash stood to stretch his legs. A picture hanging on the wall caught his eye, and he moved in for a closer look. One of the guys was definitely Pete, although it had clearly been taken quite a few years ago. Fewer wrinkles. More hair. Pete had his arm around the shoulders of another guy, and they were holding up a huge fish, broad grins on their faces.

"That's my dad with Pete," Natalia said, startling him. He hadn't heard her come back in. She held two steaming mugs of tea in one hand and a half-empty bottle of whiskey in the other.

"Here, let me help you," he said, taking the mugs from her and placing them on a table.

She put the whiskey down next to the tea and walked over to the picture. "They loved fishing. Used to be out for hours." She let out a soft sigh, and he had to clench his fists to stop himself putting his arms around her. He sensed she wouldn't welcome the attention, and he didn't want to scare her away just as he might be getting somewhere.

"You must miss him terribly."

"Every day," she said, glancing sideways at him before facing the picture once more.

Cash left her reminiscing and picked up the whiskey, adding a dash to his tea. When she came to sit beside him, he waved the bottle at her. "Want some?"

"No, thanks." She picked up her mug. "You were saying, about when you were twelve...?"

He scrubbed his chin with his hand and shuddered as he recalled the painful, repressed memories. "My dad began drinking. He'd tried to expand the business, and a takeover deal had gone sour. He'd got himself into shitloads of debt, and he turned to the bottle as a way to help numb the pain of what he saw as his abject failure. We ended up having to sell the house and move somewhere smaller. Dad wanted me to give up tennis—it's an expensive sport, you see—but Mum wouldn't have it. She saw my potential, knew I was on the cusp of making it.

"One night, Dad came in steaming drunk, and he and Mum began arguing, yet again, about how my tennis coaching was costing too much. I remember Mum screaming at him that if he wasn't so greedy, always wanting more instead of being happy with what he had, they wouldn't be in this mess. That was the first time he hit her."

Natalia's hand shot to her mouth, and her eyes widened. "The first time?" she said, the sound of her voice muffled through her fingers.

"Oh, yeah," he said bitterly. "There were *many* times after that. And each one worse than the last."

"Did he hit you too?"

Cash shook his head. "He would drag me out of the way when I'd stand in front of Mum to protect her, but he never hit me. She became his whole focus when he lost his temper, although I've never shaken the guilt that he only ever lost it because of me."

Natalia's hand closed over his, and she gently squeezed. He put his other hand over the top of hers, his thumb lightly brushing her skin. It felt so good to touch her again, although when she tensed beneath his grip, he let go immediately.

He swallowed and blinked a couple of times before continuing. "Mum took a part-time job at a local restaurant so she could keep my coaching going, but the cuts and bruises became harder to hide, and she had to give it up. Without that extra income, she decided to sell her jewellery to pay for my tennis lessons. When Dad found out, he went ballistic. That night, he put her in hospital."

Natalia closed her eyes before slowly opening them, her head moving slightly from side to side. After so many years of burying his childhood, refusing to revisit the awfulness of it all, witnessing Natalia's horror brought the memories rushing back.

"Oh, Cash," she said, her eyes brimming with tears. When one spilled down her cheek, he brushed it away with his thumb.

"Don't cry. It kills me when you cry."

She pulled a tissue from a box beside her and blew her nose. "Didn't the police do anything?"

"The hospital called them, but Mum wouldn't press charges. She still loved him, even after everything he'd done. He put her in hospital many nights after that as though, in his head, a line had been crossed, and now he knew she wouldn't prosecute..." Cash shrugged.

"Didn't anyone else try to help?" Natalia said, a tinge of bewilderment in her tone. "Teachers, family doctor?"

He scrubbed his face with his hand. "No one knew. Both Mum and I became experts at hiding the truth. The only person I ever told was Rupe. He kept me sane and made me believe that the horror I was living through wouldn't last forever."

Natalia smiled fondly. "He's a good friend."

"The best," Cash said, nodding. "And he turned out to be right because when I was fourteen, I won a scholarship to attend a residential tennis academy in Spain. I can't even begin to explain how relieved I was to escape home. I guess I hoped if I wasn't around, then maybe Dad wouldn't get as mad. After all, it had been the arguments about me that had started the physical abuse. If I wasn't there as a constant reminder of their troubles, they might patch things up."

"You know it wasn't about you, though, right?"

Cash shrugged and ignored her comment. "I began to make quite a name for myself on the junior tour. I beat pretty much any opponent put in front of me, and I almost forgot about the nightmare going on at home.

"Then right before my fifteenth birthday, I won the Wimbledon juniors title. I followed that up with the US Open, and the Australian the following year. I rarely went home, and when I did, after a day or so, I couldn't wait to leave. The atmosphere was horrendous, what with Dad permanently drunk and Mum covered in bruises. I begged her to leave him and come away with me, but she wouldn't. No matter what I said, she defended him." He pressed the heels of his hands into his eyes. "This is even harder than I thought it would be."

"If you want to stop--"

"No. If I don't get this out now, I'm not sure I ever will." He got to his feet, desperate to escape the mixture of sorrow and dismay on Natalia's face. He dug his hands deep into the pockets of his jeans and gazed out of the window.

"A couple of months before my sixteenth birthday, I'd travelled to Italy to play in a grade-A-listed tournament when Stone Phillips approached me. Stone was—and still is—one of the best coaches of juniors on the tour, and he agreed to take me on pro bono. With him in my corner, I knew I had a great chance of making it. Stone has a proven history of managing the transition from being a junior to successfully breaking into the seniors. The first person I wanted to tell was Mum, because if it hadn't been for her dogged determination and many sacrifices, I wouldn't have this amazing opportunity. I didn't want to tell her over the phone, so as soon as the tournament was over, I flew home."

His head was pounding, and he pressed his fingertips to his temples, closing his eyes against the bright sunshine. He jumped when Natalia laid a hand on his arm.

"Why don't we take a break? Go for a walk or something."

"No. I'm almost done. I need to finish."

"Well, at least sit down before you fall over."

Cash did as she asked but dropped his head. He wouldn't be able to carry on if he focused on her pity. Nausea churned in his stomach, and his heart thundered in his chest. Twelve years was a long time, and yet, as he told Natalia everything, the memories were so fresh, so painful that the events could have happened yesterday.

"I let myself in and dumped my bags in the hallway. I could hear loud music being played in the living room, a heavy bass beat making a thudding sound, which was weird because neither of my parents were into that type of music. I called out, but there was no reply, probably because they couldn't hear me over the noise. I made my way down the hall, and when I walked into the living room..."

Cash covered his face. "Oh, God," he muttered as pain flooded his chest.

Natalia's hand squeezed his arm. "I'm here for you."

Her soft voice soothed him like no other. He dropped his hands into his lap and raised his head.

She pressed closer. "Tell me," she whispered.

He closed his eyes. When he opened them, he made sure his gaze was averted. "Mum was on the floor, curled into a ball, and Dad was kicking the hell out of her. The thudding noise I'd heard hadn't been the music at all. It had been his foot striking her body and her head."

Natalia gasped, but Cash rushed on, anxious to get this over with. "I flew at him and grabbed him around the neck. I tried to stop him, but he was too strong, and he shoved me in the chest. I fell backwards and hit my head on the doorframe. I remember blood from a gash above my eyebrow dripping into my eyes, and the room began to spin. I managed to stagger to my feet. I ran back into the hallway with the intention of going next door to ask for help. That's when I saw Dad's golf clubs."

His voice broke, and for the first time in years, tears spilled down his cheeks. "I grabbed one out of the bag and ran back into the living room. I swung it as hard as I could. I hit my father on the side of the head, and he fell."

Only then did he lift his eyes to hers. "I murdered him, Natalia. I murdered my own father."

4

————

Tally bit down hard on her lip to stop her own tears from joining his. The sight of Cash crying made her even sadder. The knowledge that someone so strong and proud had shared such a private, tragic event made her heart ache. And even though she still didn't have a clue who Gracie was, or why he seemed convinced he hadn't cheated, the need to comfort him overtook everything else.

She shuffled closer and wrapped her arms around him, pulling him into her body. Tremors ran through him as he returned her embrace, his arms holding her tightly.

"I've missed you so much," he mumbled against her neck. When she didn't push him away, he eased back, his hands cupping her face. Gently, he pressed his lips to hers, and she repressed a soft moan. Being in Cash's arms again almost erased the constant agony she'd lived with the past few weeks, but at the back of her mind was the gnawing doubt that he still hadn't fully explained himself. She gripped his wrists and pulled his hands away from her face.

"Don't," she whispered. "Please don't."

"Sorry," he mumbled. He began to repetitively tug his bottom lip between his thumb and forefinger. It made her wish they were still kissing.

"No, I'm sorry. I started it."

"I knew it was a risk telling you," he said, refusing to look her in the eye. "How can you ever see me the same way now you know I'm capable of murder?"

Tally's mouth fell open, and she ducked her head until he was forced to meet her gaze. "You don't really believe you're a murderer? Cash, you were a child trying to protect your mother, and for all you knew, he could have turned on you next."

He gave a weak shrug. "I know. Doesn't stop the guilt, though."

"Jesus." She brushed a stray lock of hair off her face. "What happened next? What about your mum?"

His shoulders dropped. "After I hit him and he fell, I called for an ambulance. I was terrified they'd put me in prison. When the ambulance crew arrived, they took one look at the scene and phoned the police. Mum was barely alive, and I guessed Dad was dead when they covered his face with a sheet and loaded him onto a stretcher, although no one told me he'd died."

"Dear God," Tally muttered, astounded at the sheer callousness of such a thoughtless act and the impact it must have had on a terrified child.

"The police arrested me and took me to the station. They wouldn't let me go to the hospital with Mum. I didn't know who to call, so I phoned Rupe. His dad sorted out a solicitor and stayed with me during questioning."

"That was good of him."

"Yeah." He stroked his scruff with his fingertips. "I was a fucking mess, barely able to string a sentence together. I kept asking the police how Mum was doing, but they wouldn't tell me. They made me go over what had happened so many times I began to doubt myself. Eventually, they bailed me without charge until they'd carried out a full investigation. As soon as they let me out, Rupe's dad took me straight to the hospital."

"Your mum?" she asked again, almost afraid to hear the answer.

He lifted his head. His eyes were watery, his face pained. "She was alive. Barely. She had massive head injuries and internal bleeding. By the time I got there, they'd already operated and placed her in intensive care."

"I can't even imagine what you must have gone through. You were fifteen." Outrage swept through her on behalf of a teenage boy she hadn't known then but still felt an overwhelming urge to protect.

"It was grim," he said. "It took the police two weeks to decide I wouldn't be charged."

"But they'd have known it was self-defence, surely?"

"It could have gone either way, but I guess I got lucky." Cash gave a bitter laugh. "If you can call it that."

"Where's your mum now?" she dared to ask.

His gaze was steady on hers, and he clutched her hand. "This is where Gracie comes in."

Tally almost stopped breathing. *Now* they were getting to the crux of it, the cause of all their issues. Gracie—the woman he'd been kissing in the pictures she'd been sent, though the sender was still a mystery.

"I wondered if you were going to mention her."

"Gracie is my mother's carer. Well, one of them."

Perplexed, Tally stared at him. *His mother's carer.* "Your mum made it?"

"Yes, but she's been in a coma since it happened. Gracie and three other wonderful women live with Mum and provide round-the-clock care for her, but Gracie is the one I deal with mainly. The house in those photographs you were sent is one I had built for Mum. It has everything she needs, all the latest medical equipment."

"Oh, Cash, what a woman your mother is—to still be hanging on after all these years."

Cash nodded. "There have been plenty of times when her doctors recommended withdrawing her feeding tube. They were certain she would never regain consciousness and all I achieved by insisting they keep her alive was to drag out her inevitable death. But I couldn't do it. I always had hope." He smiled then. "Remember the photograph of me and Gracie kissing?"

Tally dropped her gaze as a sharp pain shot through her heart. "How could I forget?" she mumbled.

"That was the day my mother regained consciousness."

Tally's head snapped up. "She's awake? Alert?"

"Yeah." His smile lit up his eyes for the first time since he'd arrived earlier in the day. "Her doctors are saying it's a miracle. Not quite, based on the research I've done, but extremely rare all the same. On the day those photographs were taken, Gracie had called to tell me Mum had woken up. I raced around to the house. It's not far from mine. You can imagine how ecstatic I was. When Gracie came running out to greet me, I wasn't thinking of anything other than my mother and how, after all these years, she may finally recover. I gave a brief peck to someone I consider a friend and a confidant."

Tally tilted her head to one side. "And the photographer just happened to snap at the right time?"

The smile drained from his eyes. "I don't think it was a random paparazzi. I think someone was following me, waiting for a chance to make something out of nothing. To break us up."

She frowned. "Who would do such a thing?"

He shrugged. "No idea. An ex-girlfriend, a journalist with a grudge. Could be anyone."

"Kinga?" she asked, tensing at the thought of Cash's old agent, who'd hated her on sight. Kinga had wanted Cash for herself, and then Tally came along and ruined her plans to be Mrs Gallagher someday. The two women had an argument that ended with Kinga punching Tally in the face. Cash had immediately sacked her.

He nodded. "It crossed my mind too, so I did some digging. She was telling the truth about getting help when she turned up at the house. Remember on the Saturday we went riding? She'd already had a couple of one-on-one counselling sessions, and after our altercation, she signed herself into a residential facility in London the same day."

The enormity of what Cash had told her suddenly hit, and Tally covered her face with her hands. She'd been an idiot. A jealous, stupid, crazy idiot who'd caused all this angst. And for nothing. "You kept telling me to trust you," she whispered through her fingers.

Cash eased her hands away from her face. "Yes, I did." He grimaced. "I should have told you as soon as you showed me the photographs, but I panicked. I couldn't tell you who Gracie was without spilling the whole sordid truth—a truth I've avoided talking about for so long... I'm sorry, baby."

"You telling me what happened is the bravest thing I've ever seen." She shook her head in astonishment.

"If it means you'll give me another chance, I'd do it again. Ten times. A hundred times." He rubbed her upper arms, his hands tender but firm as they caressed her bare skin. "I have to know, Natalia. Can you forgive me? Do we have a future together?"

She gave him a playful bump with her shoulder. "You don't start with the easy questions, do you?"

His smile in response to her teasing was full of hope mixed with a tinge of fear, which flattened the corners of his mouth rather than lifting them. "Baby, it's the only question that matters."

Tally studied his face. She knew it as well as her own, and the man behind it was the only one she would ever want. But her heart had too many cuts to simply paper over the cracks, and healing would take time. "I can't go straight back to where we were, Cash. I feel battered and bruised."

He offered her a faint smile. "However long it takes, I'll wait."

She dropped her head. "I thought I'd lost you."

He tilted her chin up, encouraging her to meet his gaze. When she did, he was wearing *that* look—the one that made her knees shake and her body scream with hunger.

"I would have never given up on you. We belong together. I didn't think I was capable of loving anyone until I met you. It took me far too long to admit it to myself, let alone to you. And when I did finally manage to blurt it out..." His lips twitched at the corners. "Well, my timing was shit."

Tally laughed, the stress of the last few weeks diminishing. "It could have been better, ace."

His eyes brightened. "Have I ever told you I love it when you call me that?"

A sudden longing to be close to him led to her pecking him on the lips, but as he moved to deepen the kiss, she pulled back. Her body was urging her to do one thing, but her mind was yanking her in the opposite direction and was winning the battle. Disappointment flickered across his face, but he didn't push.

"Let's go for a walk," she said, rising from the sofa. "And if you're good, I'll let you buy me lunch a bit later."

Cash grinned at her ribbing, but as she led the way out of the living room, he stopped her. "I need you to keep this between us. If what happened to my father gets out, it could ruin my career. I trust you implicitly, but—I'm sorry—I don't feel the same way about Emmalee and Pete."

Tally shook her head. "They won't hear it from me."

"They'll want to know why you're letting me within ten feet of you, though."

"I can handle them," she said firmly.

The tension in his face receded, and when he clasped her hand, a deep-seated longing sprang up inside her. But her heart had been broken, and she needed to learn to protect it much better. Another break, and she doubted it would ever heal.

5

"Nice place," Cash said when they reached the typically English pub with a thatched roof, colourful window boxes, and whitewashed walls. He held the door open for Natalia and ushered her through.

The inside matched the outside with traditional low-hanging beams and stone floors. The place was packed, but luckily, Cash spotted a table tucked away in a corner close to where an open fire burned in the grate. He pointed it out to Natalia, and she sidled past tables full of diners, murmuring an apology whenever she had to ask them to tuck their chairs in.

"Here," Cash said, passing Natalia a menu once they'd sat down. "What do you want to drink?"

She scanned the drinks selection on the back page. "Think I'll have a glass of the Pinot."

"Why don't I get a bottle?"

She glanced up. "Are you trying to get me drunk?"

He laughed. "It's me who's going to get drunk. After the morning I've had, I need it. What about food?"

"I was thinking of having the chicken salad," Natalia said while reading the menu.

"I'd rather you chose something with more calories."

She frowned at him. "I like chicken salad."

"Humour me. You've lost a lot of weight. I don't want you getting ill, especially when it's my fault." He waved the waitress over. "Hi, can we order?"

"Sure. Welcome to the Kings Head. What can I get for you?"

"A bottle of the Pinot Noir and two glasses."

"White Pinot for me," Natalia said.

Cash smirked before glancing up at the waitress. "Whatever the lady wants, and I think I'll have the salmon. Natalia?"

She raised her chin. "The fillet steak with garlic butter, please. Oh, and fries."

Cash chuckled under his breath as the waitress made a note. He'd missed the way Natalia challenged him. If anyone else acted as she did, he'd have quickly put them in their place and enjoyed doing it. But when Natalia asserted herself, it was a treat he relished.

"Anything else?" the waitress asked, a slight dip between her brows forming as she gave him the same curious look that strangers often directed at him when trying to place where they'd seen him before.

"No," he said, handing her both menus. "That's it."

"Happy with my meal choice, dear?" Natalia said as she rubbed her chin thoughtfully.

Cash repressed a smile at her barely veiled sarcasm. "Very. I'm worried about you being this thin."

"Really?" she purred, fluttering her eyelashes for maximum effect. "Surely, all I'd have to do now is dye my hair blond, and I'd fit right in with your preferred type."

For some reason, she was trying to wind him up. He chuckled. "You're my preferred type whether you're thin or curvy. As long as you're happy, it's fine by me. I just want you to be healthy."

She held his gaze, and when her tongue swept over her bottom lip, his stomach tightened. It had always been easy for

Natalia to turn him on. She only had to be present and breathing.

"Careful," he said. "You remember how insatiable I am, right?"

Underneath the table, she rubbed her leg against his, and it took all his willpower not to groan out loud.

"Oh, I remember."

He was thinking about kicking the flirting up a notch when a couple appeared at their table.

"It is you," the man said, looming over Cash, while the woman bobbed from foot to foot and grinned inanely at him. "You're Cash Gallagher, aren't you?"

Cash inwardly cursed. He wanted to say something sarcastic like *Last time I looked*, or even better, *Yes. Now, fuck off. I'm busy.* Instead, he pasted on a false smile.

"I am," he said shaking the man's outstretched hand.

"Do you mind if we get a picture?"

Yes, I fucking do mind. "No, not at all."

The man nudged his wife. "Go on, Sarah. Get in there." After his wife squeezed in beside Cash, he took several photographs.

Cash ground his teeth and prayed for them to hurry up, but when the guy stuck a beer mat virtually under Cash's nose for him to sign, his patience ran out.

"I don't mean to be rude, but I'm in the middle of lunch with my girlfriend. Do you mind?"

The man peered at Natalia as if he hadn't noticed her before. "Oh, sorry, love," he said, his loud voice drawing unwanted attention from nearby tables. "Guess you get used to sharing him. You don't mind if he signs a few things for us, do you? The wife adores him."

Natalia took one look at Cash's face and drew herself upright. "Actually, I do mind," she said, hitting the guy with her best icy stare. "Cash has kindly posed for pictures, and now I'd appreciate it if you would leave us alone so we can enjoy our lunch in peace."

Intense pride flooded Cash's chest. What a woman. The man gaped at Natalia before his wife managed to tug him away, muttered apologies tumbling from her mouth.

After they'd gone, Natalia grinned at him. "Who needs Isaac?" she said, referring to Cash's burly security guy. She leaned back in her chair and reached for her wine, but as she lifted it to her lips, her hand froze. "Oh, shit. Why aren't you in the States? You've missed Indian Wells."

His breath stalled as he gaped at her. "You think I could compete when my head's all over the place? I'm a fucking mess."

"But your rankings?"

He let out a frustrated sigh. "Screw the rankings. I don't care. All I want is to win you back and for my mother to regain a semblance of a normal life. Nothing else matters."

Natalia began to say something then seemed to decide against it, choosing to drink her wine instead.

"What is it?" Cash said.

She lowered her voice to barely above a whisper as she leaned across the table. "How come no one knows? I've done hundreds of hours of research into you, reading everything I could get my hands on. And yet... nothing. It's a miracle you've kept all this quiet what with social media and the Internet. It's virtually impossible for normal people to keep things private. For a celebrity, it's almost inconceivable."

The waitress dashed over, holding two plates aloft. "Okay, my lovelies. Who's for the steak?"

Cash pointed at Natalia, who was glaring at the waitress with barely veiled annoyance at the untimely interruption. He waited until they were alone once more. "When it happened, I was still a minor in the eyes of the law, so my arrest, the investigation—all of it is in sealed records." He picked at his salmon as his appetite waned.

"Of course," Natalia said, nodding. "And your mum's carers have never let anything leak?"

Cash shook his head. "They've never let me down. They're all discreet, professional ladies."

She fixed her gaze on him, her beautiful blue eyes filled with empathy, and his stomach clenched. He ached to touch her, to get back to their earlier flirting, but the moment had passed.

"I'm glad it hasn't come out," she said. "It is strange, though. Why the dislike of journalists if you've managed to keep this under wraps?"

Cash popped a spear of broccoli into his mouth and chewed thoughtfully. "Fear, maybe. And worry if I opened myself up, or allowed anyone to get close to me, I might let something slip. Or an innocent remark may lead one of the more inquisitive reporters to delve a little deeper. It's far from impossible to find the truth if one has the right motivation."

"You let me get close."

"Yeah," he said with a grin. "And look where that's got me."

"Lucky for me," she said, returning his smile.

His spirits lifted, the aching void in his chest getting smaller —not disappearing entirely but at least reducing in size. Maybe he did have a chance at forgiveness.

"What happens now?" he said as she cut into her steak.

She glanced up at him. "Fancy giving me a lift back to London?"

6

"Cash, stop the car."

Tally spotted Cash's puzzled look, but he pulled over two streets from her and Em's flat in London. Cutting the engine, he twisted in his seat.

"You okay?"

"Yeah. I'm getting out here."

"Why?"

She unfastened her seatbelt. "I don't know whether Em's at home or not. Better if she doesn't spot me with you until I've had a chance to explain."

Cash grimaced. "It's not going to be easy to explain when you have to withhold the truth."

"It'll be fine," she said, trying to come across as indifferent because she didn't want Cash to know how worried she was. Trying to explain why they were getting back together when she couldn't tell Em and Pete the full story would no doubt result in judgemental stares and difficult questions. Though she was Tally's best friend, Em could be fearsome when she wanted to get to the bottom of something. She would have made a great journalist, apart from the fact she could barely spell her own name.

"Are you sure you don't want me with you?"

Tally snapped her attention back to the present. "No. It's better this way."

They got out of the car, and Cash lifted her suitcases from the boot. He set them on the pavement and kissed her cheek. "Call me as soon as you can. I'll be at the Dorchester."

He climbed back into the car and drove away. Tally frowned as she watched him disappear around the corner. Apart from the couple of kisses they'd shared in Brighton, he hadn't tried to push her into anything more, although she shouldn't have been surprised. After all, she'd been the one to pull back when they kissed, and the one to tell him she wanted to go slow. Except did she really want to go slow, or did she want to hurtle headlong into life with Cash once more? Admiring from afar was very different from being in the centre of the storm, and yet, the last three weeks without him had been torturous.

Argh! The swaying from one thing to another was making her head spin. Why couldn't life be simpler?

She turned in to her road and bumped her suitcases over the kerb as she crossed to the other side. At least Em hadn't moved out of the flat yet. Tally let herself in and left her cases inside the door of her old bedroom. A few of her things were still dotted around, although she'd put most of it in storage before fleeing to Brighton. At the time, she hadn't anticipated returning to her old home, but the familiarity of the place was exactly the comfort she needed, sort of like wrapping herself in an electric blanket on a cold winter's day.

Em wasn't at home, so she decided to cook them some dinner. She needed something—anything—to take her mind off having to break the news to Em that she and Cash were getting back together. Without a decent explanation, she was going to look like one of *those* women who tolerated cheating and forgave their significant others time and again, turning a blind eye to affairs.

Sure, it wasn't true in her case, but that was exactly how it would seem.

Em's cupboards were virtually empty, but Tally managed to rustle up a chicken stew using a few leftovers. Once the stew was bubbling away, she reduced the heat on the stove and ducked round to the local off-licence. She picked up a bottle of Pinot and a half-decent Prosecco advertised as the offer of the week.

Light had begun to fade when the front-door lock rattled. Bracing herself, Tally wandered into the hallway as Em stumbled through, lugging several makeup bags and boxes, the cord from a pair of GHDs trailing behind her. She tripped over the cord and cursed.

"Nothing changes," Tally said.

Em jumped before a flash of surprise crossed her face. "You scared the shit out of me," she said as Tally removed one of the boxes from her friend's overflowing arms. Em dropped the rest of her stuff on the floor and gave her a warm hug. "What are you doing here?"

"Nice welcome," Tally said dryly, one eyebrow slightly raised.

"You know what I mean. I'm supposed to be visiting you this weekend. Are you sure it's okay to be here? I wouldn't put it past that bastard to have a private dick watching the flat in case you turn up."

Tally stifled a grin at just how close to the truth Em was. "I've made a stew. And you had no wine in the flat. Not like you."

Em raised one shoulder. "It's no fun drinking alone. I'm serious, though, Tal. Are you sure you should be here?"

"Stop worrying." Tally strolled into the kitchen, trying to give an air of nonchalance. She lifted the Pinot and the Prosecco out of the fridge. "Which one?"

"Bubbles first." Em wandered over to the stove and stuck her nose in the pan. "That smells fab. I'm starving."

Tally passed the Prosecco to her. "You open that, and I'll put the potatoes on."

"I was right, then." Em poured the sparkling wine into two champagne flutes. She passed a glass to Tally.

"About what?" Tally said, giving Em a confused look.

Em looked her up and down. "You haven't been eating properly. How much weight have you lost, babes?"

Tally shrugged. "A few pounds, that's all. Nothing I couldn't afford to lose."

A flare of anger crossed Em's face. "It looks like more than a few pounds to me." And then she must have realised how harsh she sounded because she broke into a smile. "Let's see what we can do to load some of it back on tonight."

With her bowl full of steaming hot stew, Tally followed Em into the living room and tucked her feet up on her favourite chair. She began eating and steeled herself for the inquisition. It didn't take long.

"What's changed?"

"What do you mean?" Tally said, mouth half-full as she locked gazes with Em.

"Oh, come on," Em scoffed. "When I spoke to you on Saturday, you were in a right state. And now, even though you're as thin as a rake, you don't have the appearance of someone whose heart is broken."

"My heart was broken," Tally said, her voice small and wary.

Em snorted. "Don't play grammatical gymnastics with me. Even I know past tense when I hear it."

"Em," she said with a sigh. "Let's not do this right now. I want to eat my dinner in peace and find out what you've been up to."

"He's got to you, hasn't he?"

Tally swallowed a piece of potato and let the silence linger. She was better than her friend at this game, but Em surprisingly kept her mouth shut and let the question hang in the air.

Tally lifted her head, a half-embarrassed smile tugging at her lips. "It's not what you think."

Em dropped her bowl of stew on the coffee table and folded

her arms across her chest. "Really? Do tell me what I'm thinking, Tally."

Tally gnawed on the inside of her cheek. "Cash found me. In Brighton."

Em hissed through gritted teeth. "I knew it. The slimy fucking toad. You told him to sod off, right?"

With her appetite rapidly waning, Tally set her stew down next to Em's and wandered over to the window. The streetlamps had come on, casting weak light onto the road and the pavement. A man and a woman were walking their dog, taking turns to hold the lead. *Must be a novelty.*

"*Right*, Tally?"

Tally glanced over her shoulder to find Em watching her intently. She dug her hands into the back pockets of her jeans. "He didn't cheat on me, Em."

"For fuck's sake, Tal." Em dragged her fingers through her shoulder-length bob, tugging hard when she reached a knot. Several broken strands of hair fell on the arm of the sofa, and she brushed them to the floor. "I knew he'd win you round. You've been obsessed with him for too long."

"He didn't cheat on me."

"So those photos of him kissing that woman. Photoshop?"

"No."

"Then he did kiss her," Em said, her tone triumphant, derisive.

"A peck. That's all. The photographer caught it at exactly the right moment."

"Convenient. Who is she?"

Tally hesitated. She didn't want to lie to Em but couldn't tell her the truth. "An employee," she finally said.

"And what is she employed to do? Suck his cock when you're not available?"

Tally threw her hands out wide. "Emmalee! You're not listening."

Em snorted again. "Wake up, Tal. What kind of boss sweeps his employees into his arms and kisses them on the lips? The cheating bloody kind, that's who."

Tally sighed as she faced the window once more. Em was only giving her a hard time because she cared, but she didn't understand. How could she be expected to when she only had half the story?

Tally sensed rather than heard her leaving the room, but Em was back a minute or so later with the half-empty Prosecco bottle and her mobile phone.

"Here," Em said, thrusting the bottle at her. "You top us up, and I'll call Pete and get him over here to knock some bloody sense into you."

Tally shook her head in despair. "Don't call him, Em. Not yet."

Em jinked a hip to the side. "Give me one good reason why not."

Tally filled their glasses and took a sip. "Because you haven't let me explain properly."

Em tossed her phone on the coffee table and collapsed onto the sofa. "I'm all ears," she said, waving her hand in the air.

Tally took a deep breath. "Cash came to Brighton to explain himself, and unlike last time, I listened to what he had to say. Once I heard the full story, I chose to believe him."

"Well, go on, then. What's his brilliant excuse for kissing another woman?"

Tally grimaced as she smoothed a hand over her hair. "I can't tell you."

Em reached for her phone.

"Do you trust me?" Tally said.

Em let out a terse sigh, hand hovering over her mobile. "Babes, you know I do. But I also know you love Cash so deeply he could pretty much spin you any yarn, and you'd suck it up."

"It wasn't a yarn."

"Then why won't you tell me?"

"Can't, Em—not *won't*."

She shrugged. "Same difference."

"No, it's not." Tally shuffled to the edge of her chair and leaned forwards, her forearms resting on her thighs. "I can't tell you because what Cash chose to share with me is private and not something either of us want splashed across the front pages. The more people who know, the more likely his private life will make it into the papers. That's why he asked me to keep it confidential, and I agreed."

Em made a frustrated noise. "But don't you see, Tal? It's classic control-freak behaviour. He tells you something that makes you believe he's not a cheating rat, but conveniently, you can't tell anyone else with a bit more distance who might be able to pick holes in the story."

"He was telling the truth," Tally said with dogged determination.

"I hope he was. For your sake." Em pressed her lips together in disapproval, and then her whole face softened. "I don't mean to be hard on you, babes, but I love you to death. Living through your pain was almost as bad for me as it was for you, you know."

Tally stood up and nestled beside Em on the sofa and leaned her head on her friend's shoulder. "I know, and if there ever comes a time when I can tell you, I will. Promise. But until then, you're going to have to trust my judgement."

"For you, I'll try." Em rocked her shoulder, making Tally lift her head. "When are you moving to Ireland?"

"I'm not," Tally said, secretly pleased when a flash of surprise crossed Em's face. "I told him he'd hurt me too much to simply pick up where we left off. We're going to take it slow and see what happens."

Em chuckled. "Bet he loved that."

Tally grinned. "Got him eating out of the palm of my hand."

"I believe you. Do you want to move back in here for a bit?"

Relief hit her hard. She hadn't planned out what she'd do if Em didn't want her to move back in.

"You haven't sorted another place yet?"

"Nah," Em said. "Without you flat-hunting with me, it all seemed a bit of a faff. Mum's been helping out with the rent."

"Then I'd love to move back in."

As the earlier awkwardness melted away, Tally picked up her plate of stew and ate in silence, well aware Em letting her off the hook might only be a temporary reprieve. And God only knew what Em would say to Cash the next time she saw him.

"I'm stuffed," Em said, dropping her plate on the coffee table. She rubbed her belly. "Boy, I've missed your cooking. It's the real reason I'm letting you move back in."

Tally laughed. "It's a good job I can rustle something out of nothing. There was hardly any food in the fridge. And you accuse me of not taking care of myself."

"I can't be arsed cooking for one. I've been buying M&S microwave meals. Is that sad or what?"

"I'll do a shop tomorrow."

"Are you going back to the paper?"

Tally shook her head. "I've decided to stick with the original plan to freelance. It's a bit risky, but I've got some savings, and Pete will help out, I'm sure."

"But you are going to talk to him. About Cash."

"Yeah." Tally groaned and looked skyward as dread spread through her gut. "Telling you was bad enough. He's going to do his nut."

"Probably," Em said. "But he loves you. He'll huff and puff. Then, like me, he'll try to trust that you know what you're doing. And if it doesn't work out..." She shrugged. "We'll always be here to pick up the pieces."

Tally winced. It had to work out because a second breakup would tear her apart.

~

"Have you lost your mind?"

Redness spread across Pete's face as he paced around his office like a caged tiger. Tally began to worry about his blood pressure. She'd seen Pete angry like this before, and bitter experience had taught her it was better to let him get it all out rather than interrupt him midflow. His anger would dissipate more quickly that way.

When she didn't reply, he slammed his hands on the desk. She jumped. If she had eyes in the back of her head, she'd have probably seen the rest of the floor jump as well. Perhaps her decision to tell him at the paper hadn't been the most inspired idea. She'd banked on Pete having to keep a modicum of professionalism and hoped to turn her news into a quiet, sensible discussion.

Yep. Her strategy had worked a treat.

"Pete," she said in what she hoped was a mild, conciliatory tone. "Calm down, and let me explain."

"Calm down?" He glared at her and clenched his jaw tight. Tally braced for round three—or was it four? But then his energy seemed to evaporate, and he wearily sank into his chair. "He came to see me."

Tally's eyebrows shot up. "When?"

"Day before yesterday. Boy, that fucker works quick. I want to kill him for the way he hurt you, yet here you are, ready to forgive and forget as if nothing happened."

"I don't think I'll forget in a hurry, but there was nothing to forgive. It was all a huge misunderstanding."

Pete expelled a terse sigh. "Yeah, such a misunderstanding that you refrain from enlightening me with the details."

"I-I can't. Please trust me. I can't tell you."

Pete gave her a rueful stare. "You used to tell me everything."

Talk about layering on the emotional blackmail. "I can't tell you this. Look, I'm not an idiot. I know when someone is blatantly lying to me. All I can say is when I stopped long enough to let Cash explain those photographs, I believed him one hundred per cent."

"What stopped him telling you at the time?"

"He had his reasons. He thought he was doing the right thing."

Pete snorted. "You're a grown woman, and I can't stop you doing anything you choose, but I think you're making a huge mistake."

She let out a soft sigh. "Please, Pete. I need your support."

He leaned across his messy desk and patted her hand. "You'll never have anything else, my darling girl. But you tell that fucker I'm watching."

Tally laughed. She couldn't help pitying Cash the next time he came into contact with her wonderful uncle Pete.

"Did I tell you I'm moving back in with Em?"

Pete's eyebrows almost disappeared into his receding hairline. "You're not moving to Ireland?"

"No. I've told Cash I want to take things slow, and he respects that."

"I should fucking think so." Pete rose from his desk and wandered over to the coffee percolator in the corner of his office. He poured two cups before handing one to her. "When do you want to come back to work?"

She took a sip of her coffee, peering at him over the rim of the mug. "I want to stick with the original plan. To freelance."

He paused then nodded. "I see. So when you are ready to move in with Cash, you're all set."

She narrowed her eyes at him. "Didn't you hear what I said? We're taking things slow, but I've had plenty of time to think these last few weeks. I quite like the idea of freelancing. I don't know whether things will work out between Cash and me, but if they do, then it would be good to have an established freelance career. I hope you're still willing to push a few things my way. I'm going to need all the help I can get."

Pete gave her his first genuine smile since she'd walked into the office. "I'll always be here to support you. Your dad would be proud of you, kid."

Tally held her breath, waiting for the familiar bolt of pain whenever anyone mentioned her dad, but instead, a surge of happiness rushed through her. She was striding out on her own towards an uncertain yet exciting future.

She'd finally taken control—and it was liberating.

7

C ash glanced at his watch for the tenth time in the last hour. Apart from one brief text from Natalia the night before, he'd heard nothing. Patience wasn't something he had in plentiful supply. Waiting to find out if Emmalee and Pete had convinced Natalia to kick him to the kerb was driving him crazy. He was well aware they had the power to talk her round, and the fact that he'd asked Natalia to keep the truth about Gracie private wasn't going to help his cause.

He jumped at a knock at the door then remembered he'd ordered room service even though he wasn't all that hungry. He opened the door and ushered the waiter in, instructing him to leave the tray on the dining room table. The food turned his stomach, but the glass of wine did the opposite. He began to pace. Unable to wait another second, he sent Natalia a text:

What's happening? You okay?

He glared at the screen as if willpower alone would make a comforting text appear before him. After five minutes and *still* no reply, he threw the phone on the couch. Goddammit! He had a bad feeling about this.

Cash drifted over to the window and peered through the

blinds. Beneath him, busy Londoners sped, going about their business, each one oblivious to his mental torture. He *knew* Pete and Emmalee would win. He should have refused to let her go it alone. If he'd been there, he would have been able to control the situation.

His phone rang, and he lunged for it, speaking breathlessly into the speaker. "Natalia?"

"Jesus, bud. You lost her again already?" Rupe said in his usual sarcastic tone.

Cash groaned. "Not exactly."

"So what has happened? We only spoke yesterday."

"She wanted to tell Pete and Emmalee on her own."

"And you let her?"

Rupe's incredulity spoke volumes, and not for the first time, Cash wished he'd tried to be more persuasive. "You know how stubborn she can be. When she makes her mind up, that's it."

"And you think they've changed it for her?"

Cash scuffed a hand over the top of his head. "I don't know what to fucking think. She texted me last night after she'd spoken to Emmalee and said everything was fine. Pete was on today's agenda, and I haven't heard a thing since."

"Are you at the house?"

"No. The Dorchester."

"Then check out, and get your arse over there. I'm coming home."

"I told Natalia I was staying at the hotel. I don't want to leave until I've spoken with her. I'll bring her over tomorrow."

"Okay. I'll call you when I land. And try to chill the fuck out."

Without anything changing, he felt a whole lot better. Rupe had a knack for grounding him. He was the brother Cash had longed for as a child, and Cash adored him, even if Rupe could be an annoying bastard at times.

He tossed his phone on the coffee table as a text notification pinged. His heart jolted at the sender. He swiped at the screen and read her message:

Be there shortly.

Relief surged through him. He sank into the nearest chair. *Thank fuck for that.* Even if Pete had put doubts in her mind, she was still coming over, which meant Cash stood a chance of pleading his case and trying to reverse any damage done.

He called down to room service and ordered a bottle of wine. The wine arrived at the same time as Natalia. He kissed her cheek as she entered and then signed for the wine.

"Started without me?" She pointed her chin at his empty glass.

He grimaced. "Needed something to take the edge off." He poured her a glass of wine and topped up his own. "Pete didn't lock you in the tower, then?"

"Not quite."

Her lips twitched in an almost smile, and he put his arms around her, holding her close to his body. When she made a soft, contented sound, his fears evaporated.

"Rough, was it, baby?"

"You have no idea," she said, her voice muffled as she spoke into his shoulder.

He clipped a finger under her chin, tipping her head back. "I'm here to listen, sweetness." He sat her down, more than a little concerned with how pale she was. "Have you eaten?"

"No."

He glanced over at his half-finished carbonara, decided that wouldn't do at all, and passed her a room-service menu, pressing it into her hands when she shook her head.

"Order something, please."

She gave it a cursory glance. "Okay, I'll have the chicken soup. Honestly," she said when he opened his mouth to disagree, "I'm not very hungry."

For the third time in less than an hour, he called room

service. It crossed his mind to add a sandwich or a burger to the soup order, but he knew ignoring her wishes would piss her off, and he didn't want reconciliation to end in a row.

"Food will be thirty minutes," he said, hanging up the phone. "What went down?"

A tired frown drifted across her face. "There's not a lot to say. There was amazement, followed by shouting. Lots and lots of shouting. And finally, acceptance. They love me, I guess." She gave a half-shrug then grinned. "You, on the other hand, are persona non grata."

He laughed. "Sweetness, have I ever occupied any other position with Pete? I don't care what he or anyone else thinks. Only your opinion counts." He hesitated before spitting out what was on his mind. "Are you still willing to give me that second chance?"

She curled into his side and leaned her head against his shoulder. "You even need to ask?"

He exhaled on a shudder and rested his chin on top of her head. "One thing I've learned since being with you is to never take anything for granted."

He felt rather than saw her smile. "Glad to see I'm keeping you on your toes."

"Baby, I spend so long on my toes these days my calf muscles are three inches shorter."

She burst out laughing, but then just as quickly, her face fell. "Cash?"

"Yeah?" He frowned, wondering what had ruined her happy mood so suddenly.

"I want to meet your mum."

TALLY WASN'T sure whether Cash was scared or surprised as he drew himself upright. His eyes were wide as he faced her. If she'd spooked him by her request, then maybe it *was* all a lie.

No, surely not? It would take a hell of an actor to fake the level of emotion Cash had shown in Brighton. And if he *was* the sort of person who could make up such a terrible story, then she didn't want to be part of his life, regardless of how much she loved him.

He tapped his forefinger against his bottom lip, brows drawn low. "I'm not sure that's such a good idea at the moment," he said, adding a good dose of fuel to her fears. "She's doing great, but there's a long way to go. I don't think she's up to visitors yet."

"Okay," Tally said quietly. "I understand."

He lifted his chin, his gaze searching hers. Then he closed his eyes and sighed. When he opened them again, they were full of sadness and hurt.

"You don't believe me," he said with a slow shake of his head.

"I do," she said a little too quickly. "Of course I do."

"I don't blame you," he said, his understanding tone making her feel even worse. "I haven't exactly given you a lot of reasons to trust me."

"I'm sorry. Forget I asked."

"No. You're right." He cupped her face with both hands, his thumbs skimming over her cheeks. "You are the most significant person in my life. You should meet my mother. I'd planned on going back to Ireland soon anyway." He gave a half-smile that didn't reach his eyes. "You can come with me and tell her what a pain in the arse I am."

Tally kicked herself. This hadn't exactly gone according to plan. "I don't want to make you do anything you're not comfortable with, but I want to share all parts of your life. The bad bits as well as the good ones. I shouldn't have pushed. Your mum is still seriously ill, and I totally understand you wanting to protect her."

"I don't deserve you," he said in a hushed tone. His hand curved around the back of her neck, and he touched his lips to hers. The instant their mouths connected, a knock at the door interrupted them.

"Why is it that room service always has impeccable timing?" he said with a grimace.

Cash carried the tray inside, and as the smell of rich, warm chicken soup wafted over, her stomach growled in anticipation. He placed the tray across her knees and watched as she wolfed the lot down in five minutes flat. Once she'd finished, he picked up the tray and dropped it in the hallway outside the door.

"I can order something else if you're still hungry."

She shook her head. "No, honestly, that was lovely, but I'm fine for now."

"Okay, but I'm taking you out to dinner later. No arguments. And you are going to eat a proper meal."

"Yes, boss," she said with a grin. "But let's go somewhere simple, not to one of your posh affairs."

He raised one eyebrow. "My posh affairs?"

"Yeah, you know, those places where if I dribble down my chin, the waiter gives me that look. The one that says how dare I darken their Michelin-starred door."

Cash chuckled. "Okay. I hear you."

"STOP HERE PLEASE, ISAAC," Cash said. As Isaac pulled the car into the kerb, Natalia looked out of the window.

"Gourmet Burger Kitchen?" she said, looking at Cash over her shoulder.

"You wanted down to earth, and their burgers are amazing."

A trace of a smile graced her lips. "Cash Gallagher, you never cease to amaze me."

As they walked inside, a few heads turned his way. Diners nudged each other, and muffled whispers reached his ears. Nothing he didn't live with every day. He picked a booth by the window, and once they'd made their meal choices, he placed their order at the counter. Natalia had picked a sizeable burger as well as a vanilla milkshake, and he hadn't been able to hide his pleasure.

When he set Natalia's milkshake in front of her, she gave that coy little smirk she wore when something amused her.

"What's that look for?" he said.

"You're as comfortable here as you are in those swanky places."

He laughed, reaching across the table to grab her hand. He loved the feel of it beneath his own. The touch of her skin soothed him.

When she'd finished every bite on her plate, including half his fries, Cash began to hope she'd regain her healthy appetite. Before he'd met Natalia, most of the women he casually dated preferred to mess with their food instead of eating it. It always pissed him off. He didn't see the point of ordering a meal to then spend half an hour pushing it around the plate with a fork. Natalia had been such a refreshing change. She *loved* eating. It was one of the many things he adored about her.

She yawned widely as the waitress cleared their plates. "Sorry. I don't know why I'm so tired."

"Want to go?" he said.

"Yes, please." She yawned again.

They left the restaurant hand in hand. He rubbed the pad of his thumb over her knuckles, and she smiled up at him before resting her head against his shoulder. Happiness rushed through him. He'd won her back. It was more than he deserved.

As Isaac spotted them walking towards the car, he immediately jumped out of the driver's side and opened the back door.

"Thanks, Isaac," Cash said, ushering Natalia ahead of him. "Miss McKenzie's place, please."

She glanced over her shoulder and frowned but said nothing. Only when the car began moving did she turn to face him. "You're taking me home?"

"Yes. You're tired."

"I'm not too tired if you want to go for a drink somewhere."

Cash shook his head. "It's been a long day. Get some sleep. We'll be seeing each other tomorrow." He broke into a grin as he remembered Rupe was coming home.

She tilted her head to one side. "What's that mischievous grin for?"

Cash tapped the side of his nose. "You'll have to wait and see."

Ten minutes later, Isaac pulled up outside Natalia's apartment building. Cash walked her to the front door and drew her into his arms. He was almost scared to kiss her. He worried that he wouldn't know how to leave it there—that his need for her would overwhelm all his good intentions, and he'd end up going too far when she wanted to take it slow. But there she was, her beautiful face turned up to his, her amazing midnight-blue eyes reading his soul, and her soft, full lips parted ever so slightly. Those lips begged to be kissed.

As his stomach tightened, he buried his hands in her hair and lowered his head. He paused a millimetre from her mouth, desperately wanting to savour the moment. The brief kisses they'd shared in Brighton had been full of worry and regret. This one felt different. *Was* different.

He stifled a moan as their mouths met, desire spreading out from his chest, the tips of his fingers prickling. But instead of feeling satisfied, he wanted more. Much more. He leaned into her, pinning her to the door. He moved his hips in a circular motion, and when she returned the pressure, he lost all reason.

His hand crept underneath her skirt and inched over the smooth skin of her thigh before moving higher. He cupped her fabulously tight backside, the silk of her underwear a prequel to what he knew to be the softness beneath. Slipping his hand inside her knickers, he tentatively touched her wet sex. He groaned as he slid one finger inside her, his erection lengthening as she tilted her pelvis upwards and began to move back and forth against his hand.

Oh, fuck. He was going to lose it.

Using every ounce of self-control, he tore himself away. The pounding of his heart caused a roaring rush in his ears, like the fast running water of a stream after a week of torrential rain.

"I'm sorry," he said, smoothing her skirt into place.

"What for?" Natalia's chest rose and fell, her face a mixture of confusion and frustration.

He could empathise with the latter, but he'd agreed to take it slow. Yet there he was on their first date since making up, almost fucking her outside her front door. He wasn't sixteen, for Christ's sake.

Cash leaned forward and kissed her quickly on the cheek. "Goodnight, babe."

He strode as fast as he could to his waiting car—and didn't look back.

8

Tally stared after Cash as the Mercedes sped away, her whole body trembling with desire and frustration. When he disappeared from view, she let herself in and threw her keys on the hall table.

"Em," she yelled down the hallway. "Are you here?"

When nothing but silence greeted her, she muttered, "Guess not," and stomped into the kitchen. The more time that passed, the more pissed off she became. She should have demanded Cash come back and explain himself, or run after him, or something. Anything. Instead, she'd let him put his hands all over her and then leg it without following through.

And she'd so badly wanted him to follow through.

She spotted a note on the kitchen table, reminding her Em was staying at her brother's that night. Damn, she'd forgotten. She could have done with chatting to Em about what had happened. From the time she and Cash had first slept together in Paris right up until when they broke up, sex had been the one thing that made her feel secure about his feelings. Yet now he didn't seem to want to take that final step. They'd spent all evening together, but apart from outside just then, he'd barely touched her.

Tally yanked open the fridge and poured herself a glass of wine. She wandered into the living room and flicked on the TV, but after channel surfing with nothing catching her attention, she switched it off.

Noticing she'd already finished the first glass of wine, she poured herself an ill-advised second and headed off to bed.

TALLY WOKE the next morning still in the clothes she'd worn the day before. She must have fallen asleep without getting changed for bed. She rolled onto her side, groaning as her eyes fell on the empty wine glass on her bedside table. Cursing her decision to drink that second glass, she slowly sat up, her stomach churning and queasy.

She switched on her phone and spotted two texts from Cash:

I'm sorry I left the way I did. I want to respect your wishes, but I'm only a man after all. I love you, C. xxx

I'll pick you up at ten. I've got a surprise for you. xxx

She glanced at the clock. Nine forty-five. *Shit!*

She raced into the bathroom and managed to shower and dress in record time. She dragged a brush through her hair—she'd have preferred to wash it—added minimal makeup, and was in the middle of putting on her shoes when a knock at the door interrupted her. She finished fastening the buckle, her heart thumping out of her chest as she stepped over to the door. She wasn't sure whether anticipation or all the rushing around had made her out of breath.

She opened the door and got her answer when she felt her pulse jolt.

He'd dressed casually but still pulled off a style that would rival most models. Her gaze raked over his chest, the flat, hard muscle visible through the navy-blue T-shirt, which he'd matched with a pair of boot-cut jeans that clung to his defined thigh muscles. Even with a baseball cap pulled low over his forehead, his eyes were still visible—soft grey, sparkling with mischievous thought.

He curved his hands around her waist and leaned down to kiss her. "Morning, sweetness," he said, his lips still tantalisingly close to hers. "Did you get my text last night?"

"No, not until this morning. I fell asleep."

"I'm sorry with the way I dashed off, but..." He left the sentence hanging, and she was about to question him when he gave her a boyish grin. "So... ready for your surprise?"

Deciding now wasn't the right time for a heavy discussion about sex—or the lack of it— she smiled back at him. "I am."

"Okay, let's go."

"No Isaac?" she said as they walked across the street to where he'd parked the car.

"Not today." Cash unlocked the doors. "You'll have to make do with me."

Tally rolled her eyes as she climbed in. "Bummer."

Cash laughed as he filtered the car into the flow of vehicles. The light traffic was unusual for a workday. As they headed out of the city, the traffic became even sparser. They'd been driving for about thirty minutes when Cash pulled up outside a large country-style house and cut the engine.

"I recognise this place," she said, peering out of the window. "This is where you brought me that first day."

"I did," Cash said, his eyes shining as they met hers. "How times have changed."

They got out of the car, and as he walked around to her side, he knitted their fingers together. The door was already unlocked, and Cash pushed it open.

"We're here," he shouted down the hallway. Resting his hands on her hips, he steered her in front of him towards the kitchen. When she spotted her surprise, she squealed.

"Rupe," she said, throwing herself into his outstretched arms.

"Hello, my darling girl," Rupe said, briefly hugging her before holding her at arm's length. "What the fuck has happened to you? It's like cuddling a skeleton."

She scowled. "You sound as bad as him," she said, jerking her head backwards.

"Well, as much as it pains me to admit it, he's right. For God's sake, we need to get a few pies down you."

She waved her hand dismissively. "When did you get back?"

"This morning. Clearly, I need to be around to make sure he doesn't fuck it up again."

"Thanks for the vote of confidence," Cash said, giving Rupe a playful punch on the arm.

"So this is your house?" Tally said to Rupe as she shot a glance over to where Cash had kissed her. He caught her eye and cheekily winked, and her stomach tightened as she remembered how he'd made her feel when he'd touched her the first time.

"Yep. Come on, I'll give you the guided tour."

Rupe looped an arm over her shoulder and led her out of the kitchen. The house was huge and traditional in style. It didn't have the homeyness of Cash's place in Northern Ireland. Cash's house was enormous but still managed to be cosy. Rupe's had the stiff feel of old-money English aristocracy.

"Did you rent this place out to film *Downton Abbey*?" she said with a grin.

Rupe laughed. "I should have. I'd have made a fortune."

"What do you do with all this space?" she said as Rupe opened a door to yet another living room.

"To be honest, I can't remember the last time I was in this room."

Tally tilted her head to one side. "Then why do you live here?"

"I don't really. I just use it as my London base. I prefer to spend time on the boat."

"You've got more money than sense," she said.

Rupe nudged her shoulder playfully. "Wouldn't be hard, darling. I don't have a lot of sense."

She laughed as he led her back to the kitchen. "Shall I make us something to eat?" she said, relieved when Cash and Rupe agreed instantly. After the queasy start to the day, she didn't fancy trying out her stomach's resilience on one of their creations.

They sat down to eat at the kitchen table. Cash and Rupe were bantering like brothers who pretended they despised the other. Enormously contented, Tally watched them score points off each other and smiled at the one-upmanship. God, she'd missed this.

"When are you going back on the circuit?" Rupe said out of the blue. She'd been dying to ask that same question but hadn't yet plucked up the courage.

Cash's gaze locked on hers. "That's up to Natalia."

Her jaw slackened. "Me? Why me?"

"Because I want to make sure we're okay before my career takes over my life again."

Her skin prickled, the sensation reaching her fingertips. If she'd ever questioned his love, that single statement smashed those doubts into a million pieces. As Tally scrabbled around for an appropriate response, considering they weren't alone, Rupe must have read the situation because he got to his feet and said, "I'll leave you to it," before disappearing into the hallway.

Tally gave Cash an embarrassed grin. "Poor Rupe, being chased out of his own kitchen."

Cash pushed his chair back but remained seated. He patted his leg. "Come here."

She stood up and straddled his thighs, lowering herself into his lap.

"Kiss me," he murmured.

She curved her hands around his face, his scruff tickling her palms. She lowered her mouth to his, but as she tried to increase the intensity, she felt him holding back. She broke off their kiss. "Cash, don't you want me anymore?"

His hand stilled from where he'd been rubbing her back, and a frown flickered across his face. "Are you crazy? Of course I do."

"Then why did you leave the way you did last night?" She winced at the desperation in her voice. "And why are you holding back now?"

He caressed her cheek with the back of his hand. "Baby, you said you wanted to take it slow."

Her fingertips teased his hair. "But not physically. I want you, Cash. I *need* you. If you want to make sure we're okay, that's the way to do it."

His right thumb skated over her bottom lip, and she parted her mouth in anticipation. He leaned in and kissed her, his tongue slowly twirling with hers. Her insides twisted, and she moved closer. He grew hard, and she rocked against him. When he groaned into her mouth, warmth spread throughout her chest.

She broke their kiss and gazed into his eyes. The depth of feeling he showed humbled her. And then she knew. She held his fragile heart as tightly as he held hers. They were bound together by love. Both would be easily destroyed should that love be torn away.

Cash tipped her off his lap and clasped her hand. As he headed towards the stairs, Tally tugged him back.

"Where are we going?"

He glanced down at her. "I'm going to show you how okay we are."

Despite the thrill of desire that swept through her body, she hesitated. "We're at Rupe's."

"So?"

"We can't."

"Sure we can." He held onto her hand and took off upstairs.

When they reached the top floor, which she hadn't explored with Rupe earlier, Cash pushed open a door that led into a bedroom decorated in Edwardian style. The inside was fresh and light, a complete contrast to the dark interior of the rest of the house.

"I'm here so often Rupe finally gave me my own room," Cash said by way of explanation. "Although when I had it redecorated, he moaned like a bitch because it didn't go with the rest of the house." He shrugged. "Shouldn't have told me it was my bloody room."

Tally chuckled, but as Cash snaked his arms around her waist, kicking the door closed with his foot, she stopped laughing. His face grew serious, and as his gaze slowly grazed her body, she shuddered in anticipation.

She half expected him to lunge at her, but instead, he feathered his hands up and down her sides before burying them in her hair. He pulled a lock over her shoulder and twisted it around his finger before letting go of the curl he'd created and moving on to the next one. His eyes never left hers. Her breath hitched when his knuckles skimmed her cheek, the touch tender and soft.

"I almost lost you," he whispered.

His mouth cut off her intended reply. His kiss began in a slow, almost exploratory way as his lips moved over hers. She wrapped her arms around his neck and hitched her legs over his hips, his answering groan exactly the response she was looking for. His hands curved around her backside, holding her in place as his tongue surged into her mouth. As she rubbed herself against his erection, he tore his mouth from hers, his lips fastening onto her neck instead.

"I thought I wasn't good enough, ace," she said. "That you'd changed your mind about us getting back together."

His lips stilled, and he eased her legs to the floor. As he tilted his head backwards, his grey eyes were stormy, and he quivered with... anger? Annoyance? Irritation?

"Jesus," he muttered, sweeping a hand down the back of his head. "I fucking hate myself right now."

"No." She cupped his face, her thumbs caressing his cheeks. "This is my issue, ace. Mine. Not yours. I..." She shrugged. "It doesn't matter."

He exhaled on a shudder, and he shook his head slowly. Her hands fell to her sides. Why hadn't she kept her bloody mouth shut? If she had, they'd still be kissing. Instead, she'd ruined what would undoubtedly have been mind-blowing make-up sex by voicing hang-ups that Cash had done nothing but reassure her about. *What the hell is wrong with me?* Sometimes, she swung along the spectrum from certainty to doubt so fast it made her head spin.

"Come with me," he said, ignoring her confused look and leading her to the far side of the enormous bedroom. He pushed open an already-ajar door and stepped into a dressing room. He drew her in front of a period-design full-length cheval mirror mounted on a rectangular base. He reached around her and tilted the mirror backwards until they were both visible. His hands briefly rested on her shoulders before moving to deftly unfasten every button on her shirt. As his fingers brushed her skin, she trembled, and her lips parted. He tossed her shirt to one side and then fell to his knees and peeled off her jeans. Her underwear quickly followed until she was fully naked. She bit down on her lip, the pain momentarily distracting her from wanting to wrap her arms around herself.

He clasped her shoulders. "Why can't you see how beautiful you are?"

She shrugged. "I don't know."

Cash sighed softly, blowing warm air onto the back of her neck. "There have been times I thought we made progress, then something happens and you start up again with thinking you're not good enough for me. I blame myself fully for the latest relapse in your confidence."

As she opened her mouth to speak, he pressed his forefinger to her lips and fixed his gaze on hers in the mirror.

"I love you so much, more than I ever thought myself capable of loving anyone. I'm barely half a person without you in my life. I want you to stop with the self-loathing, because when you attack yourself, you attack me and the depth of my feelings for you."

Tally forced air into lungs that seemed to have collapsed. Her eyes fell closed, but they snapped open again when Cash tugged hard on one of her nipples. Their gazes collided in the mirror, and his smile came slow and sexy.

"Eyes open. I'm going to show you what I see when I make love to you."

Her core involuntarily tightened, and she squeezed her thighs together. A moan tumbled from her lips as Cash cupped her breasts and twisted her nipples between his thumb and forefinger. A rush of liquid heat pooled between her legs, and her head rocked onto his shoulder as she arched her back, desperate for more.

"Eyes on the mirror, Natalia," he demanded.

She lifted her head and met his gaze once more. He'd shucked his clothes, although she didn't know when, and his muscles rippled beneath his skin. His erection was hard against her backside, and she shimmied against him.

"Witch," he whispered with a chuckle.

His hand slid south, moving slowly over her ribcage, her stomach. He pressed his thumb hard on her clit as he slipped his middle finger inside her. Every nerve in her body sparked to life, and she clenched around him. A hiss left his lips as his eyes trailed over her body, scorching her, branding her with his gaze. Slipping a second finger inside her, he kept up a relentless rhythm, and the eroticism of watching his fingers disappearing and reappearing brought her to the cusp of orgasm. She moaned softly.

"Keep your eyes open, baby," he said. "I want you to see what you look like when you come."

Embarrassment swamped her, but she fought the urge to close her eyes. He repetitively circled his thumb against her clit before pressing down hard, and like a volcano erupting, she climaxed, her muscles rippling against his fingers.

"Oh, God," she murmured as an intense warmth raced down her legs. She curled her toes, and her knees trembled. A faint sheen of sweat broke out on her brow as he increased the pressure, making sure he drew every ounce of pleasure from her. As her breathing slowed, she met his smile with one of her own.

"Admit it," Cash whispered in her ear. "That was hot."

Heat rushed to her cheeks, but when she nodded in agreement, the look of pride and pleasure on his face swept away her embarrassment. He circled her waist and pressed his thumbs into the small of her back.

"Lean forward, and hold onto the mirror. Don't worry about it falling. It weighs a ton."

His fingers gripped her hips, and he lifted her backside in the air and, in one thrust, pushed himself inside. The aftershocks of her orgasm were still pulsing through her body, and Cash groaned, his teeth lightly grazing her shoulder as he drilled into her. Their eyes met in the mirror. Cash clenched his jaw tight. A steady pulse beat in his cheek, and a faint tinge of red bled into his skin with the effort of controlling himself.

Tally tightened her grip on the mirror and pushed backwards as he thrust forward. The noise he made thrilled her. She loved how much she could turn him on. During these moments, all her worries and fears melted away, and she could allow the person beneath to shine. She clenched her core hard, and when he responded by almost painfully digging his fingers into her hips, she knew he was close.

"Let go," she said.

A long, drawn-out groan spilled from his lips as he climaxed.

He buried his face in her neck, his lips searingly hot against her skin. Tally released her grip on the mirror and reached around to caress his hips before dropping her hands to his arse. She squeezed.

He laughed, the sound rumbling through his chest as he pulled out of her. He eased her around to face him. His hands curved around her waist, and he grazed her lips with a brief kiss. "Are we okay?"

She nodded. "We're okay. Now, promise me you're playing Monte Carlo."

Cash nuzzled her neck. "I'm wherever you are, sweetness."

"Oh, good. I've always wanted to go to Monaco."

9

"Aren't you fucking ready yet?" Cash stood by the front door, jangling his keys and tapping his foot. If someone broke the news to him that Rupe was a woman, he wouldn't be surprised, based on how long his friend took to get ready.

"Almost," Rupe said, trying to balance on one foot while putting on his shoes. "You only saw her a few hours ago. I'm sure you can survive being five minutes late."

Cash held back from saying what he thought, but if Rupe didn't get his shoe on in ten seconds, Cash would bloody do it for him. He rolled his eyes as Rupe hopped about, finally letting out an irritated sigh. "For fuck's sake, sit down, and put them on."

"All right, all right. Don't get your knickers in a twist." Rupe finally managed to lace up his shoes and headed for the front door. He cocked his head. "You coming or what?"

Cash ground his teeth. "You are one irritating bastard."

"And you're a grumpy fucker, but you don't hear me complaining every five minutes." Rupe held the door open, giving Cash a shove as he walked through.

Isaac dropped them off at Natalia's flat a little after eight. Despite his driver's protestations, Cash insisted he take the rest of the night off. Cash and Rupe could easily get a cab home, and Isaac's daughter was in town for a few days. It would do the man good to catch up with his family, especially as he'd soon be away from home for weeks at a time when Cash went back on the circuit.

Natalia must have been watching out for them because by the time they'd climbed out of the car, she was already standing at the front door.

"You're late," she said with the special smile she seemed to keep only for him. A warm glow spread through his body, and his fingers itched to touch her.

He leaned forward and gave her a quick kiss. "You're hot."

"You're excused," she said with a soft giggle. "Anyway, I bet it was Rupe's fault you're late."

"And how do you figure that?" Rupe said.

"Because she knows you well." Cash pressed Rupe through the door first, which allowed him to sweep his hand over Natalia's backside in private. "I can't wait to get my hands on you," he whispered in her ear. "Let's hope these two get on so we can leave early."

She wrapped her arms around his neck, standing on tiptoes to reach his lips. Her kiss was light but full of promise, and he shuddered.

"I'd like that," she murmured.

Cash took her hand as Emmalee appeared in the hallway. Natalia's flatmate scowled at Cash, but her face smoothed as she greeted his friend.

"Hi, I'm Emmalee—Em. You must be Rupe."

"Yeah." Rupe ignored her outstretched hand as he moved in and gave her a kiss on the cheek instead. "Thanks for inviting me over."

A faint tinge of red bled into Emmalee's cheeks at Rupe's

trademark overfamiliarity. "Well, technically, I didn't. Tally did. But regardless, you're welcome. Come on. Let's get you a drink."

She studiously ignored Cash as he and Natalia followed them into the kitchen. Natalia headed to the stove and gave something a stir.

"Smells good," Rupe said, sniffing the air.

"Paella." She held out a spoonful, her free hand underneath the cutlery to catch any drips. "Here, taste."

Rupe slurped at the spoon before smacking his lips. "More pepper."

Natalia grabbed the peppermill and added more to the pan. Her backside wiggled as she stirred the contents, and Cash struggled to avert his gaze until Emmalee coughed. He dragged his attention away from Natalia's perfect arse to find Emmalee glaring at him. She stole a surreptitious glance at Natalia, who was busy joking with Rupe, before leaning across the table.

"Don't think all is forgotten," she whispered in a low enough tone to keep it between them. "Just because Tally's forgiven you doesn't mean I have."

Cash raised an eyebrow. "Good to know," he drawled.

Her expression darkened. "Just as arrogant as before, I see," she hissed.

Cash expelled an irritated sigh. "Look," he said, leaning closer. "I get it. You're pissed, and you have every right to be. She's your friend, and I hurt her. I know you don't like me, but unfortunately for you, Natalia does. So you and I are going to have to find a way past this before we put unfair pressure on her."

Emmalee opened her mouth to come back at him, but Natalia chose that moment to glance over her shoulder. A frown drifted across her face. Emmalee must have spotted it, because she straightened and passed him a bottle of red wine and a corkscrew.

"Here, make yourself useful and open that."

Cash gave the label a cursory glance. A half-decent Merlot.

He opened it and took a sniff. Not bad. He poured four glasses and handed them round.

"Em, pass me those plates, would you?" Natalia held a hand out behind her without looking around. "I hope no one minds eating straight away. The rice will overcook if I leave it for much longer."

Cash stared pointedly at Rupe, who flashed a wry grin. "No problem for me, darling," Rupe said as he sat at the table and held his knife and fork upright, like an expectant child.

"No shit," Cash said. "Especially as it was your fault we were late."

"What was the problem?" Natalia said, placing two dishes of paella in front of him and Rupe.

"Rupe's a woman in disguise," Cash said. "Takes about three hours to get ready, although looking at him, you'd wonder why."

Natalia giggled. "You should give him a few tips, Em."

Rupe threw his hands in the air. "What's this—pick on Rupe night?"

"You make it too easy, buddy," Cash said.

As the evening progressed, the tension between him and Emmalee lessened, although he could tell her softening was more for Natalia's benefit than any real truce. On the other hand, Emmalee and Rupe got on so well they could have known each other all their lives. Cash watched for signs of a budding romance, but it seemed much more of a brother-sister relationship than anything else.

"Are you going back on tour soon, Cash?" Emmalee asked, glancing between him and Natalia. She seemed to be gauging Natalia's reaction, although Cash couldn't be sure.

"Yeah. Monte Carlo in a couple of weeks, but I'm taking Natalia to Northern Ireland with me first."

"You are?" Natalia said, dropping her dessert spoon with a clang.

"Yes." He tilted his head, mirroring her posture. "I made you a promise, and I'm going to make good on it."

Emmalee sighed heavily, her arms crossed over her chest. "She's only just got home, and now you're dragging her off again."

"Emmalee," Natalia said with a tinge of warning in her tone. "That's enough."

Cash covered her hand with his and squeezed. "It's okay, sweetness." He fixed his gaze on Emmalee. "If you've got something to say, then let's hear it."

Temporary truce over, Emmalee's cold stare locked onto his. "I'm just interested in what's so urgent in Northern Ireland. What did you promise her, Cash? Not to go around kissing strange women anymore?"

Natalia caught her breath as Cash shot a furious look at Emmalee. Even Rupe decided fiddling with the edge of the tablecloth was preferable to making eye contact with anyone.

Emmalee's cheeks reddened as she realised she'd gone too far. "Shit. I didn't mean that. It just slipped out."

Natalia fidgeted beside him. She kept threading her napkin through her fingers, undoubtedly waiting for him to explode. He clutched her hand, stilling her.

"Be careful judging what you don't understand, Emmalee," he said, purposely keeping his tone even, though he'd gladly have strangled her.

She ducked her head, the blush spreading to her neck. "Sorry. Never did know when to keep my mouth shut, did I, Tal?"

Natalia didn't respond. Instead, she turned to him. "When do we leave?"

He brought her trembling hands to his lips and kissed first one, then the other. "Tonight."

Natalia nodded and got to her feet. She gathered the dishes together as Emmalee scrambled out of her chair and followed her to the sink.

"I'm sorry, babes," she said, rubbing Natalia's arm. "Really, I am."

Natalia wrenched her shoulder upwards, and Emmalee's arm fell to her side. Natalia spoke over her shoulder. "Can you both give us a minute?"

Cash nodded and cocked his head at Rupe. "We'll be outside."

ALTHOUGH THE DECISION TO fly to Ireland immediately had been impulsive, Cash knew it was the right one. Natalia hadn't shared what she'd said to Emmalee, but given the grim expression on her face when she'd joined him outside, he was thankful Emmalee had been on the receiving end of her wrath rather than him.

As the plane descended, his stomach churned, and he squeezed his eyes tightly shut.

"Almost there, ace."

He briefly smiled at the nickname and gripped her hand as the plane sank another few hundred feet.

"Fuck," he gritted out as his stomach rolled. He squeezed her so tightly she winced. "How close?"

She glanced out of the window. "Two thousand feet max. Won't be long now."

He didn't let go of her hand throughout the rest of the descent, although he did loosen his grip. After about ten minutes, the wheels touched down. As the captain throttled back, the engines screamed, and the momentum threw him forward slightly in his seat.

"Maybe we should get you on one of those fear-of-flying courses."

"Done 'em," he gritted out. "Did fuck all for me."

As soon as the captain switched off the seatbelt sign, Cash bounded from his seat. He never could wait to get off planes, although at least he didn't have to suffer commercial airlines. Trying to cope with other passengers at the same time as his fear of flying? *Urgh*. The thought made him shudder.

Patrick, a driver he occasionally used when Isaac wasn't around, was waiting at the bottom of the steps as they descended. The driver was okay, but he didn't know Cash nearly as well as Isaac did. Talked shit a bit too much for Cash's liking. Isaac always managed to tune in to Cash's moods and act accordingly, whereas Patrick seemed to have only one mood—too fucking happy.

"Mr Gallagher," he enthused. "Great to see you, sir." His gaze fell on Natalia and lingered. "Miss," he finally said.

Cash set his jaw. "If you've finished staring rather inappropriately at my girlfriend, Patrick, perhaps you can put the bags in the car."

Patrick's face reddened, and he muttered, "My apologies, sir," before grabbing the bags.

Cash seized Natalia's arm as she glared at him, her eyes full of reproach. After they'd climbed into the car, Cash slammed the door and immediately put up the privacy screen.

"Was there any need to embarrass him like that?" she said, folding her arms across her chest.

"Yes, there was. And next time, if there is such a thing, he'll know his fucking place."

Natalia cast him a withering gaze and turned to stare out of the window, her shoulders set in disapproval. Cash let out a soft sigh. Maybe he had been a little rude to Patrick, but he couldn't help the surge of jealousy whenever anyone looked at Natalia, especially the way Patrick had. Cash was the only person allowed to look at her like that.

He switched on his phone, and it immediately pinged with an incoming text from Emmalee. He swiped the screen, and his eyebrows shot up as he read her message:

Cash, I'm sorry my big mouth made you both leave so soon. Tally's forgiven you, and if she can, then so can I. Friends? Em xx

P.S. Tally's bloody mad at me. Can you use some of your famous charm and calm her down a bit?

P.P.S. Rupe is an absolute card. I love him.

Cash began to laugh.

Natalia glanced over at him, her face still set with exasperation. "Who's that?"

"Emmalee." He showed her his phone, and despite her annoyance, she chuckled when she read the texts.

"I had a feeling those two would get along. Peas in a pod."

"Yeah," Cash said. "Or pains in the arse."

"I didn't exactly hold back before," she said with a grimace. "Em's intentions are good, but sometimes she treats me like I'm five."

"She loves you," he said with a shrug, typing out a quick text in return. "I've told her she's forgiven, and she's welcome to keep Rupe."

"I'll call her tomorrow."

Cash knitted their fingers together. "Am I forgiven too?"

Her mouth creased in thought. "You can be very cutting at times. The poor man didn't know what to do with himself."

"I didn't like the way he looked at you."

She let out a sigh. "Are you going to embarrass every man who glances my way?"

"Yes."

Her lips twitched. "What am I going to do with you?"

Cash grinned. "Not sure, sweetness. But regardless, you're stuck with me."

When they reached home, Cash helped Natalia out of the car. Patrick kept his gaze well averted. Cash dismissed him with a curt nod, grabbed their bags, and opened the front door.

"Tired?"

Natalia nodded, yawning on cue. It was already past midnight, and a fun night had turned rather quickly into an unexpectedly stressful one. Cash dropped their bags in the hallway.

"We can unpack tomorrow," he said. "Let's go to bed."

They trudged upstairs, and Cash flicked on the bedside lamps as Natalia wandered over to the window. She stared into the blackness, her shoulders bowed in defeat.

He followed her and wrapped his arms around her waist. "You okay, babe?"

She sighed softly. "I've had better evenings."

He rested his chin on her shoulder. "I don't like it when you're sad."

She twisted in his arms. "I'm not sad. I just don't like arguing with my best friend."

He bent his head and brushed his lips over hers, desire spreading through his chest when she kissed him back.

"Your pace, Natalia," he murmured against her cool lips, which were chilled from the night air. "You decide."

She stepped away and, holding his hands, backed towards the bed. "If only every decision was as easy."

10

When Tally woke the next morning, it took her a few seconds to remember where she was. She rolled onto her side and squinted. Cash was lying beside her, one arm flung over his head, fast asleep.

That's right—I'm at home.

Her eyes opened wide. Home? *Is that what I really think*? She flopped onto her back and shifted her gaze to the ceiling. Her mind turned over and over. As much as she'd told Cash she wanted to take things slowly, her insistence was because she *thought* she should, rather than being what she *actually* wanted. Now that they were back together, she realised she didn't want to take things slowly. She wanted to rush headlong into the unknown with all the worry and risk and excitement that would bring.

Swinging her legs over the side of the bed, she scanned the room for her stuff before remembering Cash had left the bags downstairs the previous night. She wandered into his dressing room and threw on one of his shirts. She loved wearing Cash's clothes. They made her feel even closer to him than she already felt. She sniffed the sleeve, savouring Cash's unique scent, which reminded her of thyme mixed with citrus fruit. When she walked back into the bedroom, he still hadn't woken, so she decided to go downstairs and grab a coffee.

Cash's kitchen was exactly as she remembered—large but welcoming. Tally put the kettle on and began opening cupboards. On the fifth attempt, she found a jar of instant coffee. She put a couple of heaped spoonfuls into two mugs and grabbed milk from the fridge. She was midpour when a light tap on the kitchen door made her spin around, spilling the milk in the process.

"Shit," she said, glancing around for something to mop it up with.

"Here, allow me." A woman in her early sixties with short, greying hair wandered over to the far side of the kitchen and removed a few sheets of kitchen paper off a stand. She bent down and mopped up the spillage.

"You must be Anna. Cash's housekeeper."

"I am," Anna said, speaking in the same warm Irish lilt as Cash. She had kind eyes and a homely face. She smiled and held out her hand. "And you must be Natalia."

"Tally, please," she said, shaking Anna's hand. "Sorry, I wasn't expecting anyone to be here. Otherwise, I'd have dressed more appropriately." She shifted from one foot to another, tugging on the tails of Cash's shirt.

"Not at all," Anna said as she crossed to the waste bin and tossed the milk-soaked paper towel inside. "I'm the one who's intruding. Can I get you anything?"

"No. I'm only making coffee, then I'll be out of your way."

Tally couldn't help feeling self-conscious. She'd never been around staff and didn't know how to behave. She willed the kettle to boil faster as Anna busied herself around the kitchen.

As Tally set off with two mugs of coffee, Anna smiled brightly. "Shall I make breakfast for you and Cash?"

Tally mumbled something about him not being awake yet and shot out of the room.

When she nudged the bedroom door open with her hip, Cash was lying on his side, his palm holding his head up. He gave a slow, sexy smile that made her knees tremble.

"Morning, baby." He raked her with his gaze. "Nice outfit."

"I've met Anna," Tally said in a reproachful tone. "You could have warned me she'd be here."

"And where's the fun in that?" He waited for her to put the mugs down before snagging her around the waist. He pulled her horizontally across his body, and she giggled as he covered her face and neck in kisses. "I never get sick of seeing you in my clothes. It's almost as good as seeing you out of yours."

"Well, if Anna wasn't here, I might parade around like this all day." She slowly trailed her toe up and down his leg.

"In that case, I'll send her packing."

She chuckled. "What do you have planned for us today?" she said, knowing lazing around doing nothing wasn't Cash's style.

He tilted his head to one side. "I thought we might go and visit Mum."

Tally inhaled quickly. Although visiting Cash's mum was the sole reason they'd come to Ireland the night before, she hadn't expected him to suggest doing it quite so soon. Nerves gripped her insides, and her palms became clammy. What would she find to say to a woman she didn't know—and who'd been in a coma for almost thirteen years?

"Are you sure?" she said, her voice barely above a whisper.

"Totally. Let's find out if she approves," he said with a wink.

Cash's attempt at a joke did nothing to calm her down, and she must have been wearing her fear on her face because he clipped her under the chin.

"Stop worrying. She'll love you like everyone else does."

"Kinga didn't," Tally said with a grimace.

"Don't put me in a bad mood by mentioning that woman," Cash said, his brows knitted together in a deep frown.

"Have you heard from her at all?"

He shook his head, his lips pressed into a firm line. "Lucky for her."

Tally shuddered. Cash could be fearsome when crossed, and now that he'd shared the story of his violent childhood, she completely understood his reaction to Kinga hitting her.

"Come on," Cash said, bounding out of bed. "Let's get ready, and then you can meet the only woman, apart from you and Anna, that I give a shit about."

A MODERN RED-BRICK house came into view, familiar only because of the photographs of Cash kissing Gracie. Tally's teeth repetitively grazed her bottom lip until Cash cradled her chin, stopping her. "You worry too much."

He helped her out of the car, his arm comfortingly around her waist. They walked towards the front door, but before they got there, Gracie appeared.

"Hi," she said with an affectionate sweep of her hand down Cash's arm. "Someone is going to be happy to see you." She turned to Tally and smiled. "You must be Natalia. I can't tell you how delighted I am to meet you."

Tally glanced out of the corner of her eye at Cash and tilted her head. He caught her confused look and shrugged.

"You too," she said, shaking Gracie's outstretched hand.

"How is she?" Cash asked.

"Making improvements every day. She continues to astound her doctors. Your mother has the most immense strength, Cash. Come and see for yourself."

Cash's hand was warm and steady at the base of Tally's back as he ushered her through the door.

Tally bit back her surprise at the normalcy of the house. She wasn't sure what she had expected, but as they walked down the hallway, she spotted a large kitchen, a living room, and a fully kitted-out office. And at the back, overlooking a pretty garden with colourful borders and a neat lawn, was a bedroom that would have fit right in with an exclusive private hospital.

Over by the window, half-sitting up in a bed with guardrails on either side, lay Cash's mum. She must have heard them as soon as they entered, because she twisted her head, her eyes shining as her gaze fell first on Cash and then on Tally.

"At last," she said, her voice stronger and more assured than Tally had expected. She lifted her hand off the bed in a half-wave, and Cash inhaled sharply.

"She couldn't do that last time I visited," he whispered.

Tally squeezed his arm as tears pricked at her eyes. She'd assumed visiting Cash's mum would be quite emotional but hadn't been prepared for the intensity of it.

Cash pulled a couple of chairs close to the bedside and nodded for her to sit. He reached over and kissed his mum on the cheek. "Mum, this is Natalia. My girlfriend." The pride in his voice as he introduced her made Tally's heart soar.

"Hi, Mrs Gallagher."

"Rachael," she said. "*Mrs Gallagher* makes me feel about a hundred."

Cash glanced over at Tally. "I'm sure Mum wants to hear all about you. I'll leave you two to have a chat, and I'll grab a couple of coffees."

"That would be nice," Rachael said.

Tally gave Cash a hard stare as a wave of panic gripped her, but he simply clasped her shoulder and then left the room.

"It's awful, isn't it, meeting parents for the first time?" Rachael said, gracing her with one of the most sincere smiles Tally had ever seen.

"Yes, it is."

Rachael patted her hand. "Don't be nervous. Tell me how you two met. Cash has mentioned but not in any detail. Men," she added with a roll of her eyes.

Tally laughed, instantly relaxing under Rachael's warm gaze. "I'm a journalist, and I was asked to cover an event Cash was holding as a fundraiser for his foundation. Well, 'asked' is a bit of a lie. I begged my editor to let me do it. I knew Cash hated journalists, so I used my press pass to gain entry. Once inside, I hid it in my bag."

Rachael chuckled. "I like your creativity."

"When he found out... well, let's just say he made his feelings clear. But he forgave me in the end, and here we are."

Rachael nodded sagely. "Do you like being a journalist?"

"Yes. It's all I ever wanted to be growing up, although"—she shrugged—"I'm not so sure it's as important to me as it once was."

Rachael squeezed her hand. "It's crucial to have something other than a man in your life. I can tell you love my son, but don't make your relationship with him the centre of your universe." Her eyes lost focus for a moment, then she shook her head. "I did that. It was a mistake."

Tally chewed the inside of her cheek, unsure how to respond. "Meeting Cash is the best thing that has ever happened to me, but I studied hard for too long to ever give up journalism."

"Good," Rachael said.

"I do love him, though. I want you to know that."

Rachael's whole expression softened. "He's easy to love."

"He is. Complex, and difficult to get close to, but once you dig beneath the face he shows the world, he's one of the warmest and most caring people I know." She cracked a smile. "He has a fearsome temper, though."

"He was the same as a boy. He'd get these flashes of frustration, usually when he was trying to do something he was having trouble mastering, but they never lasted long."

Tally kept quiet. Cash's temper was more than flashes of frustration. The boy Rachael had known must have been different from the man he became, and Tally wouldn't have been surprised if the guilt he felt had a lot to do with his anger issues.

"He never stops talking about you when he visits or calls. I think my boy's in love," Rachael said.

A warm glow spread through Tally's limbs, making her skin tingle deliciously. "I'm the luckiest girl in the world."

Rachael pushed herself a little more upright, waving Tally away as she stood to help. "So tell me about your family."

Tally held back a wince. "My dad died when I was sixteen. Cancer."

"Oh, that's terrible. That must have been very difficult to deal with at such a young age."

She nodded. "I still miss him."

"And what about your mum?"

Tally clamped down on the usual flood of pain her mother's abandonment caused. "She walked out on me when I was four," she said in a matter-of-fact tone.

Rachael covered her mouth with her hand. "I'm so sorry."

She shrugged. "It's old news. It was harder on my father than me, I think. I don't remember her at all."

"How are my two favourite ladies getting along?" Cash's timely appearance stopped the conversation from taking a melancholy turn. He handed a cup of coffee to Tally.

"Famously," Rachael said.

Cash took over the talking. Tally sat back and listened as he filled his mum in about his plans for getting back on the tennis circuit. After an hour or so, Rachael's eyelids began to droop, and as if she had a sixth sense, Gracie swept into the room.

"Time for her nap now, Cash. You can come back tomorrow."

"Okay." He leaned down and kissed Rachael on the cheek. "See you in the morning, Mum."

Rachael's eyes briefly flickered open before closing again. "See you tomorrow," she murmured, a half-smile gracing her lips as she fell asleep.

Cash was quiet as they drove back to his house, and Tally left him alone with his thoughts. She'd learned that when he became introspective, it was better to give him space until he was ready to talk.

When he pulled up in front of the house, he cut the engine but made no move to get out of the car, his gaze firmly fixed on a faraway point in the distance. Tally patiently waited, and after a second or two, he unclipped his seat belt and twisted his body around to face her.

"I know what I said about respecting your wishes to take it slow, but visiting Mum today reaffirms how fragile life is."

His hands reached around the back of her neck, and he eased her close until their foreheads were touching. "I can't bear the thought of being separated from you even for one day. Move in with me. I'm begging you."

Tally exhaled on a shudder. "Yes," she said, vocalising the decision she'd already made. "I'll move in."

11

A s Rupe's yacht moored in Monte Carlo harbour, Emmalee's excited squeal made Cash wince. He covered his ears and scowled at her.

"Oh wow, this is awesome," Emmalee said, leaning over the side of the boat, completely oblivious to Cash's black stare. "What a view."

Cash glanced over at Natalia standing beside Emmalee. No better view than that. The curves she'd lost when they'd split were finally coming back. His forehead smoothed as he swept a gaze over her bottom—tucked into a pair of faded denim shorts —then up and over her flared hips and firm breasts. Memories of that morning invaded his thoughts. His girl sure knew what to do with her body to drive him crazy.

She caught his eye, and he beckoned her over.

"Thanks for suggesting I bring Em this week," she said, her soft lips brushing his cheek with a kiss.

Cash curved an arm around her waist. "It'll be good for you to have company while I'm on the practice court. I'm going to have to put in some serious hours to avoid disgracing myself next week."

Her face fell, and Cash sighed as he clipped a finger under her chin. "How many times, Natalia? This is *my* fault. Not yours. *My* decision not to play the US. Besides, at least it will give the others a slight chance."

She grinned, the moment of angst over. "You know, ace, I'm thinking of getting you a How to Build Your Self-Esteem and Confidence course for your birthday."

He laughed. Natalia often teased him about his supreme self-esteem, and she was right. He rarely lacked confidence, although he did have concerns about this week. He hadn't played competitively in almost two months. The time off court was bound to have an impact, but he couldn't exactly voice his concerns to Natalia.

"Okay, lovebirds. Let's hit the town." Rupe disembarked, quickly followed by Emmalee.

Cash only had that day to enjoy Monte Carlo, and he needed to make the most of it, because starting the next day, Brad and Jamie were going to kick his arse from there to Ireland. His body was already softer, lacking muscular depth, and he knew from experience his sharpness was off. Monte Carlo was a fiercely fought tournament, attended by the best of the best, and if he didn't work his bollocks off in practice, he'd be humiliated on court.

For the first time ever, he'd allowed his personal life to eclipse his professional one. Natalia and their breakup, his mum coming out of the coma, the stress of winning Natalia back again—all of it had affected his tennis. Tomorrow, he had to start to focus again. He'd worked too hard to let another fucker be number one.

He was number one.

"Oy, Cash," Rupe shouted. "You coming or what?"

All three had already disembarked and were waiting on the quayside, Rupe with his arms folded and a look of exasperation on his face.

"Fuck's sake, Witters. Keep your hair on," Cash muttered as he took his time disembarking, much to Rupe's further annoyance.

Like most places in the world, Monte Carlo wasn't new to Cash, but as he watched Natalia bounce along, her hand tucked in Emmalee's arm, her face flushed with excitement, he was transported back to their first date in Paris. She'd given him the best gift imaginable—new eyes to see the world through.

Later, as the four of them walked back to the boat after a long day of sightseeing, Rupe said, "What should we do tonight? Casino?"

Cash glanced down at Natalia and raised an eyebrow. When she eagerly nodded, he looked over at Rupe. "Casino."

CASH'S STOMACH clenched when Natalia walked out of the bedroom into the living quarters of their stateroom. He spun his finger in the air. "Turn around."

She did a quick twirl, a soft giggle bubbling from between her lips. "I've never been to a casino. Will I do?"

The fitted navy cocktail dress clung to every inch of her curvaceous body. She'd left her hair down, which she knew he loved, and her face glowed from spending the day in the sun. He inwardly cursed Rupe's idea of going to the casino. He'd rather take her to bed, spend time peeling that dress off her before kissing every inch of her sun-kissed skin, then make love to her over and over again.

"Cash?" she said, bringing him back from daydreaming.

"Fuck the casino." He wrapped his arms around her, a low groan easing from his throat when her body melted into his. He bent his head and took her mouth. He never got tired of kissing her—they fit together perfectly in every way. His tongue tangled with hers, and he sucked hard, spurred on when she moaned softly.

"How much time have we got?" he murmured, kissing the dip where her neck met her shoulder.

"Not enough for what you've got in mind."

"And how do you know what I've got in mind?"

She giggled. "Because I can feel your *mind* pressing into my stomach."

He gyrated his hips. "You mean this?"

She giggled again. "That's the one."

"You sure we don't have time? I'll be quick."

She waggled a finger in front of his face. "Later. You'll ruin my hair."

"Spoilsport."

His lips traced a leisurely path from her neck to her collarbone, and she tilted her head to the side.

"You're not playing fair."

"I never promised to, sweetness."

"Rupe and Emmalee will be waiting."

"Let 'em," he said, bending his head lower until his mouth was level with the top of her breasts. "God, I love your body. I could spend hours exploring every single inch."

"Is that all you want me for—my body?"

He lifted his head. "Of course. Did you think otherwise?"

She lightly punched his arm and twisted out of his embrace. "Well then, I'll make you work for it, ace."

She headed for the door, but he managed to catch up with her before she opened it. He wrapped an arm around her waist and pulled her against him, her back to his front.

"The harder the better," he said, grinding his erection against her backside.

She chuckled. "Come on, we'd better go."

"Wait." He eased her around, a smile spreading across his face when he spotted the earrings he'd bought for her last Christmas dangling from her earlobes. *The first of many things I want to give this woman.* He wanted to gift-wrap the world and hand it to her on a plate. "I have something for you."

"What?" she said, the soft skin between her eyebrows furrowing into a shallow frown.

He wandered over to the dressing table and picked up a long, thin box. He held it flat on his open palm.

Her hand trembled as she reached for it. "What's this?"

"Open it, and you'll find out."

She flipped the lid, and her eyes widened. "Cash, I can't. This is too much."

He rolled his eyes. "Yes, you can." He lifted out the platinum necklace. At its base was a single teardrop sapphire, the colour of the ocean, and a perfect match for her deep velvet blue eyes. "Turn around."

She did as he asked, lifting her hair out of the way as he fastened the clasp. She dropped her hair back into place.

"I love it," she whispered, her fingers tentatively touching the gemstone.

"And I love you, baby. I'll never stop loving you."

12

Tally glanced up at Cash as he steered her through the casino to the VIP area. Multiple stares bit into the back of her head. Cash's fame was something she'd always have to deal with, along with the envy it brought. It was hard, though, to ignore the hunger in the eyes of a few women whose greedy gazes followed him wherever he went. And because he looked particularly handsome that night, those stares seemed even more intrusive.

But after what he'd said before they'd left Rupe's yacht, she felt secure in his love. She touched the sapphire stone nestling perfectly in her cleavage. It was just like Cash to buy an exorbitant gift, and although his extravagance sometimes made her a little uncomfortable, she knew it was his way of showing the depth of his feelings.

"This is fucking mint. How the other half live," Emmalee whispered in her ear. And then she nudged her. "Correction, how you live now. Don't think the rock around your neck has escaped my notice."

Tally grinned and slipped her arm through Em's. It was great having her there. She'd miss Cash when he started training the next day, and having Em and Rupe around for company would take the edge off her loneliness.

The concierge led them into a private room with a few gaming tables in the centre. A dozen or so patrons were already playing, chips stacked in piles in front of them, frowns of concentration drawing their brows low. Tally didn't have a clue how to play cards, and she glanced around, hoping to spot a couple of slot machines, or at least a roulette wheel. Even she could manage that. But this was clearly where the serious gambling happened. No slots here.

"What's the matter?" Cash said.

"I don't know how to play," she said, pointing her chin at the tables. "I was hoping for roulette."

Cash curved an arm around her waist and kissed her temple. "Rupe wants to play a few hands of poker. Let me humour him, and then we can go through to the main casino."

"Oh, no. It's fine, honestly. Don't do anything special for me."

"But you are special, sweetness."

"Jesus Christ," Emmalee said. "If he blows any more smoke up your arse, we're going to have to get the door widened to get your bloody head through."

Tally stuck out her tongue as a waitress appeared with a tray of champagne, and even though it sometimes gave her a raging headache, she gambled that one glass wouldn't hurt.

Cash and Rupe wandered over to one of the spare tables, and a croupier dealt the cards. As they casually tossed chips into the middle of the table, Tally's eyes bugged at how much they were betting on each hand.

"High rollers or what?" Emmalee whispered. "That's more than I make in a year."

Tally nodded. This was wealth on a whole different scale. Even though she knew Cash had money, seeing the price of each of those chips—and how cavalier he was about spending them—

brought into focus exactly how much money he had. An uncomfortable feeling stirred in her chest.

"Hitting home, is it, babes?" Emmalee said with a squeeze of her arm.

Tally's answering smile was brief. "You know me so well."

"I knew it would eventually. For you, that is. Me? I was born to be rich."

"You don't get much richer than him." Tally nodded her head in Rupe's direction. He had won a hand and was attempting to high-five the dealer, whose annoyance at his exuberance was barely hidden beneath her polite smile.

"I know." Em sighed. "I wish I was attracted to him, but I'm not. He's great company, funny, good-looking, but there's no spark. It's so frustrating."

Tally laughed. "I can imagine."

"Whatever you do, don't mention him to Mum. She'd have me married off in five minutes flat, and sod the chemistry. But me, I need the *feeling*," she said, emphasising her point with air quotes. "Like you've got with Cash, even though watching the two of you together is sickening."

As though he knew they were talking about him, Cash glanced over his shoulder and cocked his head, signalling for Tally to join him.

She wandered over and rested her hands on his shoulders. "How's it going?"

"Awful," he said, briefly putting one hand over the top of hers. "I need my lucky charm. You."

She watched him play, trying desperately to follow what was going on. His muscles were tense, the stress he was under having nothing to do with losing money. For Cash, it was all about winning the game, and at the moment, Rupe had the upper hand. She dug her thumbs into the base of his neck and massaged gently.

As the game went on, she began to figure out the rules. On

the fifth hand, Cash's luck seemed to turn. From that moment on, Cash's whole body language changed. The average person wouldn't have noticed the difference in him, but Tally did. His shoulders dropped, and he lounged in his chair, his legs splayed wide—a sure sign of confidence.

After half an hour, Cash had won back all the money he'd lost, and he gained a fair bit besides. But his success was to the detriment of Rupe, who lost every round and ended up significantly down. Rupe simply shrugged it off, swigged back the remainder of his third glass of champagne, and hit her and Emmalee with a winning smile.

"Okay, ladies. Who's for the slots?"

"Ooh, yeah," Em said, linking her arm through Rupe's. They headed out onto the main casino floor, but as Tally began to follow them, Cash gripped her elbow, stopping her.

"You okay, ace?" she said.

"I am now. I like to win."

"You don't say."

He tilted his head. "Are you mocking me, sweetness?"

Tally held her thumb and forefinger in the air, about half an inch apart. "Maybe just a tad."

He laughed and slipped an arm around her waist. "Right. Let's go and play roulette." Cash pocketed his chips and led her to the nearest roulette table. The croupier swapped his chips for different-coloured ones.

"Why did she do that?" Tally asked, nodding at the stack of chips Cash put in front of her.

"You mean swap? Because everyone needs a different colour. Otherwise, how would they track which ones belonged to which player? See, yours are red. Mine are blue."

"Oh, yeah. I hadn't thought of that." She picked one up and turned it over in her hand. "How much is each chip worth?"

Cash pressed his lips together in a slight grimace. "Two hundred and fifty euros."

Her eyes widened as she did a quick count of the chips. "Cash, this is far too much money," she whispered, pushing the majority of the stack over to him. He moved it back.

"It's peanuts."

"Peanuts?" she choked. "For you, maybe. Not for me."

He leaned down, his mouth close to her ear. "Yes, for you. You've moved in. What's mine is yours now. Get used to it."

She shook her head. No point arguing with him—at least not here—but sometime in the not-too-distant future, they were going to have to discuss the thorny issue of money. Although she'd let Cash pay for everything since they'd got back together, the main reason was that she wasn't earning at the moment. But she planned to put that right soon. Pete had already asked her to write an article for an upcoming feature in the paper, and she only had to say the word for him to put the feelers out for more work. As soon as she had money coming in again, she would want to contribute, even if it was only paying for the odd meal out. Yet she knew, without even having the discussion, Cash wasn't going to be happy. Well, too bad. He'd hooked up with an independent woman—he'd have to learn to deal with it.

She started as low as she could, placing a single chip on red. The odds were two to one. Cash, on the other hand, stuck a wedge on three different numbers. The croupier spun the wheel, and once it had reached a certain speed, she tossed in the ball. Tally watched it go round and round, and eventually, the ball dropped onto the track. It bounced a few times before settling on red twelve.

"I won," she exclaimed, shaking Cash's arm.

"You did. Well done, baby," he said as the croupier cleared away the losing bets, including all three of Cash's, and passed her two chips. Easy as that, she'd doubled her money. She'd never been a gambler, but she could see the allure and how simple it would be to get drawn in.

She played a few more rounds, her excitement as well as her

risk-taking increasing with each spin of the wheel. But when she noticed the stack of chips reducing in size, she decided to cut her losses.

"Sure you don't want to play a little more?" Cash asked. When she declined, he swapped their chips, and they went off in search of Em and Rupe. After a few minutes walking around the casino, Tally spotted the two of them at the craps table. A huge crowd had amassed, and from Tally's limited vantage point, Em was doing pretty well and had certainly enchanted the onlookers.

Tally watched as Em blew on the dice and held them up in front of Rupe. He blew on them too, then Em threw the dice down the table. They bounced at the end before coming to rest. There was a slight pause before a huge cheer went up.

"Guess she's won," Tally said to Cash over the noise. He nodded and eased his way through the crowd, towing her behind him. When Em spotted them, she waved madly.

"There you are. Come on, Tally, give it a try."

Tally shook her head and pressed the dice back into Em's hands. "No, you go."

Em shrugged and threw the dice once more, launching herself at Rupe when she won again, the two of them whooping and hollering like a pair of kids.

Tally grinned up at Cash. This was such a fun night. The smell of the casino, the noise of the crowd, and Cash's firm body close by all contributed to the excited fizzing in her stomach.

After they'd watched Em and Rupe for a while, Cash's arms snaked around her waist, and he tugged her gently away from the crowd.

"Let's go," he whispered.

"Okay, I'll grab Em."

"No," he said, his teeth gently grazing her earlobe. "Leave them. Rupe will take care of her."

Tally leaned into him, intense need unfurling in her

abdomen. Cash's hot tongue traced a path from her earlobe, down her neck, and she held back a groan.

"Come on. I've had to wait hours to do what I wanted to do ever since you walked out of the bedroom in that dress."

"And what's that?" she teased.

"Sweetness, don't tempt me, because you know I have no boundaries."

She clenched her core in an attempt to control the flood of desire. Cash didn't wait for her to agree. He simply swept her out of the casino. When he flicked his wrist, a car pulled up, and he eased her inside.

13

Cash grabbed a copy of the *Belfast Telegraph* and a juice and wandered up on deck. It was already quite warm. He found a shady spot and settled down to read the paper.

He flicked to the sports pages, delighted to see Harlequins had beaten Armagh 32-10 the previous day. He quickly scanned the football results. As he turned to the financial section, Rupe appeared on deck with bleary eyes and dishevelled hair.

"What the fuck happened to you last night?" he said with an exaggerated yawn.

Cash shrugged. "Decided I'd had enough."

"You could have told us. We spent about half an hour looking for you before we realised you'd fucked off."

"Sorry, darling," Cash replied. "Didn't realise I had to report in."

Rupe flipped him the bird and took a swig of Cash's juice before Cash swiped it back. "Get your own."

"It is my own."

Cash laughed. "Fair point."

"Where's Tally?"

"I left her sleeping. She's knackered."

Rupe rolled his eyes. "I'm not surprised with you fawning over her every five minutes."

"Fawning?" Cash raised an eyebrow. "Have you been reading the *Times* again?"

"There's nothing wrong with expanding your vocabulary."

Cash snorted loudly. "Since when?"

Rupe ignored his sarcasm. He added a healthy amount of cream to the coffee he'd been brought by one of the deck hands and sank into a nearby chair. "What time are you off today?"

"Have you ever thought about low-fat milk?" Cash said, nodding at Rupe's cup.

"Tastes like shit."

"Better for your ever-expanding waistline, though."

"Screw you, oh holier-than-thou wise one. Please tell me you're off to practice soon."

Cash grinned and glanced at his watch. "A couple of hours." He snagged an apple from the fruit bowl. He'd need to eat something soon but wanted to wait for Natalia. He wouldn't see her all day as it was. He'd told her not to come to practice––he didn't need her to witness his humiliation––so she was going shopping with Emmalee instead.

After half an hour, when she still hadn't appeared, he wondered if there was something in Rupe's earlier dig. He'd always had a voracious sexual appetite, but it had significantly increased since he'd met Natalia. Maybe he needed to back off a bit.

Hmm, no. That won't work. He could barely keep his hands off her as it was, let alone touch her less.

"Where's Emmalee?" he said to Rupe, who was throwing fish food over the side of the boat. "I thought she'd be up by now."

Rupe brushed the remains of fish food off his hands. "Already up and out. Went for a run."

"She's keen," Cash muttered. He'd kept a close eye on

Emmalee, expecting her to have another dig at him about why Natalia had chosen to forgive him. He couldn't stop the nagging doubt that Emmalee would put Natalia under so much pressure she'd buckle and tell Em about his past, although Natalia hadn't mentioned any probing.

Cash went back to reading the paper, but it didn't last long. He sensed Natalia before he saw her, and he slowly raised his head. She hadn't bothered getting dressed, instead deciding to cover up in a floor-length satin dressing gown. If she was naked underneath, he definitely approved.

"There you are," he said, patting the seat next to him. She sat down and rested her head on his shoulder.

"You should have woken me. I didn't mean to sleep this late."

"You needed it."

"Yeah, but I won't see you all day." Her bottom lip stuck out in a pout.

Cash laughed and bent his head, sucking her lip into his mouth. "Plenty of time later, sweetness."

"For real?" Rupe said, holding his hands out to the sides, palms up.

"Where's Em?" Natalia asked.

"She's gone for a run," Rupe said.

"A run?" Natalia laughed. "Em doesn't run. I bet she spotted a guy she fancied on the quayside and decided to stalk him."

"Poor bastard," Cash said, earning a dig in the ribs from Natalia. "You hungry?"

"Yeah."

"What do you want?" he said, beckoning to Rob, one of the deck hands.

"Porridge and fruit."

"Ham and cheese omelette for me, please, Rob. And a protein shake. Rupe?"

Rupe shook his head. "Still recovering from last night."

Rob disappeared below deck as Emmalee arrived back on the

boat. There wasn't a bead of sweat on her, although she'd dressed for running.

"You just missed the breakfast order," Cash said. "If you run, you'll catch Rob."

"Unless you think you've already done enough running for the day," Natalia said with a giggle.

Emmalee raised an eyebrow. "What are you trying to say, Tal?"

"Did you catch him?"

Emmalee laughed. "You know me too bloody well. It's rather annoying."

"Well, did you?"

"As a matter of fact, I have a date tonight. You need to help me find something fabulous and a little bit slutty when we go shopping later."

She spun around and headed below deck, presumably after Rob.

Cash leaned towards Natalia. "Here," he said, passing her his credit card. "Feel free to buy something fabulous and a little bit slutty for yourself too."

She shook her head. "I can't take your money, Cash."

Cash held back from rolling his eyes. "It's not *my* money."

"Yes, it is." She sighed, and her head flopped against the chair.

"What's the problem?" He couldn't keep the hard edge out of his voice. He did not understand her stubbornness on this issue.

"If you two are about to have a domestic, I'm going." Rupe wandered off in the same direction as Emmalee. He had never been subtle but had always been able to read Cash.

"You agreed to move in."

"Yes. But I didn't agree to being a kept woman."

Cash let out an exasperated sigh. "Oh, come on, Natalia. Don't make a big deal out of this. Just take the fucking card."

"Cash," she said, her tone low but firm, as if she was talking to an errant child who'd chucked his crayons on the floor in a fit of pique. "I value my independence, and you pushing your money on me makes me feel as though that freedom is being taken away. Pete's already put a couple of freelance jobs my way, so I'll be getting back to work soon, and that means I'm perfectly capable of contributing."

He crossed his arms over his chest. "And I'm supportive of you getting back to work. It was my idea that you freelance, remember? But no matter how hard you work, you'll never make enough to live the kind of life I want for you. I've never had anyone to lavish my money on except myself. And believe me, that becomes fucking boring after a while." He uncrossed his arms and picked up her hand. "I want you to have the world, Natalia, and I want to be the one to give it to you."

Her mouth creased in thought. "You're not going to fight me on the work thing?"

He frowned. "Why on earth would I do that? I'll always support your career. I know how much being a journalist means to you, and freelancing is the best of both worlds. I get to have you travel with me, and you get to do what you love."

Her face broke out into a huge grin. "I do love you, Cash Gallagher."

He waved the credit card in the air. "Then take this. Please, babe. It'll make me happy. This is Monte Carlo, and everything costs a fucking fortune. Go with Emmalee, have a good time, and you can tell me all about it later."

He watched the conflict play out on her face, showing her caught between pleasing him and still feeling in control of her independence. He knew he'd won when she whipped the card from between his fingers.

"Okay. But I'll still be hunting for the bargains."

He grinned and kissed her cheek. "I wouldn't expect anything less."

14

Em and Tally left for the shops not long after Tally had waved Cash off to Roquebrune-Cap-Martin, where the Monte-Carlo Masters would kick off in less than a week. For the first time since they'd met, his supreme confidence appeared to have slipped, although he was doing his best to hide it from her. Two months away from competitive tennis had to seem like a lifetime. She'd bet the fact he was going into the tournament without being seeded first—something he hadn't done in years—was preying on his mind. She'd have to try and find a gift to cheer him up, although she didn't have a clue what to buy. What could she get for the man who already had everything?

"Where should we head first?" Tally said. She'd never been to Monte Carlo. Em, though she'd never been there either, would have it all planned out. She was the queen of buying anything and everything—the perfect consumer. Tally, on the other hand, rarely shopped unless she needed to.

"Carré D'Or, of course," Em said with a twinkle of mischief in her eyes.

"And what's so special about Carré D'Or?"

"It's where the rich shop, babes. Think Rodeo Drive or Champs Élysées."

"Neither of us can afford to shop there," Tally said.

"You can."

"No, I can't." Tally let out a huff of frustration. "I've told you— I might have Cash's credit card, but I'm not taking advantage."

Em rolled her eyes. "Come on. It'll be fun. Even if we don't buy anything, we can press our noses up against the windows of the posh shops and piss off the staff."

"How do you know about Carré D'Or, anyway?"

Em shrugged. "I asked Rupe."

Tally chuckled. "Perhaps you should have asked Rob. He might have been able to suggest somewhere a little more in our price range."

Em linked her arm through Tally's. "Why should I do that when I have you? If there's a bargain to be had, you'll sniff it out."

With Google Maps on their phones, they made their way to Carré D'Or. Tally didn't need to read the street sign to know when they'd arrived. Sleek shop fronts, pristine streets, and stylish architecture—the place oozed money.

"I was born to be rich," Em said, peering through a window filled with clothes she couldn't afford. "If I won the lottery, I wouldn't be one of those people who says, 'Nothing's going to change—I'll still work, still get my clothes from Primark,' blah, blah, blah. I'd change *everything*."

"Yeah, well, you're not rich. Bad luck."

Em playfully bumped her shoulder against Tally's. "Cash is wasted on you. At least his money is. If I nabbed a rich guy, I'd know exactly what to do with all that lovely wonga." She rubbed her thumb over the tips of her fingers.

Tally laughed. "Maybe your date tonight will work out, and he'll whisk you off to live in a mansion overlooking the Mediterranean."

"Doubt it. He's a student doctor."

"Aww, never mind. Come on—let's try to find some shops that sell stuff we can afford."

Em reluctantly followed, although Tally did have to stop several times when she realised her friend had been tempted by yet another ridiculously priced dress and was lagging behind, her nose pressed up against a tinted window.

"You're like a magpie," she said, hauling Em away. "You see something shiny, and you're gone."

Em grinned unashamedly, and after a few more unplanned stops, Tally managed to coax her away from Carré D'Or.

They wandered around for about half an hour, eventually coming across a narrow street full of unique one-off shops and without a chain store in sight. *Now, this is more like it.* Thrilled with her find, Tally ignored Em's grumbling and dragged her friend into a few clothes shops, all of which Em turned her nose up at, before they came across one that looked quite promising. It had lots of one-of-a-kind designs at reasonable prices.

"Here," Tally said, holding up a fitted knee-length teal dress with a plunging neckline and a scooped back. "This would be perfect on you." Em wouldn't be able to wear a bra with it, but she didn't have the same problem as Tally in that department.

"Ooh, that is lovely." Em glanced at the price tag and nodded in approval. "I knew you'd sniff out the bargains."

"Go and try it on."

Five minutes later, Em peeked around the curtain of the fitting room and waved Tally over. "What do you think?" she said, pushing the curtain to one side.

Tally whistled. "Wow. You're a *knockout*. Buy it."

Em smoothed her hands over her hips and stood on tiptoes. She turned to the side and frowned into the mirror. "You think?"

"Yep. Makes your legs look fantastic, and you've got the figure to pull off a dress like that."

"As do you."

Tally snorted. "With these"—she pointed to her chest—"I need the support."

"That's what tit tape is for."

"Hardly. Duct tape more like."

They burst into laughter. It had been ages since Tally had been shopping with Em, and she'd forgotten how much fun it could be.

Em bought the dress, and they headed off to find matching shoes. Em decided on a pair of skyscraper heels in nude, which went perfectly with the dress but would mean she wouldn't be able to walk properly for a week afterwards. Still, Em seemed to think the overall look would be worth the sacrifice.

"Fancy lunch?" she asked Tally as they wandered back onto the street.

"Do you mind if we visit a little shop I spotted down there first?"

"Don't tell me you're finally going to buy something?"

"I saw a perfect gift for Cash in the window when we were passing earlier."

Em rolled her eyes. "Seriously? What about a little gift for you?"

"I haven't seen anything I like."

"Okay, let's go. On one condition."

Tally narrowed her eyes. Em's conditions usually involved something Tally wouldn't like. "What's that?"

"You might not have seen anything, but before, I spotted a fabulous dress you'd look gorgeous in. So here's the deal. We'll go to the shop. You buy whatever it is you've spotted for Cash, then you have to come with me, try the dress on, and promise to keep an open mind."

Tally nibbled on her lip. "Oh, Em, I'm not sure."

"If it makes it easier, think of it as another gift for Cash," Em said with a giggle.

Tally's eyebrows shot up towards her hairline. "How hot is

this dress?"

"Babes, it'll blow his mind."

She laughed. "You're incorrigible."

"That sounds like a yes."

"Do I have a choice?" Tally said, already regretting giving in when Em flashed a wicked grin her way.

As they walked into the gift shop, the bell above the door tinkled. Tally headed straight for the window display and picked up a pair of silver cufflinks.

"Can you engrave these?" she asked the shop assistant, holding them in her outstretched hand.

"Certainly, mademoiselle. Did you have something in mind?"

Tally dug a pen and paper out of her bag and drew what she wanted. Em leaned over her shoulder.

"He's going to love those."

"Do you think so?"

"Yep. I like the design too."

Tally tweaked her drawing slightly before handing it over. "Will it take long?"

"No, mademoiselle."

"I'll wait, then."

While the cufflinks were being engraved, Tally took a look around. She wasn't a big clothes shopper, but sifting through knickknacks and one-off items was her idea of heaven.

"Here we are, mademoiselle." The shop assistant passed her the engraved cufflinks. Tally examined her work. They'd turned out better than she'd imagined they would.

"I love them," she said, handing over her own credit card. She worked out she'd still be within her credit limit once they were charged. They were her gift to Cash, and it didn't seem fitting to use his money to buy them. But she needed to get back to work soon. Her statement would be due any day, and she'd only have a couple of weeks to pay it. She *had to* get going on the article for Pete later.

"Just you to sort now," Em said.

The place Em had in mind was only a five-minute stroll away. Em headed straight for a rack at the far end of the store and rifled through.

"Aha, here it is."

She held up a floor-length dark-red dress with a low neckline and a slit up the side. Tally's mouth fell open.

"What do you think?" Em said.

"You have got to be kidding. I can't get away with that."

"You promised to try it on. Trust me." She thrust the dress into Tally's reluctant hands and pointed to the fitting room. It took Tally about five minutes to figure out how to even get the damned thing on, but when she did, she glanced in the mirror and gasped.

"Em," she croaked. "You there?"

"I'm coming in." Em slipped around the curtain, being careful not to expose Tally to the whole shop. "Oh, wow. Fuck, I'm good."

"I can't pull this off," Tally said, tugging the parted material over her exposed breasts.

"Yes, you can." Em turned her around. "A bit of tape here and there, and you're good to go."

"But it's so... so..."

"Hot."

"I was going for *tarty*."

"Rubbish," Em scoffed. "You've got an amazing figure, Tally. I've told you this, like, a hundred times, and I, for one, am glad to see a bit of meat back on your bones. When you're ninety and wrinkled, you'll wish you'd shown your curves off a bit more while you still could."

As Tally handed over Cash's credit card, she could have sworn the assistant flashed a look of amazement as she wrapped the dress in tissue paper, as though to say *Really, honey?*

Tally was inclined to agree.

15

Every year that Cash had played the Monte-Carlo Masters, he'd always jogged to and from practice. That day, for the first time, he grabbed a cab back to the harbour. Exhaustion swamped him. Two months off the court had put a serious dent not only in his fitness but also his sharpness—how well he saw the ball. All of it, bound together, made him dread the next week.

Brad had killed him on court, and Jamie had murdered him in the gym afterwards. His body ached all over. He'd need an ice bath and a massage to stand any chance of moving the next day, let alone being able to do it all over again.

Climbing up to Rupe's boat was a feat of sheer willpower. It had to be, because he had nothing left in his legs. He managed to make it back to the stateroom without bumping into Rupe, who loved it when Cash struggled physically. It made Rupe feel better about his own piss-poor fitness levels.

Cash staggered into the stateroom and dropped his bag beside the door. Natalia was lying on the couch, reading a book, her feet resting on the arm. She glanced up and smiled, one of those smiles that instantly lifted his spirits.

"Hey, how was it?"

He moved her legs, wincing as he eased himself into the space next to her, and placed her feet in his lap. "Fucking awful."

"Want me to run you a bath?"

Cash shook his head. "I need an ice bath."

She pulled a face. "Rather you than me."

"It's the only way I'll be able to move tomorrow."

"Brad didn't go easy on you, then?"

"I think he upped the ante on purpose. He's certainly made his point." Cash painfully climbed to his feet, already feeling stiffness in his hamstrings. "Best get this over with."

He called down to the kitchen and asked for a couple of sacks of ice to be brought up. While he waited, he filled the bath halfway with cold water. When the ice arrived, he tipped it in, stripped down to his boxers, gritted his teeth, and stepped into the tub. He hissed and clenched his jaw as the freezing water bit into his skin. His teeth began chattering, and after five minutes, he couldn't feel his feet.

Natalia poked her head around the bathroom door, her expression one of concern. "Cash, what do you need when you get out?"

"Warm clothes and a hot drink."

"How long do you have to stay in there?"

"Fifteen long fucking minutes."

She disappeared for a few moments. When she returned, she sat on the edge of the bath and began massaging his shoulders. He groaned and pressed closer to her. "That feels good."

As soon as the alarm went off, Cash flew out of the bath and grabbed a towel.

"I've put some clothes on the bed," Natalia said. "I'll pop to the kitchen and fetch you a coffee. Get under the covers."

"Now you're talking," he said.

She shook her head slightly. "You have a one-track mind."

By the time she returned five minutes later with a large mug of coffee, Cash had burrowed under the quilt. His teeth had stopped chattering, but his body still felt cold.

"Here," she said, passing him the mug. "Can't you take a hot shower?"

"No. I need to warm up slowly."

"I've never seen you take an ice bath after training."

He sipped his coffee. "I don't usually need to. Brad's a bastard."

She laughed. "He's got your best interests at heart. How was it really?"

He grimaced. "I'm not as sharp as I should be." When worry crossed her face, he squeezed her hand. "There's plenty of time. How was your day?"

"Yeah, good. We got Em a dress for her date tonight."

He waggled his eyebrows playfully. "And what did you get?"

She tapped the side of her nose with her forefinger. "You'll have to wait and see. I left your credit card on the dresser."

"Thanks," he said, making a mental note to get her added to his account and have a second card sent out. He finished the coffee, put the mug on the bedside table, and flung the bedcovers to one side. "Get in. You'll have me warmed up in no time."

RUPE HAD AGREED to go ashore for the evening, and with Emmalee on her date, Cash and Natalia would be alone. She was getting ready in Emmalee's room because, apparently, she needed Emmalee's help to get into the dress. She still hadn't shown it to Cash, but he hoped she'd gone with *less is more*.

He headed up on deck, still stiff but not as sore as earlier. The ice bath and deep-tissue massage must have been working their magic. Spring had arrived in the Mediterranean, and he'd asked the staff to set up a table outside where they could dine and appreciate the spectacular view of Monte Carlo.

He corked a bottle of champagne—one glass wouldn't hurt too much—and took a sip. For once, Rupe's taste lived up to his bank balance. Cash glanced at the label. Jesus, Rupe had gone all out.

A gentle cough sounded behind him, and he turned around. It took a moment or two to find his voice. Rupe wasn't the only one who'd gone all out.

"Wow." His breathing quickened as Natalia walked slowly towards him.

She grazed her teeth over her bottom lip. "Is it too tarty?"

"Are you kidding?"

The dress was the colour of a fine burgundy, rich and dark. It plunged down to her navel, giving him a good eyeful of her magnificent cleavage, and a long side slit showed off one very shapely leg. Around the middle, a thin gold belt cinched her waist. She'd left her hair loose and kept her makeup light. Every part of him ached to touch her.

"Come here." He held out his hand. She put her silver clutch bag on the table and took it. "You look stunning. If this is what you come back with, I'll send you shopping more often." He pulled her into his arms, and they began to dance around the deck.

"There's no music," she said. He began to hum out of tune, and she laughed. "Oh well, I guess you can't be good at everything."

He chuckled and spun her around. He loved to dance. It reminded him of happier times with Mum, before everything turned to shit. He shook the negative thought from his head. His mother would dance again. He was certain of it.

"I missed you today," he said, pressing his cheek to hers.

"Missed you too."

He pulled back and tilted his head to the side. "But you had a good time with Emmalee?"

"We had a great time."

"Are you hungry? Rupe's had the staff go the extra mile."

"Very." Her lips brushed his ear. "And not only for food."

Cash's stomach was tied in knots. He could barely force the food down, what with Natalia dressed in the sexiest outfit he'd ever seen, and the fact she kept rubbing her calf against his leg and touching his hand, his arm, his face. All he wanted was to rip the damned dress off and make love to her right there on the deck. He was about to suggest it when she gave him a flirtatious glance.

"Do you want your present?"

He slowly raked a gaze over her body. "I thought I already had it."

"I bought you something else. With my own money." She wrinkled her nose. "Well, the bank's money. But it's kind of the same thing."

A rush of excitement made his pulse jump. "I never get gifts."

Melancholy darkened her face. "That's so sad."

He shrugged. "Doesn't matter. I'm about to get one."

"You are." She pushed her chair back and walked across to the table where she'd left her bag. Intrigued, Cash followed. She pulled out a small square box and held it in the palm of her hand. "Open it," she urged, pressing her palm closer to him.

Cash took hold of the box and flipped the lid. Inside, nestled on dark-blue satin, lay a pair of silver cufflinks in the shape of tiny tennis rackets. "Oh, wow, baby. They're great."

"Turn them over. Look on the inside."

He did as she asked, and his heart flipped. She'd had them inscribed with the letter C intertwined with four points of the letter N. He lifted his eyes to hers.

"I love them."

"Honestly?"

"Yes." He removed the cufflinks he'd put on earlier and replaced them with the ones Natalia had bought, thrilled with the thought behind the gift. His hands curved around her waist, and he pulled her towards him. "Why didn't you come into my life sooner?"

She gave the secret smile she kept only for him. "Because you weren't ready for me until now."

16

T he buzz of the crowd was as loud as Tally remembered from the last match she'd attended, or maybe even more so. There was an enormous amount of interest in Cash's first match on the circuit in almost two months. He'd received a bye for the first round, and this second-round match against a fairly unknown qualifier would usually see the stadium about three-quarters full, maximum. But not that day. Even corporate ticket holders had managed to drag themselves away from the lure of the free bar.

Tally's right leg jiggled vigorously until Em clamped down on her knee.

"You're doing my head in, babes. Chill out. He'll smash it."

"I feel sick," Tally said.

"Don't you dare ruin my first-ever tennis match by throwing up. I'm super excited."

Rupe laughed. "You're all heart, Em."

She grinned and dug her elbow in his ribs. "Don't you side with her."

Tally tuned out their banter as she scanned the stadium. She winced at the occasional handwritten sign that told the world what that particular person thought of her boyfriend. Jealousy flared within her—pointless jealousy that Cash did nothing to encourage but her body involuntarily expressed anyway. At least she was smart enough to know that listening to tabloid gossip was a sure-fire way of wrecking a relationship. It would be easy to believe the mindless lies they printed. Tabloids had caused a split in more than one celebrity relationship by identifying a single thread with little substance and turning it into a sensational exclusive.

Tally continued scanning the crowd, more to take her mind off the upcoming match than out of any real interest. A woman directly opposite wearing a large fawn-coloured hat drew Tally's attention. Those poor spectators behind her. They wouldn't be able see a thing.

She'd half turned away when something made her take a closer look. A good portion of the woman's face was hidden behind enormous Jackie O sunglasses, but even so, she seemed vaguely familiar.

No! It couldn't be. Tally leaned forward, as if the extra six inches would make all the difference, and squinted. Jesus. She was right.

"Rupe," she said a little more sharply than she intended, interrupting his ribbing of Em.

"What's up?"

"Directly ahead," Tally said, pointing her chin. "Woman in the big hat. Tell me I'm wrong and that isn't Kinga."

"You mean Rocky Balboa's had the nerve to show up?" Em said, peering in the same direction as Rupe.

"Fuck me," Rupe said. "It is. Christ, that woman's got more front than Blackpool prom. She'd better hope Cash doesn't spot her. Knowing him, he'll aim a hundred-mile forehand right at her head."

A sense of dread crept across her skin. *What the hell is Kinga doing here?* Tally instinctively knew it wasn't to watch a game of tennis. No, Kinga wanted to see Cash. But for what reason?

Nervous fluttering in her abdomen gave her an empty, hollow feeling. Not only did she have to manage her fear of Cash bombing in his first match back on the tour, but now she had the additional worry about what Kinga's agenda might be. Tally stared in her direction, willing her to glance over, but Kinga's gaze was firmly fixed on the corner of the court—the same corner Tally expected Cash to appear from in about five minutes.

"Don't sweat it, darling," Rupe said with a comforting squeeze of her hand.

"Don't sweat what?" Brad said as he and Jamie slipped into their seats. "You panicking again, Tally?"

Rupe glanced over his shoulder. "Kinga's here."

Jamie and Brad shared a look.

"You're fucking kidding," Brad said.

"Wish I was. Twelve o'clock."

He peered over Tally's shoulder, an expelled hiss sounding in her ear. "Shit, that's all we need. If Cash spots her, it'll turn his concentration to shit."

"Can't we get her ejected or something?" Em said.

"On what grounds? This is just like Kinga. She never did know when to quit."

Tally twisted in her seat. "How's he doing?"

Brad pulled a face. "Honestly, hon, I'm not sure how this is going to go. Problem is we've only had a week to work with him, and when you don't play for a while, it's the sharpness that goes. You end up a millisecond behind where you need to be, and that's all it takes at this level. Granted, his opponent is a qualifier, but often they're worse."

"Why?"

Brad shrugged. "Nothing to lose."

She swallowed down her fear. Once more, her gaze fell on

Kinga, but as the players came on court and the noise level increased significantly, Tally forced herself to look away.

As Cash appeared, dressed in his customary black, his eyes met Tally's, and his lips twisted into a wry smile, a sure sign he wasn't one hundred per cent confident. Even though Brad had told her he wasn't in the best shape, seeing it for herself was much worse. She wouldn't be teasing Cash about overconfidence that day.

"You got this," she mouthed and gave an encouraging smile.

His face softened, and he winked before waving to the crowd. Tally watched as he went through his normal routine. He placed his racket bag beside him, laid a towel over the chair, and set up various bottles of liquid, each one containing a different set of nutrients.

He took a sip of water, lifted out his first tennis racket, hit it against his hand to test the tension, and walked on court for the warm-up. The crowd cheered, whooped, and hollered, but Cash didn't acknowledge them this time. Tally knew this look. He'd gone within himself, focused on the task ahead.

It gave her hope.

Cash won the toss and elected to serve. A hush descended on the crowd as he prepared to play the first game. He was a speed player: a couple of bounces of the ball, serve, win the point, and repeat. It was one of the reasons he was successful—opponents couldn't deal with the pace at which he drove the game. And yet that day, Tally counted ten bounces of the ball before he served. She held her breath as he tossed the ball in the air, his back arching, tennis racket behind his head.

He hit an ace—and acute relief hit her.

He served out the game to love, and the whole match was over in less than an hour. Tally scanned the crowd for Kinga, but she'd disappeared. Maybe she had just come to watch Cash play.

"Is that it?" Em said. "I was hoping for a bit more."

"Longest hour of my life," Tally said. "But thanks for wanting to stretch out my agony."

"Oh, you know what I mean, babes. What happens now?"

"Wait for Cash to do his post-match interviews, then we get the hell out of here and go somewhere that will pour me a large glass of wine."

Jamie kissed her cheek. "Tell Cash well done from me, and I'll see him on the practice court tomorrow."

"Aren't you joining us?" Tally pushed her sunglasses on top of her head and squinted up at him.

"I cannae today." He winked. "Got a date. Fine wee lassie she is too."

Tally grinned at Jamie's retreating back as she followed Brad and Rupe off court. She held onto Em's hand to prevent her from skipping off after anything that caught her eye. Tally did not want to spend ages trying to track her friend down.

"We'll meet you in the lounge," Brad said and then headed off towards the locker room.

Tally nodded. "Okay."

"Don't we get to go in the locker room, too?" Em asked in a disappointed tone.

"No."

"Shame. Cash's opponent was pretty hot."

Tally glanced over her shoulder. "One man not enough?" she said, thinking of the student doctor Em had been seeing pretty much every day since they arrived.

"Keeping my options open, babes."

Tally shook her head. Em was a law unto herself.

They arrived at the players' lounge, and Tally pushed open the door. As she walked inside, her gaze fell on the person sitting opposite. A wave of despair swept through her chest. Tally tried to find her voice, but *she* beat her to it.

"Hello, Natalia," Kinga said.

17

Tally fished around, trying to make a sound—any sound—while Rupe sneered at Kinga.

"Who did you screw to get in here?" he said, his hands resting low on his hips.

"Nice to see you again, Rupert. It's been too long." Kinga pinned a stray blond hair into her favoured chignon before slowly getting to her feet. "Please sit down, Natalia." She waved towards the chair she'd vacated, but Tally's feet refused to move.

Em stood in front of Tally, momentarily blocking her view. "Keep your orders to yourself, lady," Em said.

"It's okay, Em," Tally said, relieved to have found her voice. "Why don't we all sit down?" Tally impressed herself with how gracefully she brushed past them all and pulled out a chair at the table. Kinga sat directly opposite, Em on her right, Rupe on the left.

"I'm sorry to turn up unannounced," Kinga said, eyes firmly on Tally.

"What do you want, Kinga?" Tally said.

"My job back."

Rupe snorted. "Cash is the same guy, you know. Still the

sharp-tongued stubborn son of a bitch he always was. I'd scarper before he gets here if I were you. Safer all round."

Kinga's gaze didn't even flicker in Rupe's direction. It was as though he hadn't even spoken. "I owe you an apology."

Tally tightened her grip on the arms of the chair. Outwardly, she was presenting an air of calmness. Inside, her stomach muscles cramped uncomfortably, and her heart was beating far too fast.

"You could have texted me."

Kinga laughed, the sound tinkly and light, very unlike the harsh, sarcastic laugh of the old Kinga. "I think apologies are much better made in the flesh, don't you?"

"Depends on who's making the apology."

The smile drained from Kinga's eyes. "I am sorry, Natalia. I never should have hit you. It was... I wasn't myself."

"Are you still obsessed with him?" Tally said.

A flash of surprise crossed her face, and then she shook her head. "No."

"Why should I believe you?"

Kinga's gaze dropped to the floor. "My deluded infatuation with Cash wasn't healthy. My counsellor has helped me to see that. I'm a different person now, and I want to make amends."

Both Rupe and Em opened their mouths to speak, but Tally shot them a warning glance. "What's so different?"

Kinga lifted her chin and took a slow breath. "It's difficult to explain."

"Try."

Tally surprised herself with how clipped and harsh her voice sounded, but she wasn't about to let Kinga off lightly. The woman had belted her, after all. Tally was allowed to feel aggrieved.

Kinga's gaze lowered again. "Cash had become my entire life," she said, unease etched into the stiff line of her jaw. "But the price I paid was to lose myself. These past couple of months, I've been able to find *me* again." Her hand clasped a small cross she wore around her neck, and she drew it back and forth along the chain.

"I've met someone." Her face softened, and her eyes took on a misty glaze. "His name's William. He's a marketing executive for Nike. With William's help and my counselling sessions, I've been able to see clearly for the first time in a very long time."

Tally drew her teeth across her bottom lip. Kinga appeared sincere, but as the woman had shown nothing but animosity towards her since their first meeting in Paris back in February, Tally couldn't quite bring herself to believe the presented image.

"Please, Natalia, forgive me. If you can forgive me, then I have a chance of Cash doing the same thing. I want my career back."

Tally held her gaze for a moment or two before looking over at Rupe. "How do you think he's going to react?"

Rupe considered her question. "Badly," he finally said.

Tally fixed her eyes on a spot on the table before glancing between Rupe and Em. "Can you leave us?"

Em's eyebrows shot up. "Are you sure?"

Tally laughed. "I think I'm safe."

Rupe glared at Kinga as though sending her a silent warning. He got to his feet, patted Tally's arm, and cocked his head at Em. "Come on, Fallon. I'll buy you lunch."

Tally's gaze followed Em and Rupe as they left the players' lounge. She leaned back in her chair and crossed her legs, picking a stray bit of fluff from her skirt.

"Okay, Kinga. You want a chance to talk to Cash, fine. But be prepared for what he might say."

Kinga's sigh of relief was unmistakeable. "I want you to know how truly sorry I am," she said, sincerity leaching into her tone. "I've never hit anyone in my life, and certainly not over a man." She chuckled, clearly hoping for a bit of female solidarity.

Tally nodded but kept her manner cool as she tried to sort through her feelings. Cash needed someone looking after his considerable interests, and despite Kinga's faults, she had never failed him in that department. If he hired someone new, it would take years to build up to the level of trust he had with Kinga, financially at least, and by that time, his career would be over. The problem would be persuading Cash that taking Kinga back was in his best interests.

"Was it difficult?" Tally said. "The counselling, I mean?"

Kinga stared at her hands. "Yes." After a few seconds, she lifted her head. "All sorts of things came up, from years ago. Long before I met Cash." Her eyes fixed on a faraway point in the distance, and for a few moments, she seemed to have been transported elsewhere. Then she blinked and shook her head. "It's not easy facing up to the sort of person you've been, especially when you find out that's not who you really are—that you've been playing a part without even realising it."

A rush of empathy moved through Tally's body, but as she began to reach out to Kinga, she changed her mind. "I can't just forget that you hit me, but I do understand why. Whether Cash will... I'm afraid that's something I can't control."

"I understand. And thank you. I know what I did was unforgiveable and not just because I hit you, but because of how awful I was to you when you and Cash first got together."

Tally let out a soft sigh. "Look, I'm not the type to hold grudges. I think having you on the team again would be good for Cash, and that's why I'm willing to support you when you talk to him. If he agrees"—she shrugged—"then we'll take it from there."

EVEN AFTER CASH had showered and changed, adrenaline still coursed through his body. He hadn't wanted to admit how shit-scared he'd been before stepping out on the court, not even to himself. Now the game was over, he could finally think about it. Two months was a long time to be away from tennis, but playing out there had been like coming home. All the pain of the last week was forgotten in the excitement of winning.

"You played well," Brad said as Cash bent down to tie his shoelaces.

"Yeah, I'm pretty pleased. How was Natalia?"

"More nervous than you, I think. I'm sure she's equally relieved."

"Is she in the lounge?"

"Yeah, with Rupe and Emmalee. They were talking about a large glass of wine last I heard."

Cash laughed. "Could do with one of those myself."

"Not on my fucking watch."

He laughed again. "I'll be a good boy. Iced water only."

"Good." Brad picked up his bags. "I'll sort these. Good luck at the press conference."

Cash groaned. He'd almost forgotten about that chore in the euphoria of the win. As it turned out, he needn't have worried. The press conference wasn't nearly as bad as he'd feared. Surprisingly, most reporters seemed pleased to have him back on tour, and the questions focused on the match rather than his personal life or the reasons for his absence.

After twenty minutes, he managed to escape. He couldn't wait to see Natalia. She'd tried her best to hide her fear before the match, but he knew her too well. He'd be getting her that glass of wine. She'd earned it.

A few players stopped him on his way to the lounge, all wanting to welcome him back. He exchanged a brief word or two, relieved when he finally got to the lounge.

He pushed open the door, scanned the room, and spotted Natalia sitting alone by the window. As he walked towards her, she locked eyes with him, stood up, and almost scrambled around the table in her haste to get to him. She fastened her arms around his neck, and a kick of anxiety shot into his bloodstream at the tightness of her hold and the stiffness in her body.

"Hey, you okay?" He pulled her close, his hand rubbing comforting circles on her back. "Where's Rupe and Emmalee?"

"Stay calm," she whispered in his ear.

Confused, he tilted his head back and smiled down at her. "I have to admit, I expected 'congratulations' or 'well done.'" When she didn't return his smile, he frowned. "What's going on?"

She reached for him. "Promise me you won't do anything stupid."

He pulled her hands away from his face. "Spit it out, Natalia."

She took a deep breath and expelled it slowly. "Kinga's here."

Rage hissed through his body, surprising even him with its intensity. As blood rushed to his head, his vision grew hazy, Natalia's face disappearing behind a red mist.

"Cash, listen to me. She's saying she's changed. She wants a chance to be heard, that's all."

"Where is she?" he gritted out.

"Cash—"

"Where the fuck is she, Natalia?"

It took a huge effort to keep his voice level. He knew he was scaring her, but he couldn't stop himself. *Fucking Kinga.* He didn't want her anywhere near him or Natalia. It had taken him a long time to wake up to the fact that she was a bitter, poisonous bitch who would stop at nothing to get what she wanted.

"I'm here."

Cash spun around. As his gaze met Kinga's, he must have achieved the scathing look he'd intended, because she flinched and took a step back. He marched across the room, gripped her by the elbow and, without saying a word, propelled her towards the exit.

"Cash, stop it." Natalia grabbed his arm, but he shook her off.

"This is between me and *her*."

Natalia stepped in front of him, barring the way out. "No. It's between *me* and her," she said between clenched teeth. "I know you like to think the whole world revolves around you, but it was *me* she belted. Now, stop making a scene. Everyone is looking. Just hear her out. Think of it as closure if nothing else."

Cash glared at Kinga. He didn't know what she'd said to get Natalia on her side, but she'd need to work a hell of a lot harder to convince him she was anything other than a conniving bitch.

"You've got ten minutes."

"Not here," Natalia said. "Let's go back to the boat."

Cash glanced around. Several pairs of eyes were keenly watching the altercation.

"Fine," he bit out, and with his hand on the small of Natalia's back, he ushered her through the door, leaving Kinga trailing behind.

No one spoke on the journey back to Rupe's boat. The atmosphere was uncomfortable and strained. Cash had no idea what had happened to Rupe and Emmalee, but he guessed Natalia had told them to make themselves scarce. Sensible girl.

"Clock's ticking, Kinga," he said once they'd settled in the living room below deck. He checked his watch to press his point.

A small smile crept around her mouth. "Direct as ever, Cash."

He let out a long, drawn-out sigh. Kinga shared a look with Natalia, and Cash frowned as he watched the silent exchange between the two women.

"I have apologised to Natalia, and she has been gracious enough to accept my apology, although neither of us is downplaying how disgracefully I behaved. I was out of control, Cash, both with her and with you. I'm sorry. For everything. I've spent the last couple of months having intensive counselling." She laughed, the sound hollow and without feeling. "I've learned quite a few things about myself during that time. I'm here to ask for your forgiveness, and maybe..." She paused and tucked a stray lock of hair behind her ear. "Maybe we could even work together again."

Cash almost choked. "You and me working together again? You're fucking joking."

"Cash." Natalia squeezed his leg under the table.

"It would never work. Natalia may be able to move on from your violent outburst, but I can't. I won't."

Kinga's face fell, and she gave Natalia a pleading look.

"Cash, things aren't the same as they were. Kinga's in a committed relationship now, aren't you?" Natalia nodded in Kinga's direction.

"Yes." Kinga's face softened. "His name is William. He's good for me. Doesn't let me get away with much."

Cash glared at her. "I don't see the relevance."

Kinga winced, and her fingers gripped the cross around her neck. Seconds scraped by before she leaned forwards, elbows on her knees. "Look, I was... obsessed with you. Living in a fantasy world. The day I hit Natalia is one I will regret for the rest of my life. Meeting William and getting the help I need has taught me that although I have made terrible decisions based on shaky foundations, I'm not a violent person."

Cash widened his eyes as Natalia briefly touched Kinga's arm. Kinga's answering smile was about as genuine as he'd ever seen.

"Cash, you said yourself there was no one better at their job than Kinga," Natalia said. "And you haven't replaced her yet. You need an agent, someone to look after your interests."

He glanced between the two women as they patiently waited for him to speak. He'd always known Kinga was a bitch, but before Natalia had come along, it hadn't bothered him in the slightest. She'd been great at her job, and he hadn't cared about the rest. Even the ill-timed passes she often made at him had been easy to deal with. His anger wasn't about the things she had done to him—it was because she'd hit Natalia. Violence against women, regardless of the sex of the person committing it, was unacceptable in his eyes. And Cash didn't know whether that was something he'd ever get past, even though Natalia clearly had.

He shook his head. "I don't understand you at all," he said to Natalia. "She *hit* you."

Natalia gave him a wry smile. "Haven't we all done things we wish we could go back in time and do differently? I know I have. I'm not saying we're ever going to be best friends, but I believe that people who put the effort into changing deserve a second chance."

Cash scrubbed his face with his hands and let out a heavy sigh. Silence clung to the air around them, like humidity before a thunderstorm. Cash let it sit there, lingering. Kinga fiddled with a large ruby ring on her left hand, twisting it round and round her finger, while Natalia sat quietly beside him.

"One-month trial," he eventually said, regretting the words as soon as he'd spoken. "But be warned, Kinga. Step out of line, and this time, I'll ruin you."

18

Tally pushed open the door to Starbucks and looked around for Kinga. She spotted her at the back of the coffee shop, nursing a half-finished latte.

Tally rushed over. "Sorry I'm late. Traffic was awful. Do you want another coffee?"

"That'd be great," Kinga said with a smile.

Tally grabbed a couple of coffees and sat down with a sigh. "I hate driving Cash's car. It's too big. Took me ages to find a big enough parking space that wouldn't mean I had to climb out of the window."

Kinga laughed. "You should have got him to drop you off."

"He couldn't. Brad's over at ours," she said with a mischievous grin. "He thought Cash needed some extra practice after losing his semifinal in Monte Carlo."

Kinga grimaced. "How has he taken the loss now he's had a few days to let it sink in?"

Tally picked up her coffee and took a sip. "Surprisingly well. He recognised he was half a yard short and that's why he didn't make the finals." She grinned. "Brad had that determined look when he arrived this morning." She put her cup on the table. "So, what's up?"

Kinga tilted her head to one side. "Has anyone ever told you that you have an innate ability to read situations very well?"

Tally shrugged. "It's no big secret. When we met the other day, you looked like you had something on your mind, and so when you called this morning asking to meet up, I figured you'd decided to tell me."

Kinga minutely shook her head. "Very astute." She fixed Tally with a stare, her eyes holding a tinge of fear mingled with regret. "I owe you an apology."

Tally frowned. "You've already apologised. There's no need to keep raking over the coals every time we see each other."

Kinga gripped the cross on the chain she always wore and clenched it tightly. "No, not that. This is worse. I wasn't sure whether to tell you, but I can't keep it from you any longer. It's not right."

A swirl of apprehension began to grow in Tally's stomach, and her skin prickled. "Tell me what?"

Kinga closed her eyes and took a deep breath before locking her gaze on Tally once more. "I took the photographs. The ones of Cash with that woman." As Tally gaped at her, Kinga rushed on. "I'm guessing it was completely innocent because you two are still together, and I'm so glad you didn't break up because of me. But as I'm trying to make a fresh start, I wanted you to know."

As shock rolled through Tally's system, she covered her face with her hands and scrubbed hard. "I don't believe this."

"It was all part of my illness. I'm so sorry."

Tally narrowed her eyes. "But I don't get it. The pictures were taken on the Tuesday, and you'd already checked into that residential facility in London. Cash did some digging because it crossed his mind you might have been the culprit."

Kinga wiped a hand over her mouth, smudging her usually perfect lipstick. "I did check myself into the facility after the altercation with Cash on that Saturday, but over the next couple of days, I got more and more angry at how awful he'd been—how cold and dismissive, and how protective he was of you. I hated you both back then, and I wanted you to suffer, so I flew back to Ireland and followed him, waiting for a chance to cause trouble. I got lucky." She grimaced. "Sorry, wrong word."

As her head began to pound, Tally massaged her temples. "We did break up. For about three weeks. Fortunately, Cash managed to persuade me he hadn't cheated and the situation was completely innocent."

Kinga winced, and her hand tightened around her necklace. "I don't know what to say. Can you ever forgive me?"

"Jesus, Kinga, you couldn't have told me this earlier? Or did you keep it a secret so I'd help you get your job back?"

Kinga recoiled. "No. God, I wanted to tell you straight away when we talked in Monte Carlo, but I didn't know where to start." Her hands trembled as she wrapped them around her coffee cup. "What do you think Cash will do?"

Tally put her hand up. "Stop, please. Let me think."

Kinga fell silent as Tally ran scenarios through her mind. Cash would sack Kinga immediately. No, worse than that—he would seek revenge. He'd ruin Kinga's life, and as much as Tally could feel anger and disappointment bubbling beneath her skin, she kept coming back to the fact that Kinga had been ill. That didn't excuse her behaviour but did explain it. No, she had to keep this from Cash, at least for the time being. When the time was right, she'd tell him.

She met Kinga's anxious stare. "I'm not going to lie. I'm furious that you almost ruined the best thing that had ever happened to me, but the fact is you didn't. Cash and I are stronger than ever, but our breakup meant he missed a lot of tennis. If I tell him this now, it will destroy his focus once more. So here's the plan. I won't tell him, and neither will you. Sometime in the future, when things are more settled, I'll talk to him. Agreed?"

Kinga nodded. "Whatever you think's best."

SWEAT POURED off Cash as he prepared to face another onslaught from the ball machine. Brad was clearly trying to fucking kill him. The machine was set at top speed and the highest random oscillation, meaning Cash had to sprint side to side, go forward and backward, prepare for lobs, drive volleys, forehands, and backhands. His game was improving, no doubt about it. He'd made up the half-yard short that had contributed to his loss in the semis at the Monte-Carlo Masters, and he was almost back to his physical best.

"Okay, let's call it there." Brad passed him a protein drink and a banana.

Cash sank to the floor, groaning as his body violently protested. "I'm too old for this shit."

Brad picked up a tennis ball that had rolled to his feet. "Give up, then. About time I retired to a Caribbean island and had hot girls in skimpy bikinis bringing me all the mojitos I can drink."

"Yeah, right. You'd get bored in about ten minutes."

"Don't bank on it." Brad bounced the ball on the floor. "How did the pace feel?"

"It's there, or thereabouts. I was thinking of playing Munich ahead of Madrid."

Brad shook his head. "It's too close, the points are worth shit, and it'll tire you for the following week."

"You don't think I need a few matches under my belt?"

"No. What you need is to remember you're number fucking one, no matter what the rankings say."

Brad moved around the court, collecting stray tennis balls and popping them back into the machine. Brad knew him too well, could read that his confidence wasn't where it should be. Winning on a tennis court was as much about belief as talent. Sometimes more so. And at the moment, Cash had very little faith in himself.

"You mind if I go?" he said to Brad, anxious to catch up with Natalia to see how her meet-up with Kinga had panned out. In the couple of weeks Kinga had been back on the team, he couldn't find fault either with the level of commitment she'd shown to him or her kindness towards Natalia. Cash hadn't dropped his guard, though. He didn't trust Kinga yet, but she'd given him no reason to renege on the chance she'd pleaded for.

Brad picked up the last of the balls and tossed it on top of the others. "Nope," he said, switching the machine off at the wall. "Try and keep moving, though. Jamie will be over later to give you a massage. We need to keep you supple if we're to maintain this level of practice."

Cash nodded wearily and trudged off court. At least he didn't have to travel far—the tennis court was at the back of his own house. Three minutes later, he staggered into his bedroom and flicked on the shower. As the cubicle filled up with steam, he quickly undressed and stepped inside. Jets of hot water cascaded over his body. He leaned his forehead against the cool tile and closed his eyes. Fuck, that felt good. Even though cold water would be better for tired muscles, he craved the heat.

After ten minutes, he was briefly entertaining the thought of getting out when the shower door opened, and a fully naked Natalia slipped inside.

"Hi," she said quietly, her lips blazing a trail across his shoulders as her arms snaked around his waist.

Exhaustion forgotten, he felt his cock lengthen. He twisted around in her arms and swept wet hair away from her face.

"You're just the pickup I need," he said, bending his head to kiss her soft neck. She smelt of peaches, sweet and luscious.

"I thought you'd be exhausted after your practice session."

"I was."

"What happened?"

"You turned up," he said, manoeuvring her against the back wall of the shower, away from the pounding jets.

She shimmied against his growing erection. "You certainly seem happy to see me."

"Oh, baby," he groaned, lifting her legs and hooking them around his waist. His hands clasped her deliciously tight backside as he pushed himself inside. "So goddamned happy."

~

CASH ROLLED over in bed and ran his fingertips up and down Natalia's arm, knowing he should refrain but, at the same time, wondering whether he had enough energy for round two.

"How was Kinga?"

A flash of something he couldn't read crossed her face before she hid it behind a bright smile. "We had a good chat."

Cash frowned. "Something to tell me, sweetness?"

She shook her head. "Just girl talk. You'd be bored."

"You're probably right." He flipped her on her back, and a giggle broke from between her gorgeous lips. He rubbed the tip of his nose down hers and dropped a soft kiss on her mouth. "What do you want to do tomorrow?"

"Can we go riding?" she said, a bright smile lighting up her face. "I haven't been since... " She broke off, a frown appearing. "Since we broke up."

Cash waggled a finger in front of her face. "Oh no, you don't," he said, tugging at the corners of her mouth until she giggled. "No more guilt, baby, okay? And yes, we can go riding tomorrow."

"Great. It'll be good to get some downtime as I've got three articles due back with Pete next week."

"Just don't work too hard. I don't want you getting tired." With a waggle of his eyebrows, Cash dipped his head and brushed the seam of her lips with his tongue. Like a blossoming flower, she opened her mouth, allowing him access. His kiss was soft at first, then insistent. Writhing seductively against him, she didn't disappoint.

"Again," she demanded, her voice low and husky.

Fuck. Could my woman be any more perfect?

19

C ash parked outside his mum's house a few days later.
With the European season around the corner, this
would be the last time he saw her for a few weeks. He
wouldn't have time to come home between tournaments.

"You're quiet," Natalia said as he cut the engine.

He twisted in his seat. "I don't know how to handle this. What
do I tell her?"

"The truth," Natalia replied simply.

Cash ran a hand over his face and sighed heavily. The
previous day, when Mum had finally asked what had happened
to Dad, Cash had bottled it, made an excuse, and hurriedly left.
But he couldn't hide from that conversation forever.

He rested his forehead against the steering wheel and closed
his eyes. Natalia's warm hand rubbed soothing circles on
his back.

"It's going to be okay, Cash. It's natural for your mum to want
to know what happened, especially now she's recovering. You
owe it to her to fill in the gaps. Stay true to the facts, answer any
questions she has, and just be there for her."

He raised his head and met her gaze. Her blue eyes were soft and warm as they raked his face, looking for clues to his state of mind.

"You're pretty smart. You know that?"

"I have my moments," she said, giving his shoulder a playful nudge. "Now, stop procrastinating, and get your arse inside."

He grinned to himself as he climbed out of the car.

Gracie greeted them at the front door. "Hey, you guys." She gave Natalia a brief hug and patted his arm. "Ready?"

"Sure," he lied.

"Good. Because she's been bugging me all morning about what time you're getting here."

A horrible, sickly feeling grew in his gut. How did he begin to tell his mother he'd killed her husband, his father? He didn't have a clue. The walls began to close in, his pulse rate firing up.

"Hey." Natalia's left hand curved round the back of his neck, and she squeezed.

He kept his gaze averted.

"Hey," she repeated, more forcefully this time.

Cash lifted his head and stared into her eyes. Gradually, his breathing slowed. "What if she hates me?" he whispered.

He found himself in Natalia's arms, her embrace tight and firm. His whole body began to relax as she murmured comforting words in his ear. He didn't know what he'd do if she wasn't by his side.

"Okay, let's go."

He knitted his fingers through Natalia's and set off towards his mother's room.

"Maybe you should do this alone, Cash," Natalia said.

"No," he said. "I want you with me. I *need* you with me."

Her response was to squeeze his hand as he pushed open the door to Mum's room.

∾

TALLY DETACHED her hand from Cash's and hung around by the door as he wandered inside. Rachael's bright smile greeted them both.

"There you are," she said, holding out her arms.

Cash gave his mother a warm hug before settling into the chair next to the bed. He glanced over at where Tally was still hugging the doorframe. He frowned and cocked his head.

"Tally, come and sit next to me," Rachael said.

Despite both mother and son clearly wanting her there, she couldn't help feeling this was a conversation to which she didn't belong. But as neither seemed to be giving her a choice, she wandered over and gave Rachael a kiss on the cheek.

"You look wonderful," Tally said. "Sorry that it's been a few days since I came, but things have been pretty busy workwise."

"No matter." Rachael waved her hand dismissively. "You're here now. So," she said, fixing her razor-sharp gaze on Cash, "are we having this talk now? Or are you going to keep avoiding the situation?"

Tally glanced at Cash. In the whole time she'd known him, she'd never seen him this nervous. He tucked his chin into his chest, avoiding anyone's gaze, and his hands were clenched so tightly his knuckles had turned white. As the atmosphere grew tense, Tally had a sudden urge to escape.

"Why don't I go and make us all a drink?" Tally said. "Leave you to it."

"No." Rachael's hand shot out, her fingers curving around Tally's wrist. For someone who'd only recently come out of a thirteen-year coma, Rachael's grip was surprisingly strong. The physio must have been working. "You're family. And I want you here."

"So do I," Cash said, finally lifting his head, his eyes imploring her to stay.

"Okay," she said, a little stunned at Rachael's comment about her being family. It made her insides warm, and a fuzzy sensation spread across her skin.

"That's settled, then," Rachael said, refocusing her attention on Cash.

He squeezed his eyes shut, but when he opened them, they held a new resolve. Tally hoped confessing to his mother would enable Cash to finally let go of the past. To bury it, along with the terrible guilt he'd carried around all these years.

Rachael reached for Cash's hand as he began to talk. She didn't take her eyes off him, and when Cash told her he'd been arrested, her fingers tightened on Tally's arm, as though Rachael needed the extra support. When he finished, his shoulders sagged, and he bent his head low until Rachael gently lifted his chin.

"Don't you dare hang your head," she said.

"I killed him," Cash said, his voice so quiet Tally had to strain to make out the words. "I'm responsible."

"You're responsible for saving my life," Rachael said firmly. "If you hadn't done what you did, I wouldn't be here."

The tension clawing at Tally's shoulders evaporated. She could have hugged Rachael. Those simple words were exactly what Cash needed to hear. His hands trembled as he reached for his mother.

"So you forgive me?"

Rachael lifted her hand to his face, her touch soft and exploratory, almost as though she was using the contact to reconnect with the son she'd only known as a child, not the man before her.

"There's nothing to forgive." A sob caught in her throat, and her eyes shone with unshed tears. "I'm the one at fault. I'm the reason for everything you had to go through."

"No." Cash's response was emphatic. He pressed Rachael's hand to his cheek. "You are *not* to blame."

"I should have left him," she whispered, her chin trembling with the effort of keeping her emotions in check.

"He'd have come after you. He never would have let you go. You know that."

Rachael fell into Cash's arms, and he held her close, gently rubbing her back as she sobbed, her head buried in his chest. Feeling like an interloper, Tally quietly got to her feet and tiptoed out of the room, leaving mother and son alone.

She wandered into the kitchen and put the kettle on.

"How'd it go?"

Tally glanced over her shoulder to find Gracie leaning against the doorframe, hands tucked into the back pockets of her jeans, her brows pulled low.

"Pretty well, considering. It can't be easy hearing all that, knowing you weren't there for your son at a time when he needed you the most."

Gracie moved into the room and pulled up a chair. "Poor Rachael."

Tally poured boiling water over instant-coffee granules and passed Gracie a mug. "They've got a lot of catching up to do."

When Cash appeared about fifteen minutes later, his eyes were heavy, dark circles creating purple bruises beneath, and his mouth pinched in at the corners. He gave Tally a wan smile and nodded at her mug. "Can I get one of those?"

He sank into a chair, his head flopping backwards almost as if he didn't have the strength to hold it upright.

Tally put his drink on the table and stood behind him. She rested her hands on his shoulders, massaging the tightly bunched muscles. "How is she?"

"Sleeping. Gracie, would you mind giving us a minute?"

"Of course," Gracie said. She picked up her coffee and left the room. As soon as they were alone, Cash covered his face with his hands.

A sense of alarm crept over her as she took a seat beside him. "What's going on, ace?"

He brought his head up slowly. "We've got a problem. A major fucking problem."

Tally waited for Cash to expand on what the problem was, but as they drove away from Rachael's house, he remained tight-lipped. When Tally had left them alone, Cash's mum had been understandably upset, but they'd seemed okay. There was no point distracting him while he was driving. She would push him on the matter once they were home.

The smell of warm bread greeted them the minute they opened the front door. She grinned as she remembered Anna had promised to bake baguettes that day. Tally had told her they were her favourite—particularly when slathered in butter while the bread was still warm. Tally's stomach grumbled appreciatively.

"Hungry?" Cash said with a smirk. His mood had lightened the minute they'd walked through the front door.

Perhaps he is overreacting about this supposed problem.

"Starving. Can you smell that? Anna's a genius."

They headed for the kitchen. Their timing was perfect because Anna was removing the bread from the oven as they walked in.

"You are my favourite person in the whole world." Tally lowered her head and sniffed. "They smell amazing."

"Hold it," Anna said, slapping Tally's hand away as she tried to grab one of the baguettes. "They're too hot. Give it a few minutes."

Tally grumbled but did as she was told while Anna bustled about slicing cheese and popping butter into a dish. After a few minutes, she touched the top of the bread and nodded.

"Okay, it's all yours. I'll leave you to it."

Tally dived in, tearing a baguette in half and breaking it open. Steam escaped from inside, and she spread butter on top, which immediately melted. She piled on the cheese and took a bite.

"Oh my God," she mumbled, mouth half-full. "Don't you ever get rid of that woman."

Cash helped himself to the other half of the baguette. "It's good to see you eat, sweetness." He pinched her hip.

"I have no willpower," she lamented, making Cash laugh.

"Good." He opened the fridge and pulled out a bottle of white wine. "Want one?"

"Yes, please. Bread and cheese and wine. We could be back in Paris."

He placed a half-filled glass in front of her and wiped a crumb from the side of her mouth. "I can't wait to take you back to Paris."

"Me either. Anyway, sit," she said, pointing at the stool next to hers. "Talk to me."

He did as she asked, taking a deep slug of wine and another bite of his sandwich. He chewed thoughtfully as though playing for time.

"Mum's almost well enough to start getting out and about."

"That's good, isn't it?"

He rocked his head from side to side. "Yes and no."

She frowned. "What do you mean?"

Cash teased his beard with his fingertips as he expelled a soft sigh. "How do I explain her? I mean... how do I explain where my mother has been all these years without the full story coming out and being splashed across the front pages."

Tally blew out a breath. *Now* she got it. And he was right. It was a problem. His greatest fears were coming to fruition.

She tapped her forefinger against her lips. "Hmm, yeah."

"Hmm, yeah?"

"I'm thinking."

"Well, hurry up, because I'm all out of ideas,"

There'd be no keeping this quiet. Even if they were extremely careful, the press would find out the truth in seconds. As soon as Cash was seen in public with his mother, the digging would begin. And Rachael deserved to live a full and proper life, not one hidden behind walls.

The answer came to her in an instant. Simple and controllable. A broad smile spread across her face.

"I've got it."

"Yeah?"

She threw her hands out wide. "Give me the exclusive."

Cash's eyebrows almost disappeared into his hairline. His mouth opened and closed again. He shook his head as though he had water in his ears.

"How would that help?" he finally said.

She covered his clenched hands with hers. "Babe, there's no way you're keeping this quiet. Not now. But by talking to me, and *only* me, I can control not only the way the information gets out but also the slant of the story. Plus, you'd get full editorial rights on the finished article."

Cash repetitively drummed his fingers on the kitchen worktop as he considered her proposal. She hoped he would think it through properly and not dismiss it out of hand. It was their only real option.

"Okay." He stared at his hands, refusing to meet her gaze. "I presume you'll put it through Pete?"

"Yes," she said, a little stunned at how easily he'd come around. "And I'd like to tell Emmalee too, at least before it comes out in the paper."

Cash lifted his chin and gave the heavy sigh of a man who had struggled for years to hold on to a family secret only to have the walls he'd carefully built collapse around him. "Whatever you think's best. As long as she keeps her mouth shut."

"Cash." She rubbed her thumb over the back of his hand, absorbing his strength and giving him hers. "Everything's going to be fine. Trust me."

"You know I trust you. But this is going to get rough, Natalia. I'm going to need you now more than ever."

21

Pete surprised the hell out of Cash by not interrupting. Not even once. Apart from the odd raised eyebrow, he remained quietly attentive. Cash gave him the abridged version, but even that took a good fifteen minutes to get through.

When he stopped talking, Natalia's fingers curled around his, and he glanced down at where their hands were joined before making eye contact with Pete again.

"Well," Pete finally said. Cash expected more but didn't get it. Pete stared out of the window, his fingers thrumming on his mahogany desk, and he gnawed at the inside of his cheek. The action reminded Cash of Natalia, and he almost smiled but managed to contain it in case Pete assumed he found the situation funny. There was nothing remotely funny about the position Cash was in. When his mother had begun her road to recovery, this particular situation hadn't occurred to him. Fuck, he hated the loss of control.

"Well...?" Cash prompted, shifting uncomfortably in his chair. Anything could come out of Pete's mouth, and the last thing Cash needed was a row. But if Pete acted like a cock, a row was precisely what he'd get.

"I'm amazed you've managed to keep this quiet. All these years. That's quite impressive, particularly for someone like you."

"What do you mean, *someone like me*?" Cash snapped.

Pete made a calming motion with his hands as, simultaneously, Natalia tightened her grip.

"Take it easy," Pete said. "I meant being in the public eye, that's all. Most celebrities have trouble hiding the fact they've taken a shit, let alone a story as huge as this."

"My life is not a story," Cash bit out.

"Cash, Pete doesn't mean it like that," Natalia said, trying, as ever, to be the mediator. "Do you?"

Her pointed comment was steely, as if warning Pete the next thing that came out of his mouth had better hit the right tone.

"No, of course I don't. But come on, Cash, you're not dumb. You have to know this is coming out, and when it does, it's going to be huge."

"That's why we're here, Pete," Natalia said. Her grip on Cash's hand had tightened to the point where he was beginning to lose sensation in his fingers. He flexed his hand beneath hers, and she relaxed slightly. "Cash knows there will be questions about his mum. Where she's been. Why she was in a coma all these years. We've agreed the best way to handle the situation is to take control. Get the story out first in his own words." She paused. "We want the exclusive to be with you."

Pete's eyes grew wide in astonishment. "Here? You want to publish here?" His gaze snapped to Cash's. "And you've agreed to this?"

"Yes," Cash said, clenching his teeth together. He ignored the growing ache in his jaw.

Pete whistled through his teeth. "Smart move."

"All Natalia's idea."

"Smart girl."

"Tell me something I don't know," Cash said with a fleeting smile in her direction.

"So you're in?" Natalia asked Pete.

"Shit, yeah."

"Right." Natalia pulled back her shoulders and placed her hands flat on Pete's desk. "Here's how it's going to go. I'll write the article. Cash has full editorial privileges. If he says no to something, anything, it's no. End of story. And I want to work with Danny."

Cash flashed her a look. He'd never met Danny, an ex-colleague of Natalia's and also a close friend, although she spoke of him often. Cash wasn't sure how he felt talking with a stranger about something so personal. And painful.

"That is, if you agree," she said as if she'd sensed his unease.

"Let's talk about it later," he said, unwilling to have this conversation in front of Pete.

She nodded. "I'll let you know on the last point," she said to Pete. "But are you good with the rest?"

A slow grin unfurled on Pete's face. "Your father would be pretty proud right now, Tally. As am I. It's a deal."

He held out his hand, and she shook it, her brief look of pain at the mention of her father quickly replaced with satisfaction.

"Thanks." She smiled and glanced at Cash. "Ready, ace?"

"Yes," he said, rubbing his eyes. He wanted nothing more than to get back to the hotel and put all this shit in the back of his mind. And there was one surefire way of doing exactly that. Natalia's half-smile and twinkling eyes told him she was on the same page.

"We'll be in touch," she said, rising to her feet.

"When do you fly to Madrid?" Pete asked.

"The day after tomorrow, but I'll start working on the first draft immediately. I think we should aim for the week after next for publication."

"So soon?" Cash said, an uncomfortable feeling stirring in his chest. "That'll be right around the Madrid finals."

"Let's talk about it, decide together," she said, rubbing his arm. "But the longer we leave it—"

"The more likely it'll come out."

"Precisely."

He gave a bitter laugh. His fiercely protected privacy was about to be splashed across the front pages of a national newspaper. And even though he would be in control of the words Natalia wrote, the fallout was way beyond anything either of them could hope to regulate. He had no idea how his sponsors would react, or his fans. The next few weeks were going to be tough. He could lose his career, his lucrative sponsorship deals, and his fans, but worse than all that, those he loved the most were about to get caught in the crossfire.

And there wasn't a damn thing he could do about it.

22

E m sat in stunned silence as Tally finished telling her about Cash's mum and the story Pete was going to publish. Every now and again, Em would open her mouth to say something, but then she'd simply shake her head and remain quiet.

"So now you know," Tally said, leaning forward to pick up the cup of tea Em had made her. She took a sip and screwed up her face. Cold. She leaned back on her chair and flicked the kettle on.

"I feel *terrible*," Em said. "I gave Cash such a hard time, and yet all he was doing was protecting his mum."

Tally shrugged. "It's not your fault, but at least now you know why I was so quick to take him back. I wanted to tell you before it comes out, but please, it's just between you and me."

Em made a locking motion across her mouth. "My lips are sealed. When is Pete going to publish?"

"Not sure yet. A couple of weeks, maybe earlier. My preference is sooner rather than later."

A frown flickered across Em's face. "Why the rush? He's kept it under wraps until now."

"Well, Rachael is getting stronger all the time, and she wants to start spreading her wings, which will undoubtedly cause questions to be asked, but for me, it's more than that."

"What do you mean?"

Tally rested her chin on her hands. "Cash has carried the guilt over killing his father around for years, but he's also consumed with fear—of losing his career, his livelihood, his fans. Once his story is in the public domain, he can let the fear go. And my guess is none of those things will happen. It's all about how we manage the message."

Em nodded. "Makes sense."

Tally stood and made another cup of tea. "Want to hear my other news?" she said as she sat back down.

Em tilted forwards. "Always."

"I found out who took the photographs of Cash with Gracie."

Em's mouth fell open. "Who? How?"

Tally smirked. "The 'how' is because she confessed. The 'who'... Kinga."

Em sucked in a breath. "Oh my God." She shook her head. "I never trusted that woman."

"I know."

"Cash must have gone ballistic."

Tally chewed the side of her cheek. "I haven't told him."

Em's eyebrows shot up. "Why not?"

"He's got enough stress right now. Plus he's just getting back into playing again. The last thing I want is to knock him off course again."

Em wrinkled her nose. "Babes, I'm not sure that's the right decision."

Tally shrugged one shoulder. "Maybe not, but it's the one I've made. I told Kinga that when I gauge that the time is right, I'll tell him."

Em let out a low whistle. "What a fucking mess."

"I feel for her. She's trying to do the right thing, make a fresh start."

Em snorted. "She doesn't deserve your forgiveness, but then, you always did have a forgiving nature. Me? Not so much."

Tally laughed. "Yin and yang—that's us."

Em grinned. "The perfect team."

≈

ISAAC DROPPED Tally and Cash outside Danny's place later that evening. Danny had invited them round to dinner after Cash reluctantly agreed to include him in writing the article. Danny didn't fool Tally, though. His benevolence was only because he wanted her to meet Luke, his latest boyfriend, whom he'd described as "the one."

"Ready?" she said, weaving her fingers through Cash's.

He glanced at her, his face expressionless. "No."

Her heart cramped. If there were any other way around this terrible situation they'd found themselves in, she'd take it.

"It's going to be fine. I've already filled Danny in on most of it. He wants to get to know you a little—that's all. It'll help when it comes to the edit."

"Let's just get it over with, okay?"

She sighed and started to walk up the path, Cash trailing slightly behind. She was halfway to the house when Danny flung the door open and stepped out to greet her.

"Hey, baby girl," he said, wrapping his arms around her and rocking her from side to side. "It's been too long."

She giggled. "Danny, get off. You're making me dizzy."

He released her. "And here's the reason I haven't seen you in, like, forever. Although I'm not surprised," he said, leering at Cash with a salacious grin on his face. "If he were mine, you wouldn't be seeing much of me either."

Tally gave her friend a dig in the ribs and stole a glance at Cash. She wasn't sure how he would take to Danny. She had grown used to Danny's camp ways, but some people found him a bit much.

She needn't have worried.

"Shame for you I'm hetero, then," he said with a broad smile as he shook Danny's outstretched hand. "And you need to watch it. She's beyond feisty when she's jealous."

Danny laughed. "Oh yeah. *Vicious bitch* doesn't even begin to describe her."

Tally planted her hands on her hips when Cash chuckled, and she shook her head at both of them. "I am here, you know."

Danny looped an arm around her shoulder, tucked his hand into the crook of Cash's elbow, and hustled them inside. "Come and meet Luke. I've told him how utterly fabulous you are, so try not to let me down, Tal."

Tally glanced once more at Cash. Danny had worked his magic. Cash had completely relaxed. The worry lines around his eyes were gone, and his shoulders were no longer hunched up next to his ears.

Luke was nothing like she'd imagined. Based on Danny's previous boyfriends, she'd expected someone midheight with dark hair and a fairly lithe physique, a little bit wimpish. Luke couldn't have been more opposite. He was tall—quite a bit taller than Danny—and broad shouldered with a thick head of sandy hair that flopped over his forehead.

"It's great to meet you finally," he said, giving Tally a peck on the cheek. He was a lot more circumspect with Cash, leaving the greeting at a firm handshake. "Please, come and sit down. Let me get you both a drink. Wine okay?"

Tally and Cash nodded, and as Luke disappeared into the kitchen, Tally's eyes darted to Danny's.

"He's a bit of a departure from the norm," she said.

"I knew you'd say that," Danny whispered. "But he's amazing. Everything I could ever want. I want you to like him. It's important to me that you two get along."

"Listen, if he's good enough for you, he'll do for me."

"Good. Now shush. He's coming back."

"So what do you do for a living, Luke?" Tally said as Luke returned with bottles of red and white wine, which he set in the middle of the table.

"I design Linux systems."

Tally gave him a questioning look. "What are Linux systems?"

"They're basically IT operating systems," he said, laughing as Tally screwed her face up. "Yeah, I know. IT is boring except for geeks like me."

"IT confuses me," she said.

"You're not alone. I get confused at times."

"What made you choose IT?" Cash said as he accepted a glass of wine.

"I don't think I chose it as much as it chose me. While other kids were out playing, I was in my room building servers and desktop computers."

Cash smiled. "I guess it's a bit like me with tennis."

Luke nodded. "I've never wanted to do anything else. I love tinkering with computers, working out what the problem is when they go wrong."

Tally caught Danny's eye and nodded in approval. His grin couldn't have been any wider as he soaked up every word Luke spoke.

After dinner, Luke and Danny cleared the dishes, and once they were out of earshot, she squeezed Cash's hand. "You doing okay, ace?"

He gave her a genuine smile. "Yeah. Danny's grand. They seem like a great couple."

"Danny's the best. He'll do right by you on the article, as will I."

Cash lowered his voice. "Can he be trusted to keep his mouth shut? I don't want him sharing anything with Luke. After all, we don't know him."

She nodded. "Don't worry. I'll make it clear to Danny this is a three-way, not a four-way."

Cash chuckled. "Not sure he's my type, and you're definitely not his."

She rolled her eyes. "You could turn any innocent comment into a filthy one."

"And you love it, baby." Cash coaxed her onto his lap and nuzzled her neck with the tip of his nose.

"Stop." She half-heartedly tried to pull away.

"I'll stop when your words match your body language," he said, tracing his tongue along her collarbone. When his teeth grazed her earlobe, she hissed loudly.

"Cash, let me go. They're coming back."

She managed to wriggle out of his arms and make it back to her chair in time to save her blushes. Or so she thought.

"Don't let us interrupt you," Danny said, barely repressing a grin as he sat down. "And if you're going to try to hide the fact you've been making out, you might want to sort your hair, Tal."

He and Luke shared a look before the two of them burst out laughing.

"Bugger off, the pair of you," she said, running a hand over her hair.

"Impressive," Danny said to Cash. "We've only been gone five minutes, and you've got her all of a dither."

Tally huffed. "Oh, for God's sake, don't encourage him."

"No, do," Cash said with a grin. "My ego needs a bit of stroking."

Tally choked out a laugh. "Any more stroking, and your ego will be lying on its back waiting for me to scratch its belly."

"Now, there's an image," Danny said as he poured three coffees. "Okay, let's get on so you two can finish what you started at my dining table." Danny glanced over at Luke, who nodded.

"That's my cue to leave," he said, kissing the top of Danny's head. "I'm off to the gym. It was great to meet you both. We should do this again soon."

Luke gave Tally a hug and shook Cash's hand before heading out. Danny waited until he heard the front door slam and then switched on his iPad.

"Okay, beautiful people. Let's get to work."

23

Tally held her breath as Cash set the article down on the coffee table. She waited for him to say something. Anything. Instead, he strode across their hotel suite and grabbed a bottle of water from the minibar. With his eyes on hers, he took a long drink.

"Well?" she prompted.

He held the bottle by the neck, casually swinging it from his hand as he walked back to the sofa, then picked up the article once more and thumbed through the pages.

"It's good. Very good. A sympathetic feature for an unsympathetic man."

Tally expelled a frustrated breath. "You have *got* to get over this." She tapped her finger against the papers he held in his hands. "Every word in there is true, and the underlying meaning is exactly what I was aiming for. That's why I took over a week to draft it. It's time to leave the past behind, Cash. Don't you think you've suffered enough?"

He gave a weak shrug. "Maybe. It's difficult, seeing it written down, knowing the world will be reading those words and judging. I couldn't give a shit what they say about me, but I'm worried about Mum. She isn't ready to cope with any negativity."

Tally placed her hand over his. "Your mother is stronger than you think. We'll deal with it. Whatever happens, we'll deal with it together."

"Yeah, I guess." He took another long drink of water.

"Is there anything you want to change before I send it to Pete?"

"No. Like I said, it's good." He grinned. "Looks like I've got myself hooked up with a rather talented woman."

Tally laughed even as a slight blush heated her cheeks. "Be careful, ace. There's only room for one ego in this relationship."

Cash chuckled and tugged her to sit astride his lap. He fed a lock of her hair through his fingers before reaching up to give her a quick kiss.

"I'll grab my stuff. We need to leave in fifteen minutes."

She encrypted the file before sending it to Pete. He responded in minutes with a note saying he'd get any changes back to her before nightfall. Then she could make the final tweaks before agreeing with Pete which edition of the paper it should be scheduled for.

Cash was pensive on the way to the tournament, his mouth creased in thought, and tired lines around his eyes made his face look drawn. Tally left him alone with his thoughts. This wasn't easy for him, though he was coping remarkably well, especially with the knowledge that, in a few days, the article would hit newspaper stands, the Internet, everywhere. What happened afterwards—well, it was anyone's guess.

When they reached the stadium, Cash headed for the locker room. Tally wandered off in the direction of the players' lounge. The article kept reverberating in her mind. Cash was right—it was some of her best work—but that didn't matter in the long run. What did matter was the reaction it would spark.

She grabbed a coffee and spotted Kinga poring over a sheaf of papers.

"Hey," Tally said, dropping wearily into the seat next to her.

"Morning." Kinga tucked the papers away in a blue folder. "How's he doing?"

"A little more tense than I'd like."

Kinga shrugged. "That's Cash. He's always tense before a game." She twisted the ruby ring on her finger. "Have you thought any more about when you might tell him about the photographs?"

Tally shook her head as her insides clenched. He had enough stress at the moment. Spilling her secret would only add to that. "It's not the right time." She rested her hand on Kinga's arm. "I know you're worried, but try to relax."

"I don't deserve your compassion, Tally, but I'll take it."

Tally smiled. "Ready to go?"

Kinga glanced at her watch. "You go ahead. William is on his way. I'll wait for him and join you shortly."

Tally picked up her empty coffee cup and dropped it into the rubbish bin before heading onto court. She took her seat, ready for the quarter-final, and sent up a silent prayer that Cash would have his mind firmly on the match and not on the article. If he didn't, he'd lose.

She should have known better. Cash came on court, utterly focused, and hammered his opponent. After the formalities were over, he glanced up into the players' box and flashed a cocky grin. Tally laughed with relief at the return of his supreme confidence.

"Are you joining us for dinner tonight?" Kinga asked as they headed inside.

"I can't," Tally said. "I've got some work to do this evening."

"Not to worry. I'm sure William will keep me suitably entertained. Won't you, darling?"

"I'll do my best," William said with a smile in Tally's direction.

Tally watched as the couple walked away, William's tall, broad stature and dark, wild curls a direct contrast to Kinga's petite frame and blond, perfectly styled hairdo. Tally had got to know William quite well over the last couple of weeks and would definitely put him on the "keep" list. Kinga had changed so much, and Tally guessed at least fifty per cent was due to William's influence.

As soon as Cash had completed the obligatory press conference, Isaac drove them back to the hotel. The atmosphere in the car was completely different from earlier in the day. Cash was in a great mood, making constant jokes, and Tally began to hope he'd started to come to terms with what was about to happen.

After they arrived at the hotel, Cash disappeared into the bedroom to make a few phone calls while she ordered room service. She usually preferred to go out for dinner, but she needed to talk to Cash regarding the best time to tell the team about the article, and the last thing they needed was anyone overhearing their conversation.

When he sauntered into the living room of their suite, top button of his jeans undone, and wearing a white T-shirt that clung to his firm, muscled chest, Tally swallowed hard. He walked unhurriedly towards her, so she averted her gaze. She couldn't allow him to distract her.

"The article's being published this Saturday," she said, deciding on the direct approach. "I know that only gives you two full days to prepare, but it's for the best."

Cash sighed and sank into a chair. "I thought you only sent it to Pete today."

"I did. He'll have spent the day editing it. I'm expecting it to land in my inbox by the time we've finished dinner, and that puts us on track for the weekend edition."

Cash's fingertips played with his beard, and not for the first time, she sensed his fear. She knelt in front of him, her hands resting on his thighs. "I get it, ace. You feel like you've climbed onto a rollercoaster, and now you can't get off, but trust me, when this is out, things are going to get a whole lot simpler."

Cash laughed bitterly. "You think?"

"I know," she said firmly. "I think we should tell the team as late as possible on Friday night."

Surprise flashed across his face. "I thought you'd push for me to tell them sooner than that."

"We can't afford for this to leak. I'm not saying anyone on the team would, but the more who know…" She shrugged. "It doesn't leave Kinga much time to talk to the sponsors, but I'm sure she'll manage."

His chest heaved as he sucked in a lungful of air. "Okay," he said quietly. "I'll ask them to come here on Friday night."

24

Cash was quiet and distracted over dinner. Tally knew why, of course. He was trying to come to terms with the timing of the article and what he would tell the team. In the early part of their relationship, she used to worry whenever Cash became morose, assuming he was quietly figuring out a way to dump her. But she was a lot more secure these days. It was better to let him work stuff out in his own time. The more she pressed, the testier he would become. He'd come around. After all, it wasn't as if he had a choice.

Tally piled their dinner things onto the room-service tray and left it in the hallway. She was about to make an attempt at conversation when her phone rang. She spotted Pete on the caller ID and frowned.

"Hi, Pete. Have you managed to finish the edit?"

Cash's head snapped up, and he tugged on the neck of his T-shirt as though it had somehow tightened around his throat.

"Pretty much. Need to talk to you about a few things, though."

"Oh?" Tally said.

"Yeah. Any chance you can get a flight over tomorrow morning? It would be easier to discuss face-to-face."

Tally's skin prickled, and the hairs on her arm stood up. Something was off. "Is everything okay?"

"Sure," Pete said far too brightly. "I'll only need you for a couple of hours max. You can be back in Madrid by early evening."

Tally glanced over at Cash. "Hang on a sec, Pete." She put the phone on mute. "Pete needs me to go to London. There and back in a day."

Cash raised an eyebrow. "Why?"

She shrugged. "A couple of things about the article. He wants to talk to Danny and me together," she said, making it up as she went along. The last thing she needed was for Cash to grow suspicious. She was suspicious enough for both of them.

"The hotel can set up a video conference for you."

"Yes, I'm sure they could," she said, playing for time. "But nothing quite beats face-to-face. It's important we get this right."

His eyes narrowed. "You'll be back in time for the match?"

"Of course."

"Okay."

His shoulders fell, evidence of his unhappiness. She wasn't delighted either, but she painted on a bright smile regardless. "All sorted, Pete. Can you get Nancy to book the flights? I have to be back here tomorrow evening."

"No problem. I'll text you the flight details. See you tomorrow."

ON ARRIVAL IN LONDON, the traffic was awful, made worse by the torrential rain. It took her twenty minutes longer than usual to get from the airport to the paper, but as she jumped into the lift, she couldn't help a moment of excitement churning through her insides. It was good to be back. She waved at a couple of her former colleagues but headed straight for Pete's office. No time for niceties that day, especially as she was already late.

She knocked once on the glass before pushing the door open. Pete wasn't alone. Danny was sitting in the chair directly opposite Pete's desk, and standing off to the side was a grey-haired guy in his fifties.

"Sorry I'm late," she said, giving Pete a peck on the cheek before doing the same to Danny. "Bloody London traffic."

She laughed but stopped when no one joined in. She shot a glance at Danny, puzzled when he wouldn't look her in the eye.

"What's going on? And who are you?" she said pointedly to the stranger in the room.

"Tally, this is Doug Chavant. Doug owns several national and local newspapers here in the UK and a couple in the US too."

"Right. And that's important because...?" She glanced at Doug. "No offence."

"None taken," he said with a slight curve of his lips.

Pete sighed as he rested his forearms on his desk. "There's been a leak."

Tally stared open-mouthed at Pete before glancing at Danny, who still wouldn't meet her gaze. "That's impossible. I've encrypted every message, and you've both done the same."

Danny paled, and he covered his face with his hands. "I'm sorry, Tally. It's all my fault."

"Danny...?" Tally flashed a puzzled glance Pete's way.

"Allow me to explain," Doug said. "One of my editors was approached with a story about Cash Gallagher. A rather explosive story. Guaranteed paper seller. But the person in question wanted a considerable amount of money in return for the exclusive. Any payments over a certain amount need my approval, so my editor brought the story to me, requesting I sign off on the payment. I didn't."

Tally frowned. "Why not?"

"Because your uncle and I are old friends, and I have a lot of respect for him. I'm aware you're in a relationship with Mr Gallagher, so naturally, Pete was the first person I called to see if he knew what was going on."

"And you told him we were planning to release the same story," Tally said to Pete.

Pete nodded. "Exactly."

"How did this source find out?"

Danny faced her then. His eyes were glossy with unshed tears, and she could have sworn his chin trembled. "Because of me."

She frowned. "I don't get it."

"Pillow talk," Pete said with a hard stare in Danny's direction.

"It was Luke." Danny's voice broke under the strain. "I barely told him anything, Tally, I promise. But then he repeated it to his personal trainer."

"Who came to your editor?" Tally asked Doug.

"No," he replied.

Tally shook her head. "Okay, you're losing me."

"Luke's personal trainer also trains Victoria Kaminsky," Pete said.

"Kaminsky?" Tally threw her hands in the air. "Well, that's it, then. We're screwed. She hates me."

"No, we're not," Pete said. "Not yet. Between Doug and me, we have enough contacts to bury this story for a day or two. But we have to move quickly. I've already done the edit. Unfortunately, this situation means there's no time for you and Cash to review. I want to publish tomorrow."

"Tomorrow? But it's his semifinal tomorrow." She wiped clammy hands on her jeans. "I need to talk to Cash."

Pete nodded. "I thought you'd say that, but if he baulks at the timeline, make sure he understands this is coming out regardless. And better if it's our version than Kaminsky's."

Pete, Doug, and Danny gave her some privacy. Alone, she tried to order her thoughts, but they wouldn't get in line. *Shit, shit,*

shit. All their plans. She dialled Cash's number without a clue how to begin.

"Hi, sweetness," he said. "How's London?"

"Wet," she said.

"It's twenty-five degrees here today."

"All right, don't rub it in."

Cash chuckled. "Don't worry. You'll be back here in a few hours. Tell me, what was so important you had to go all the way to London?"

Tally closed her eyes and took a deep breath. "There's been a leak," she blurted.

"Leak?" Cash sounded confused. Then he inhaled sharply. "Fuck. It's out?"

"No. Not yet. Pete has managed to put a lid on it, but that won't last long. He wants to publish tomorrow."

Tally expected a vociferous argument, but Cash was silent. She thought they'd lost the connection, but then she heard him sigh.

"Whatever he thinks is best." His tone was quiet and considered with a tinge of defeat.

Tally's heart squeezed. "There's no time for me to review following Pete's edit. Are you okay with that?"

A bitter laugh sounded down the phone. "No, I'm not fucking okay with that. But what other choice do we have?"

"None," she said quietly.

"Do you know how it got out?"

A twinge of anxiety chewed at her insides. "Let's talk when I get back tonight."

He must have sensed her stalling because he paused. "What time's your flight?" he eventually said.

"I'm heading back to Heathrow right now. I should be with you by eight."

He sighed again. "I guess I'd better brief everyone here and get Kinga onto the sponsors. Isaac will pick you up. Call me when you land."

Tally hung up and opened Pete's door, ushering everyone back in. "We're on. I hope you're going to do something about Kaminsky."

Pete made a slashing movement across his throat. "She's done."

"Good." Tally shook Doug's hand. "Thank you, Mr Chavant. I can't tell you how much I appreciate it." She kissed Pete on the cheek but couldn't quite bring herself to do the same to Danny.

"I'll call you," Tally said to Pete.

She closed the door and was halfway across the office when Danny shouted, "Tally, please, can we talk?"

As a few interested parties raised their heads, she signalled for him to follow her outside.

"I'm so sorry."

She pressed the button for the lift. "I can't believe you did that."

His shoulders dropped. "I can't believe it either. Please just give me five minutes. Let's get a coffee."

The lift doors opened, and she stepped inside. "Five minutes," she said as Danny followed her.

He sat opposite Tally in the coffee shop across the road from the paper, the skin bunched around his eyes as though he were in pain, and although she didn't like seeing him so upset, she was more concerned with how to tell Cash, especially as he'd voiced his concerns about extending his story beyond the two of them.

"So what happened?"

Danny lifted his eyes to hers. "I don't know where to begin."

"What exactly did you tell Luke?"

Danny shook his head. "Not much."

"But enough?"

"So it seems." He gave a long, low sigh, his mouth down-turned in sadness. His eyes were brim-full of unshed tears, and he furiously blinked them away before they had a chance to fall. "Pete's furious and he's got every right to be. I'm just thankful he hasn't sacked me as well as Kaminsky. I'm so sorry, Tal."

She curved her hands around her mug of coffee. "I know you are, but jeez, Danny, I wish you'd kept your trap shut for a few more days."

Danny lowered his chin to his chest. "Can you ever forgive me?"

She blew a breath through her nose. "Danny, we've been friends for a long time. You screwing up doesn't change that, but I could honestly strangle you right now."

"I could strangle myself."

Her lips twitched, despite her annoyance. "I don't think that's physically possible."

"What do you think Cash will say?"

Tally grimaced. "I doubt it will be repeatable. I can't say I'm looking forward to the conversation."

"Please tell him how sorry I am. Luke is too. He didn't mean it, you know. It wasn't malicious."

Tally glanced at her watch. "I can't deal with this right now. I've got to go."

She left Danny with his head in his hands and caught a taxi back to the airport.

25

As Tally walked into the arrivals hall, she spotted Isaac holding up a white sign with "Natalia McKenzie" written in black marker. She chuckled to herself and waved. He hurried over, immediately lifting her bag from her shoulder.

"I'm sorry, who are you?" she said.

Isaac smiled. "It's busy here. I wanted to make sure you saw me."

"Couldn't miss you, Isaac. You tower above everyone else."

Isaac had managed to get a parking space right across the street, and within five minutes, they were on their way to the hotel.

"How's he doing?"

Isaac twisted his head towards her, while still keeping an eye on the road. "He's a little tense."

Tally laughed. "Always so polite, Isaac. You mean he's being a grouch and making everyone's life miserable."

He squirmed in his seat. "We're all glad you're back. Let's leave it at that."

"Has he spoken to you?"

Isaac nodded. "It was a bit of a shock."

He didn't expand any further, and Tally didn't press. Isaac dropped her in front of the hotel. She trudged inside, an empty feeling in the pit of her stomach as she tried to second-guess Cash's reaction when she told him Danny had shared the story with Luke. Danny, whom Cash had voiced concerns over when they'd met for dinner. She was going to have to tell Cash he'd been right. God, she *hated it* when he was right.

She drew the key card out of her bag, inserted it into the slot, and took a deep breath before pushing the door open. Cash wasn't alone. Kinga and William were sitting on the sofa, and Rupe stood off to the side, wearing an unusually grim expression. No sign of Brad or Jamie.

"Hi," she said, dropping her bag on a nearby chair. "Party started without me?"

Cash jumped up and strode across the room. "Hey, baby." He cupped her face and kissed her before glancing over his shoulder. "Thanks for coming," he said, effectively dismissing everyone. "I appreciate it."

Kinga took the hint and immediately stood up. "Of course. We'll see you tomorrow." She rubbed Cash's shoulder and kissed Tally on the cheek. "Try and get some rest. It's going to be a big day."

"Fucking understatement of the year," Cash muttered.

Tally put her arm out when Rupe began to leave. "Can you stay a minute?"

"Of course," Rupe said.

Tally glimpsed Cash's puzzled look, which she ignored. She figured Cash might need emotional support from Rupe. Even if Cash didn't, she did. She closed the door behind Kinga and William and sank down onto the sofa.

"What a day," she said, rubbing her face with her hands.

"Well? How did the almost-fuck-up happen?" Cash's tone was sharp, telling her he was close to the limit of his patience.

"Sit down."

He hesitated, but after a brief pause, he did as she asked.

She took both his hands in hers. "I know this is a day or so earlier than we imagined, but the outcome is the same."

"What happened?"

"And Kinga will help handle the press. You know how good she is at doing that."

Cash snatched his hands from hers. "Stop fucking procrastinating, Natalia, and tell me."

Tally glanced at Rupe then back at Cash. "Luke let it slip to someone he shouldn't have. Accidentally."

Cash shot her a furious stare. "Luke? Danny's Luke?" When she nodded, he threw his hands in the air. "And how the fuck did Luke find out? No, let me guess. Danny fucking blabbed, didn't he?"

Tally gnawed at the inside of her cheek. She reached for him as he jumped to his feet. "There's no actual harm done."

"No harm done? I fucking *told* you I wanted to keep this between us. But no, you *had* to do it your fucking way."

Rupe opened his mouth to defend her, but she shot him a glance. "That's not fair. We both agreed. And let's face it—the only thing that's changed is we're going to print twenty-four hours earlier than planned."

Cash clawed at the neck of his T-shirt, an expression of absolute fury etched on his face. "That's all right, then. Fuck you, Natalia. And fuck Danny."

Rupe launched out of his chair and loomed over Cash. "I'm warning you, dude. You speak to her like that again, and I'm going to give you the fucking pasting you deserve."

Cash jumped up too and shoved Rupe hard in the shoulder, causing him to stumble backwards. "Oh yeah? You won't push me right now if you know what's good for you."

"Stop it!" Tally yelled as she threw her hands in the air. "Both of you. For God's sake."

Cash's arms fell to his sides. Without making eye contact with either her or Rupe, he slumped into the nearest chair and held his head in his hands.

"Everything will be fine, bud," Rupe said, already back to his usual amiable self.

Cash lifted his chin, his face creased in defeat. "Guarantee that, can you?"

Rupe grinned. "Yeah. I got superpowers, don't you know."

Cash's lips twitched, the first time he'd shown an iota of humour. "Do you mind leaving us alone?"

Rupe met Tally's gaze, seeking her agreement.

"We'll knock for you at ten tomorrow morning," she said, standing to see him out. "You might as well travel to the arena with us."

Rupe clapped Cash on the back and then gave Tally a hug. "I'm right down the hall. If you need me, holler."

"We will."

Tally closed the door behind him. As she turned around, Cash briefly met her gaze before dropping his eyes to the floor.

"I'm sorry," he said, scraping a hand through his hair. "I shouldn't have spoken to you like that."

She crossed the room and knelt down in front of him, her hands lightly brushing his thighs. "I know you feel like you've lost control, but once this is out, things are going to get better." When he refused to focus on her, she squeezed his knees. "You *have* to trust me."

His face twisted. "Were you scared of me? Is that why you had Rupe stay behind?"

"Of course not," she exclaimed. "I wanted him here for moral support. I know you'd never hurt me."

"I'm sorry for yelling. I didn't mean to. I was all prepared for it coming out Saturday, and now it's tomorrow instead..." He gave a weak shrug. "It caught me off guard, that's all."

Tally wrapped her arms around his neck, pulling him close. He clung to her, and her heart wrenched painfully. "Whatever happens, ace, we'll face it together."

26

Cash opened his eyes on the morning of his semifinal, and for about two seconds, he forgot what was to come. Then realisation hit him, and he groaned. The day was going to be hell. Not the worst fucking day of his life, but not a barrel of laughs either.

He rolled onto his side, and his heart rate spiked. Natalia was lying on her back, her hair a wild tumble over the white pillowcase, her normally pale skin flushed. A dart of guilt shot through him at how vile he'd been to her. He'd treated her like shit, and in return, she'd offered him unconditional support.

She stretched in her sleep, a sigh of pleasure escaping her parted lips. The movement caused the bedsheet to slip, revealing the curve of one pale breast. His cock twitched, and he lifted the covers. His gaze swept over her breasts, down to the dip in her waist, which led to perfectly flared hips.

"Morning, pervert."

Cash's head snapped to Natalia's face. Her eyes were half-open and alight with laughter. He forced a grin. "Busted."

She rose up on her elbow and looked him square in the eye. "How are you doing, ace?"

"I'm sorry about yesterday," he said, tucking a lock of hair behind her ear. "I don't know why you put up with me."

"Because I love you."

His heart squeezed, and he kissed her briefly on the lips. "I don't deserve you."

"How are you feeling about today?"

He shrugged. "I'm pulling out of the tournament."

Natalia gasped. "Why?"

"Because." He shrugged again and glanced at the clock. "First edition will be out, and it'll already be online."

"But that doesn't mean you shouldn't play. Not if you want to."

"If I go out there today, I'll lose. Badly. My mind isn't on the job."

She tilted her head to one side. "Are you sure?"

"Positive."

"Have you called Brad or Kinga?"

"Not yet. I wanted to tell you first." He swung his legs over the side of the bed and wandered into the living room of their suite. He returned a few minutes later, holding his phone. "Why don't you order breakfast while I take my medicine."

Natalia smiled, although the smile didn't quite reach her eyes. He watched as she walked naked across the room to grab her dressing gown from the bathroom. His stomach cramped with pleasure, the sight of her momentarily distracting him. She'd changed so much in the last few months, her confidence in her body and in his love for her soaring. And even though he wouldn't have thought it possible, he was more attracted to her now than in the beginning.

He thought about tossing a coin to decide who to call first, but as both Brad and Kinga would likely lose the fucking plot when he told them he wasn't playing the match, the order didn't matter. He decided on Kinga, only because he wanted her to arrange a press conference for later that day. Might as well get it over with in one go. And if he was upfront with the press, maybe they'd go easy on him.

Yeah. Of course they would.

～

TALLY SLUNG ON her dressing gown and left Cash alone. She could only imagine how pissed off Brad would be, and not for the first time, she worried he would think Cash's career had begun to unravel ever since she'd come onto the scene.

She ordered breakfast for the two of them and grabbed her phone. Might as well check out the article online and see what sort of comments people were leaving. She clicked on the newspaper app. The article was at the top of the page, and she quickly scanned it. Pete was a superb editor. The story had come across as empathetic, while at the same time not sounding as though any pertinent facts had been omitted. They hadn't, but sometimes stories read as though the journalist was hiding something, which led the public to think they were being lied to.

She scrolled down to the bottom of the article. *Shit.* Already, more than one thousand people had commented, and it wasn't even nine in the morning. Taking a deep breath, she began to flick through the comments, anxiety quickly turning to euphoria. Apart from the odd troll sticking the knife in, the public was fully behind Cash. As relief washed over her, the nervous tension in her stomach evaporated. She continued to read amazing messages of love and support and couldn't stop a broad smile edging across her face.

She glanced up as the bedroom door opened. Cash's hair was dishevelled where he'd probably been dragging his hand through it as Kinga and Brad told him what they thought of his decision. The strain showed on his face.

Tally held up her phone, still open at the comments page.

"Well, ace, the public is on your side, so those journalists may have to be a bit nicer to you."

Cash reached out and took hold of her phone. His thumb flicked across the screen as he scrolled through the web pages. As time went on, a deep frown turned into a tentative smile. After a few minutes reading, he raised his head.

"Well, who'd have thought?" He handed back her phone. "That'll help the sponsors swallow the pill."

"Your fans love you."

"Shame they won't be interviewing me later."

She chuckled. "What did Kinga and Brad say?"

A trace of a smile left his lips. "Do you really want to know?"

"That good?"

Cash collapsed onto the seat next to her. "Brad called me a fucking idiot. And Kinga, well, I can't repeat what she said. Foul-mouthed bitch."

"It went well, then?" Tally said, giving him a playful nudge.

Cash grimaced. "Neither of them agrees with my decision."

"But ultimately, it *is* your decision. There's still time to change your mind."

He shook his head. "I've asked Kinga to inform the tournament director and to arrange a press conference for this afternoon. Once that's out of the way, we can travel to Rome to get ready for next week."

"What time is the press conference?"

"Kinga's going to meet with my lawyers this morning and then arrange it for two." He clasped her hand. "You'll be there, right?"

Tally swallowed past a lump in her throat. "Where else would I be, ace?"

MANIC CHATTER SEEPED through the door as Tally and Kinga peeked into the room where they were holding the press conference. It was slowly filling up. If the footfall continued at that rate, it would be standing room only in about thirty seconds.

"Ready?" she said, glancing over her shoulder at Cash.

"No. But what choice do I have?"

"Come on, ace. This isn't you. Remember how much you hate the bastards, and you'll be fine."

Cash chuckled and pulled her into his arms. "What would I do without you?"

She brushed a lock of hair from his forehead. "Lucky for you, you'll never have to find out."

He gave a heavy sigh. "Maybe I should have hired a publicist."

"Thanks for the vote of confidence," Kinga said with a smile.

"You know what I mean. This isn't exactly your job."

"My job is anything you need it to be. I'm not exactly inexperienced in dealing with the press. Just remember, only answer what you're comfortable with, and ignore the rest. Shouldn't be too much of a stretch for you," she added with a grin. She waved her hand for Cash to go ahead, but as he passed her, she tapped his arm. "Stay cool."

Cash grimaced and opened the door. Loud chatter immediately reduced to a low hum as he pulled his chair out and sat down. Isaac stood off to the left, his eyes scanning the room. Kinga took her place on Cash's right, Tally sat to his left. She almost whispered something about him being flanked by his harem, but one look at his grim expression, and she changed her mind.

"Ladies and gentleman, thank you for coming," Kinga said. "As per the briefing statement, Cash will take questions for fifteen minutes. Please, only one question per journalist to give everyone a chance." She glanced around the room, pointing at a seasoned sports reporter who worked for the BBC, who also happened to be a nice woman. "Priya, your question."

"What made you decide to go public now, after all these

years?" Priya said, pen poised to take notes even though her voice recorder sat on her lap.

Cash groped for Tally's hand under the table. "After almost thirteen years in a coma, my mother is making an excellent recovery, and quite understandably, she wants to get out and about. As questions will undoubtedly be asked if we're seen together, I decided now was the right time. Believe me, if there'd been another way, I'd have taken it."

"Was it difficult confessing to your mother?" asked the next reporter, whom Tally didn't recognise.

"Yes," Cash answered. Tally almost rolled her eyes. The guy would fail Reporting 101. Kinga picked up on Cash's irritation and pointed at the next journalist.

"How do you think this exposé on your personal life has affected your game?"

Cash raised an eyebrow. "Well, I'm here talking to you instead of playing today. What do you think?"

As the press conference continued, Cash's responses became terser, and in return, the reporters made their questions more pointed. Tally glanced at her watch. Five more minutes, and they'd be out of there.

"Can you explain in more detail what happened that night?" asked Joe Martinez, an old adversary whom Cash had previously banned from his press conferences. Tally risked a glance at Cash. His face was impassive, but beneath the table, his fingers clenched tighter around hers.

"What night?" he said in a droll tone.

"The night you killed your father."

"Can you read?"

"Yes."

"Then read the fucking article," Cash snapped.

"You don't have anything else to add?"

"No."

"That's enough, Joe," Kinga said, pointing at the next reporter.

"Why did you get your girlfriend to write the article rather than a real journalist?" Martinez said, ignoring Kinga's attempts to move the process along. "Was it because she dumbed it down, gave it the right slant to get the public on your side? Or is that the extent of her journalistic prowess?"

She tightened her grip, but Cash easily tore his hand from hers. He half-rose out of his seat. "Yeah, she dumbed it down," he said, leaning across the table to glower at Martinez. "So fuckwits like you with half a brain had a chance of following it."

Martinez laughed. "Is that the best you've got?"

Tally guessed what Cash was going to do, but she was a second too slow. She lunged for his arm, but he'd already vaulted over the table. Isaac dashed across but he, too, wasn't in time. There was a sickening crunch as Cash's fist connected with Martinez's face, followed by a collective gasp around the room.

"Oh, bollocks," Kinga said.

Talk about understatement of the year.

27

Kinga was waiting in the hotel lobby when Tally and Cash arrived back from the police station.

"What happened?" she said, clambering to her feet.

"They cautioned him. He was lucky."

Cash sucked on his knuckles, still bloodied and grazed despite Tally's best attempts to patch him up. "How did Martinez get in?"

Kinga shrugged. "We weren't vetting them, Cash."

"Well, we should have been," he said, glaring at Kinga.

"It's not Kinga's fault," Tally said, hitting him with a hard stare. "Look, everyone in the business knows Martinez is a snake. All he did today was prove it."

"Yeah, and sort out his retirement fund courtesy of yours truly." Cash shook his head. "Still," he added with a smirk, "it was worth it. Even if he gets his nose fixed on my money, I'll always have the memory of it splattered halfway across his face." He outright laughed then. "Fucker."

Kinga did her best to act as if she disapproved, but her twitching lips gave her away. "Right, well, if it's all right with you, I'm going to head off home. When are you flying to Rome?"

"Tomorrow," Cash said. "Hey, have you heard how Anatoly got on?"

"He won. Straight sets."

"Grand. I'll give him a call later."

"I bet he'll be much more interested in hearing about your exploits than talking about his." She kissed Tally on the cheek. "I should be in Rome by Sunday afternoon, but I'll let you know if I get caught up."

"Thanks for everything, Kinga," Cash said, his tone the warmest yet since she had rejoined the team. "You've been amazing."

"Seconded," Tally said.

Kinga shrugged. "I told you. My job is anything you need it to be."

Cash slung an arm around her shoulders and kissed her temple. Kinga blushed. Cash's acceptance of her as a part of the team again had given her a new confidence, and as he walked Kinga to the hotel entrance, Tally noticed she was standing taller.

Once Kinga had left, they went up to their hotel suite. As soon as they were inside, Cash waved his phone at Tally and grimaced. "Better call Mother."

"You'll need this," she said, passing him a tissue. When he frowned, she giggled. "For your bleeding ears."

Cash laughed and disappeared into the bedroom. He reappeared about five minutes later and collapsed onto the sofa, his eyes fixed on the ceiling. He blew out a heavy breath. "Did I say it was good to have a mother again?"

"Bollock you, did she?" Tally said.

"I had to remind her I wasn't a child."

"To her, it must seem like you still are."

"I hadn't thought of that." Cash's brow briefly creased. "I was holding my own until she used the *D* word."

Tally tilted her head. "What's the *D* word?"

"Disappointed."

"Ah." Tally laughed. "It's a great tactic. Pete's used it on me over the years, particularly when I was working on my degree and wasn't knuckling down. Sure does the trick."

Cash teased at his scruff with his fingertips. "Do you think I was wrong to hit him?"

"It wasn't the smartest move." She placed a hand on his arm. "I know you don't care what the press say about you, and I get that. But it's not only you anymore."

He gave a long, low sigh. "I know." He reached for her hand and brought it to his lips. "That's the last time, I promise."

"Is Rachael okay, though? Apart from having Rocky Marciano for a son."

Cash grinned. "Yeah, she's fine. Not even a sniff of the press. Isaac's all over it if any do turn up."

"I'm glad he's there."

"Me too. Guess I'll be in the papers again tomorrow."

"Yep. Steel yourself."

Cash raised his eyebrows. "You don't think Martinez is planning a cosy fireside article?"

Tally laughed. "I'm glad you're seeing the funny side."

"As long as he steers clear of saying anything about you or my mother. Because if he does, I'll make it my life's work to ruin the fucker."

Tally's eyes widened. "Is that why you went for him today? Because he made out I couldn't write for shit?"

Cash shrugged. "Of course."

"Oh, Cash." She shook her head. "I thought it was because he pushed you on what happened with your dad."

Cash's eyes sparked with annoyance. "When he said what he did, I saw red. He can say whatever he likes about me. It'll be old news soon. But I won't have him dissing you."

She rested her head on his shoulder. He might have gone about protecting her in the wrong way, but she couldn't deny the warmth spreading through her limbs.

28

As Tally eased into her seat on Wimbledon's centre court, nerves swarmed her stomach. Apart from when Cash had decided to pull out of Madrid back in May, he'd won four of the big European tournaments. And now, two months later, there they were at the Wimbledon final, and she couldn't help thinking...

All good things.

Once the day was over, they would be taking a well-earned break. With Cash's crazy tournament schedule and Pete putting more work her way, they'd barely had any time to themselves. She'd also decided to tell him about the photographs once they were on holiday. The timing felt right now that their lives had finally settled down, and she hoped the distance would help him look at the situation dispassionately without going off the deep end.

She pushed her sunglasses on top of her head and dabbed at the sweat beneath her eyes. She dug a compact out of her bag. *Great. Lovely black smudges. Waterproof mascara? What utter rubbish.*

She squeezed a bit of water onto a tissue and carefully swept away the black marks. Who would have bet on England having a heat wave during Wimbledon fortnight?

"You missed a bit." Kinga took the tissue from her and swept it under Tally's right eye. "There, that's better."

"Thanks," Tally said with a smile. She tucked the tissue in her jacket pocket and dropped her sunglasses back in place. Her leg jiggled as Em rested her hands on Tally's shoulders.

"Chill out, Tal. You're going to have a bloody heart attack at this rate."

Tally glanced behind her and placed her hand over Em's. "Thanks."

Em frowned. "What for?"

"Being here."

"Where else would I be, babes?"

Tally shrugged. "Nowhere, I guess."

Em wrapped her arms around Tally's shoulders and hugged tightly. "It's going to be fine. I know you find it hard to watch, Tal, but the form he's on? Jeez."

Tally nodded as she turned to Rachael, whose doctor had given her the all-clear to attend today's Wimbledon final.

"You doing okay?" she asked.

Rachael patted her arm. "I'm fine. I'm finally going to see my son play. Nothing could make me happier."

"If you get too hot or feel faint or dizzy or anything, you have to promise to tell me."

Rachael smiled serenely. "Stop worrying, Tally."

"He's going to win," Kinga whispered in Tally's ear. "Four sets."

"Can you make that three?" Tally said.

Kinga laughed. "You're always so nervous. He's had a fabulous season, and today he'll top that off by becoming Wimbledon champ for the seventh time. Mark my words."

"Yeah, 'cause you know everything," Em muttered under her breath.

Tally gave Em a hard look. Kinga appeared not to have heard. Em still held a grudge against Kinga even though Tally had forgiven her long ago.

Brad slipped into his seat behind Rachael. He leaned forward. "Ready, ladies?"

"Nope," Tally said.

"I'm ready," Rachael said in an excited voice. "I can't wait."

Tally twisted in her seat to face Brad. "How is he?"

Brad raised an eyebrow. "Déjà vu, Tally. He's fine. You're not. Same old, same old."

She tried to smile, but her nerves were running out of control, her stomach churning with that awful sick feeling she got before every match. Not just finals. *Every* goddamn match.

"Breathe." Brad passed her a bottle of ice-cold water. "And drink. Last thing I need is you passing out on me."

Tally took a long pull, the cold water soothing her dry and scratchy throat as the buzz of the crowd increased. She glanced around centre court. Pretty much everyone was seated now, apart from the most important members of the royal box. As she had that thought, the Duke and Duchess of Cambridge appeared. The duchess looked beautiful and immaculate as always. She watched as the duke said something to her. Tally couldn't hear them, but she managed to lip-read the duchess's response: "Yes, I'm okay."

She smiled to herself as the crowd got to their feet and clapped. Her eyes flickered to the corner of the court. Cash, dressed head to toe in white as was Wimbledon custom, walked slowly behind Anatoly, his opponent for that day. Ahead of them, two men carried their bags—another Wimbledon tradition.

"Here we go," she murmured as Kinga squeezed her hand and Em's grip tightened on her shoulders. Tally glanced sideways at Rachael. Her face was flushed with excitement, and her eyes shone as she clapped. Tally couldn't even begin to imagine how Rachael was feeling at that moment.

Cash set himself up and took out a racket, hitting it against his hand. He jumped up and down on the spot a few times, to the delight of the crowd, and sauntered onto court. Tally moved to sit on the edge of her seat and began nibbling on her nails, although after the number of games she had sat through during the European season, she didn't have much left to chew.

Cash won the toss and, as always, elected to serve. The two men posed for the obligatory photographs before sharing a quick word and a smile. But once they'd taken their places at opposite ends of the court, their faces fell serious.

The first set was close, with each man giving little away. Matches between Cash and Anatoly were always tightly fought affairs, and that day was no different. The first set went to a tiebreak, which Anatoly won.

"Four sets—I told you," Kinga whispered. "You know Cash. He uses being behind as a catalyst to up his game."

Tally nodded, but fear lodged in her throat. She couldn't shake the feeling Cash's winning streak was coming to an end.

In the second set, he changed it up, seeking Anatoly's weaknesses, and when he won six games to four, Tally jumped to her feet, clapping wildly, the tension that clawed at her shoulders subsiding. Maybe Kinga's prediction would turn out to be right.

But she'd celebrated too soon. Anatoly took the third set, giving him a two-set-to-one lead.

"Four sets my arse," Tally muttered, glancing sideways at Kinga. "Hope you didn't bet too much on a three to one."

Kinga flashed a quick grin. "Oh, ye of little faith."

"Realist, you mean."

Kinga didn't reply. She gave a small shake of her head and refocused her attention on the match.

A tight fourth set led to yet another tiebreak. Tally's stomach churned painfully, and her skin prickled with slow-onset pins and needles. She wiped clammy hands on her skirt. He had to win the tiebreak, or it was all over.

Tally focused on Cash. Apart from a slight tightening of the skin around his mouth, he did not reveal his feelings.

"Come on, come on," she muttered, chewing the last nail so far down it began to bleed. Em brushed her hand up and down Tally's arm, a soothing gesture she'd used for years when Tally got too stressed. Rachael's grip on her hand grew tighter.

At five points apiece, Anatoly hit a perfect lob, which sailed over Cash's head. Despite sprinting backwards, Cash was too close to the net to reach the ball. It landed about an inch inside the baseline for a winner and gave Anatoly championship point.

"God fucking damn it," Brad muttered under his breath.

Tally rubbed the back of her neck, her muscles tense and painful. Cash prepared to serve to stay in the match. He hit a perfect serve, which should have been an ace, and against most other players it would have been. But somehow, Anatoly got the tip of his racket on it, and curving his wrist at an impossible angle, he hit the ball cross-court for an outright winner.

Anatoly dropped his racket and fell to his knees as sorrow swept through Tally's chest.

Cash had lost.

29

W hen Cash walked into the lounge, he found Natalia and Mum standing with their heads together, chatting. Natalia jumped up the minute she saw him. Wrapping her arms around his neck, she whispered, "I'm so proud of you."

Cash leaned across the table to kiss his mother. "Sorry I couldn't win for you, Mum," he said with a shrug.

"Nonsense," Rachael said. "Today might not have been your day, but the pride I felt watching you out there..." She raised a trembling hand to her face, her voice cracking as she brushed away a tear.

Cash swallowed past a lump in his throat. Nine months before, his life had been shit, and now look where he was. His mother was thriving and living life to the fullest, despite missing out on the past thirteen years, and he had his girl, who he was more in love with than he'd ever thought possible.

"I'm going to take off," Cash said, waving at his mother when she began to stand. "No, Mum, stay. Enjoy the rest of the afternoon. Kinga, can you make sure Mum gets back to the house okay?"

"Of course I will," Kinga said. "Let's get you the guided tour."

"If you're sure," Rachael said. "I must admit I'm dying to have a nose around."

"Shall I book a table for dinner? Say, eight?" Kinga said.

"Oh yes, do," Rachael said. "Dinner would be lovely."

Even though it was the last thing Cash wanted, he kept his mouth shut. He could stomach one lousy dinner if it made his mother happy.

"Let me know where," he said to Kinga. "We'll meet you there."

"Make sure you invite Em," Natalia said. "She's around here somewhere."

"Probably chatting up some poor unsuspecting bloke," Cash said, earning a hard stare from Natalia.

When they stepped outside, Isaac already had the car door open. Cameras flashed, and fans pushed all manner of memorabilia into Cash's face. He stopped to sign a few autographs and posed for a few pictures before he finally climbed inside. Isaac closed the door behind them, the noise from outside instantly abating. Cash's head hit the back of the chair as his lids fell shut.

"I'm knackered," he said, blindly reaching for Natalia's hand as the car moved off.

"It's been a hard season. I'm not surprised."

His eyes opened a crack, and he squinted at her. "The next month is going to be hard too."

Natalia laughed at the obvious innuendo. "You haven't even said where we're going."

"Correct."

"But you've got it all planned out, haven't you?"

"Yep."

"And you have no intention of telling me."

"Correct again."

Natalia stuck out her bottom lip. "I hate surprises."

Cash snorted. "Liar. You fucking love them."

She grinned then. "You're right. I do."

He leaned his head on her shoulder, a contented sigh escaping his lips when Natalia stroked his hair.

"I wish we weren't going to dinner tonight," he said.

"Oh, yeah? What would we do instead?"

Cash lifted his head and wiggled his eyebrows. "Sweetness, really?"

Natalia glanced at her watch. "We've got a little over two hours. An hour for me to get ready. If you're not too tired, that gives you an hour to impress me with your sexual prowess."

Cash moved fast, pressing Natalia flat onto the back seat. "Then there's no time to waste," he said, cutting off her surprised giggle with his mouth.

A soft groan sounded low in her throat as Cash moved his lips over hers. He drove his tongue inside, rewarded when she thrust her hips upwards and rubbed against his crotch. Earlier exhaustion forgotten, he willed Isaac to drive faster. He didn't want to fuck her in the back of the car. She deserved to be cosseted on a soft bed and wrapped in silk sheets. But if she carried on rubbing him like that, his instincts would take over.

"We're here, sir."

Isaac's voice came through the intercom, and Cash tore his mouth from Natalia's. Like a pair of lustful teenagers, the two of them dashed inside the house he'd rented for Wimbledon fortnight.

He kicked the front door closed, lifted her into his arms, and tore up the stairs, taking them two at a time. She laughed all the way, only stopping when he laid her down in the middle of the enormous bed, and then her face became serious as she watched him drag off his clothes.

As he began to straddle her, Natalia pressed her hand against his chest. "Let me. It's my turn to look after you tonight."

A bolt of desire exploded in Cash's stomach. Although Natalia's confidence in bed had increased over the last few months, she still preferred Cash to take the lead. He rolled onto his back and held his arms out wide, palms facing up. "I'm all yours, baby."

He closed his eyes, his mouth parting as she pressed searing-hot lips to his neck, shoulder, chest, working slowly down his body. Her tongue traced warm, wet circles around his nipples and over his abdomen. She licked each pronounced muscle before moving farther down. *Oh God, yeah.* He thrust his hands into her hair to control the speed. She immediately stopped, removed his hands, and rocked back on her heels.

"Oh no, you don't," she said, wagging her finger. She pushed his arms over his head. "I'm in charge. Keep them there, or I'll tie them up."

His tongue darted out to wet his lips as a flush of desire made his cheeks burn.

Natalia briefly frowned and then smiled. "You like the idea of that?"

Cash nodded vigorously. He'd never allowed a woman to tie him up, would never have given over that sort of power. But this wasn't any woman. This was Natalia, the love of his life, the other half of his soul. He'd let her do anything she wanted, and surprisingly, the idea turned him on.

She climbed off the bed and disappeared into the adjoining bathroom. When she returned, she was threading the belt from a dressing gown through her fingers.

"Remember Paris?" she said with a shy smile.

Paris. The time she'd let him tie her up when they'd barely known each other. Cash still found the trust she'd shown in him that night humbling every time he thought about it.

"Baby, how could I forget?"

She straddled him, wrapped the belt around his wrists, and fixed it to the bedstead.

"The minute you say it's over, then it's over," she whispered, repeating the words he'd said to her that same evening.

She began the torturous journey down his body once more, licking, sucking, kissing, tracing every muscle with the tip of her tongue. When she reached her ultimate target, Cash tensed, his stomach clenching. His breath came in short pants as she swept her tongue over the head, removing the bead of moisture that had gathered on the tip. His cock twitched, and a deep growl sounded low in his throat. She looked up at him and smiled.

"More?"

Unable to trust himself to speak, he nodded, and he lifted his hips to stress the point. Natalia pressed the flat of her hand low on his abdomen and pushed him back down. She wrapped one hand around the base of his cock and closed her mouth over the head, beginning a steady rhythm of taking him deep then swirling her tongue over the tip before starting the whole process from scratch.

Cash bit down hard on his lip, barely holding on, but when she glanced up and they made eye contact, he lost it. "Oh, baby," he groaned, his hips jerking upwards through his climax. Natalia cupped his balls and gently massaged him while he poured himself into her warm, wet mouth. The whole time, she kept her eyes on his. The emotional connection drew out his orgasm until it almost became painful.

He didn't feel her removing the restraints, but suddenly, his arms were free.

She crawled up his body and rested her head on his chest. Peering up at him through half-closed lids, she smiled. "I love doing that to you."

"And that's why I only last thirty seconds every time you do. I can just about hang on, but when I look into your eyes, I'm a goner."

She twisted around to glance at the clock.

"How long have we got?" Cash said.

"Twenty minutes."

Cash smiled down at her. "Time to return the favour."

30

They arrived at the restaurant a little late, mainly due to Cash taking longer than the twenty minutes they'd had to spare. He'd certainly been thorough, and the memory made Tally shiver.

"Cold?" he asked innocently.

Tally stood on tiptoes. "You're an arrogant arse," she whispered in his ear.

He stifled a grin. "You were wonderful," he murmured. "And as stunning as you look in that dress, I can't wait to peel it off you later."

"Shhh." She wriggled out of his arms and flashed a look at Rachael who, fortunately, didn't seem to have heard.

Cash gave her an unconcerned grin and clutched her hand. "Right, let's get this over with."

"Cash," Rachael scolded. "Don't be so ungrateful. Kinga wanted to do this for you."

The restaurant Kinga had chosen had two Michelin stars. The inside was decorated in gold and crimson hues. The tables were widely spaced, each one surrounded with deeply cushioned chairs and fancy crystal centrepieces.

Tally glanced up at Cash. "I prefer GBK," she murmured.

Cash grinned. "Don't worry, sweetness. I'll be right there to wipe food off your chin before anyone notices."

They were shown to the back of the restaurant, where their table took up most of the far wall. Tally waved as she spotted Em, who waved back then pointed to the end of the table, where Rupe was busy chatting up the waitress.

Tally yanked her hand from Cash's and almost ran across the restaurant.

"I thought you couldn't come," she said, hugging Rupe so tightly he made a faux-choking sound.

"If I'd known you were going to try to kill me, I may have had second thoughts." Rupe extricated himself from her arms and rose from his chair. He clapped Cash on the back. "How you doing, loser? Sorry I missed the match."

"Thanks for the support," Cash drawled.

"Are you going to start losing on a regular basis? Because if you are, I might have to find another best mate. All this negative energy is bad for my chi."

"You're all heart," Cash said. "And what's with the fucking chi? If you turn any further into a girl, it'll be *me* dumping *you*."

Rupe made a theatrical wave of his hand then kissed Rachael on the cheek and made sure she sat right beside him. "Honestly, Mrs G, he hasn't always been this rubbish. It's a shame you missed the best bits of his career."

Rachael burst out laughing. "Only you, Rupert, could make light of the situation and get away with it. You always were shameless. Even as a little boy."

"Tal, over here," Em said, pointing to the empty chair between her and Kinga, a glaring sign of Em's dislike of Kinga that Tally couldn't fail to notice. For some reason, her friend had been spoiling for a fight with Kinga all day, making odd snippy comments that Kinga had so far ignored. If Em carried on, it would be a very long night.

Cash sat opposite Brad, and in seconds, the two of them had their heads together, minutely examining every detail of the final and where it had all gone wrong.

"Boring," Em said in a singsong voice, ignoring the glower Cash sent her way. "When are you two off on your travels?"

"Day after tomorrow," Tally said.

"Has he told you where you're going yet?"

"Nope."

Em leaned against Tally's shoulder. "I've barely seen you, and now you're off again," she said with a pronounced pout.

Tally chuckled as relief swept through her. Em's mood seemed to be improving. "You've seen me every day for a month."

"Yeah, well, it doesn't seem like enough."

When the food arrived, Cash and Brad finally stopped talking tennis and joined in the conversation with everyone else. Contented, Tally sat back and watched. These people were her family. Each and every one. She loved the way they all talked over one another, the banter relentless. Hearing Rupe and Cash tear chunks out of one another with Brad and Jamie trying to play referee, and watching Rachael roll her eyes exactly the same way as Cash did, happiness surged through her.

"You okay, babes?" Em said. "You're awfully quiet."

Her eyes filled with tears. "I'm much more than okay."

"Oh no you don't." Em waggled her finger in front of Tally's face. "If you make me cry and I end up with black streaks down my face, I'm going to be seriously pissed."

Tally laughed. "I love you." She briefly touched her head against Em's.

"Love you more," Em said.

"For goodness' sake, it's getting awfully maudlin down this end of the table," Kinga said.

Em stiffened and leaned in front of Tally. "I'm allowed to miss my best friend. You see more of her than I do."

Kinga raised her hands in the air. "Of course you are. It was a joke. I didn't mean to offend you."

"Yet you seem to manage it with ease."

"Em, let's not get into an argument," Tally said, trying to keep the peace.

"It's okay, Tally," Kinga said with a sigh. "Emmalee, I know you don't like me, and that's fine. You're entitled to your opinion. But Tally has forgiven me. Maybe you should think about that before continuing to be so hostile. "

Em bristled as she glared at Kinga. "I may have a lot of faults, but at least I'm not a bitch who tries to split people up by stalking them until the right photo opportunity pops up."

∼

Cash cut Rupe off midjoke as Kinga gasped, her hand flying to her chest. He leaned across the table. "What did you just say?" he said, his gaze fixed on Emmalee.

Natalia dug Emmalee with her elbow. "Shut up, Em," she hissed under her breath.

A dark flush spread from Emmalee's neck until it had covered her cheeks. "Nothing," she mumbled.

He turned his gaze on Kinga, whose eyes were wide, her forehead peppered with beads of sweat. Then he looked back in Emmalee's direction.

"I asked you a question," he said, his voice low and controlled even though his insides felt as though they were going through the spin cycle on a washing machine.

Natalia half-rose from her chair. "Cash, it's nothing."

He held his hand in the air, palm facing her. "I don't want to hear from you right now." When she recoiled, a twinge of guilt pinched at his insides, but he pushed it away as white spots of anger danced across his vision. "Tell me, Emmalee."

"What's going on?" his mother said, her brow furrowed in confusion.

He ignored her and refocused his attention on Emmalee, who mouthed an apology to Natalia before meeting Cash's furious stare. "Kinga took the photos of you and Gracie."

A hush descended across the table. Natalia had paled, her eyes wide and fearful while Kinga was holding her stomach as if in pain and rocking in her chair.

Cash clenched his fists as his whole body trembled. "And how do you know that?" he said, his voice dripping ice.

Emmalee grimaced. "Tally told me. I'm sorry, babes," she said to Natalia before staring at the floor.

Natalia slowly blinked. "Too late now," she muttered.

"And you," he bit out, turning his focus on Natalia. "How the fuck do *you* know."

"Cash, please…" Her voice quivered. "Not here."

"I told her." Kinga got to her feet, her shaking hands resting on William's shoulders.

"But it was my decision not to tell you," Natalia said. "I just thought—"

"I'm not fucking interested in what you thought." He surprised himself with how calm he sounded, especially as he was boiling inside. He pointed at Kinga. "You're gone."

"Wait." Natalia scrambled to her feet and came towards him. As she reached out, he stepped back. Her hand fell to her side, and her bottom lip wobbled.

"Let's talk about this, please, Cash," Kinga said. "This isn't Tally's fault."

Cash clenched his jaw because if he didn't, he wasn't sure what would spill out. He glanced down at Rupe fidgeting in his chair. "Can you sort out the bill?"

Rupe nodded. "Leave it with me. Stay cool," he added under his breath.

Cash turned to his mother. "We're leaving." He held her arm

as she got to her feet. Around the table, faces were showing varying degrees of confusion, horror, and distress, but none were as awful as the deep feeling of betrayal that had settled in his gut. He didn't know how long Natalia had kept this from him, but even one day was too fucking long.

He caught her elbow as he passed with his mother and propelled her through the door. Isaac had the car waiting outside, and he jumped out to open the back door. Cash stood back as his mother climbed in. As Natalia went to do the same, she paused. "We need to talk."

"Oh, we will," Cash said, his tone full of bitterness and hurt. "When *I'm* ready."

Her eyes glistened with unshed tears as she got in the car without saying another word.

"Will someone please tell me what on earth is going on?" his mother asked again as the car sped away.

Cash remained tight-lipped.

Natalia murmured under her breath, "Not now, Rachael."

He stared out of the window as the blood boiling in his veins turned to ice. The minute they pulled up at the house, Cash launched himself out of the car and, without waiting for anyone, stormed inside. He took off upstairs and slammed the door to their bedroom as he tried to figure out what he should do next.

31

Tally made Rachael a glass of warm milk and settled her into bed. She patted the space beside her, and Tally sat on the edge.

"Do you want to tell me what's going on?"

Tally rubbed her face as exhaustion swamped her. "I screwed up, Rachael."

Rachael tilted her head to one side. "It can't be that bad."

She blew out a breath. "When Cash and I first got together, I was always worried he'd see through me and break it off."

Rachael made a tutting noise, which caused a smile to tug at Tally's lips. "Even though he assured me that he wanted me and only me, I never truly believed it, which is why when I received some photos of Cash kissing a woman who I now know to be Gracie—well, it was very easy to jump to conclusions."

"My Gracie?" Rachael said, a hint of incredulity to her tone.

Tally nodded. "It was all completely innocent, but I didn't know about you then, and so when I confronted Cash, he couldn't offer a suitable explanation. We split up for a while until he plucked up the courage to tell me about you and his father."

"And Kinga took the photographs," Rachael said, putting two and two together and making the maths stick.

"Yeah. She confessed to me a few months ago, but Cash had so much going on, and I wanted him to be able to concentrate on rebuilding his career." She shrugged. "So I didn't tell him."

Rachael let out a soft sigh. "Probably not your best decision."

Tally gave a wry smile. "I had planned to tell him while we were away. I thought he'd be more relaxed and might not—"

"Fly off the handle," Rachael said with a grin.

"Something like that."

Rachael squeezed her arm. "Go and talk to him. The longer you leave it, the harder it becomes."

Tally nodded and rose from the bed. "Can I get you anything? Do you want me to fetch the iPad?"

"No. I still haven't quite got to grips with all this technology yet. A lot has changed in the last few years." She pulled a face. "The other day in the supermarket, they asked me if I wanted to pay contactless. I just stared at the assistant. She might as well have been speaking a foreign language."

Tally laughed. "You'll get there, and we're here to help." She leaned forward and kissed her cheek. "Lights on or off?"

"On. I've got a magazine article I'd like to finish," she said, digging a copy of *Vogue* from the drawer beside her bed.

Tally closed the door with a quiet click and let out a long breath. She began to trudge down the hallway then stopped halfway. A quick nip of something for Dutch courage wouldn't go amiss. She jogged downstairs and poured a small glass of wine. As she took a sip, her phone buzzed. She glanced at the screen. A text from Em:

I'm so sorry, babes. Are you okay?

Tally dialled Em's number, and she answered immediately. "God, babes. I'm so glad you called. I feel fucking awful."

"You have a bloody big mouth, Fallon," Tally said in a teasing tone.

"I know. How did Cash take it?"

"Badly," Tally said. "He stormed off to bed as soon as we got home, and I'm downstairs having a glass of wine before facing his wrath."

"Shit, babes. I can't apologise enough. You trust me with something, and I can't keep my trap shut. That woman winds me up like no other, but that wasn't an excuse to break your confidence."

"Forget it. I was going to tell him anyway... but you got there first," she added with a laugh.

Em groaned. "Don't be nice to me. I don't deserve it."

Tally chuckled. "I'd better go. I'll call you tomorrow."

She hung up and downed the rest of the wine before heading back upstairs. Outside her bedroom door, she paused and steeled herself for what was to come.

Cash had already undressed and was sitting up in bed reading. He studiously ignored her as she stepped inside, and Tally repressed a sigh. She unzipped her dress and let it fall in a heap on the floor. Cash's gaze briefly flickered in her direction before returning to his book.

She removed a satin nightgown from the drawer next to her bed and slipped it over her head. As she climbed beneath the covers, she looked at Cash.

"Are we going to talk about this now or later?"

Cash let the book fall into his lap, but when he met her gaze, Tally found it difficult to swallow because instead of fiery anger, he looked at her with cool appraisal.

"How long have you known?" he said, his voice unnaturally quiet.

Tally gnawed at her cheek. "Since we got back from Monte Carlo."

His eyebrows shot up. "You've kept this from me for three months."

A wave of regret washed over her at the hurt in his eyes. "Kinga confessed to me when we got back to Ireland."

Cash pinched his nose between his thumb and forefinger. "I have never hidden my loathing of being lied to, and yet you chose to keep something from me that was a terrible time for *both of us*."

"Cash—"

His hand shot in the air. "For one second, *one second*, Natalia, think about this from my perspective. You, Kinga, and Emmalee all sharing a dirty little secret."

"It wasn't like that. I was going to tell you."

He gave her a scathing look. "When?"

"On holiday."

Cash let out a sarcastic laugh. "Happy bloody holidays."

She reached for his hand, but he pulled away. Tally winced. "When she told me, you had all the stress of your mum's recovery, our reconciliation, your tennis career just getting back on track. I knew if I told you it was Kinga behind the photos, it'd knock you off kilter again. I did it to protect you."

He clutched a hand to his chest. "Well, aren't I the lucky one."

She shook her head. "If all you're going to be is sarcastic, there's no point talking to you."

"You've got that right." He threw back the covers and climbed out of bed.

"Where are you going?" she said, panic leaking into her tone as he headed for the door.

"I need space to think. I can't be with you right now."

As the door slammed, Tally covered her face with her hands and began to cry.

WITHOUT CASH BESIDE HER, Tally tossed and turned all night, and when light filtered through the curtains, she climbed out of bed and went downstairs. She put the kettle on and was in the middle of making a coffee when Cash appeared.

"Do you want one?" she said in what she hoped was a conciliatory tone.

He nodded and sat at the breakfast bar. Paying her no attention, he began tapping into his phone. She pushed a cup of coffee towards him and rested her hip against the kitchen counter.

"Where did you sleep?"

He lifted his head, his gaze cool as it fell on hers. "One of the spare rooms," he said before bowing his head once more.

Tally's chest tingled, and a sudden chill made her shiver. "Cash, I'm sorry. I made a mistake."

"Yes, you did," he said in an icy tone.

He took two or three sips of coffee before jumping down from the stool.

"Where are you going?" she said, hating the plaintive sound of her voice. He ignored her, so she followed him into the hallway. He lifted a jacket off a coat peg and picked up a set of keys. "Cash..."

He turned around. "I've heard your side of it. Now I'm going to hear Kinga's. She's meeting me at Rupe's in an hour."

She began to stuff her feet into a pair of trainers. "I'll come with you."

"No." He held his hand up. "This is *my* closure."

Without another word, he stepped outside and slammed the door behind him.

32

Kinga's eyes were wide and fearful as Cash waved for
her to sit. Dark circles framed her eyes. Evidently, she
hadn't slept much. She seemed unable to focus properly, her gaze flitting from one object to another, looking
anywhere except at him. She kept smoothing her hair, the
bangles on her wrist making an annoying tinkling sound every
time she lifted her hand.

As Cash glared at her, she dropped her hands into her lap.
Silence hung heavy in the air, like that moment before a glass
shatters on the ground. Cash kept it going—a little cruel, maybe,
but he had no intention of making this remotely comfortable
for her.

"I'm glad you called," she finally said, breaking the silence
between them.

He turned a cold, impassive stare on her. "I want to know two
things. First, when did you tell Natalia it was you?"

She wrung her hands. "After you got knocked out of Monte
Carlo. I met her in Belfast for a coffee."

At least she didn't lie about the timeframe.

"And whose idea was it to keep it from me?"

She slowly blinked. "Tally was worried you had enough on your plate. She thought if you found out, it would affect your tennis just as you were getting your career back on track."

And she didn't lie about her reasoning for keeping it from me.

"That's all I wanted to know. You can go now." He turned away.

"Cash, please. Let's talk this through."

"No." He spoke over his shoulder. "You're gone, Kinga. Out of my life. For good."

She clambered to her feet. "Please, give me another chance. Everything's different."

Cash expelled a curt breath. "I seem to remember the same argument when I reluctantly agreed to one more chance after you hit Natalia."

"But Tally and I have grown so close these last few months. And you--"

Cash spun around and swiped his hand through the air. "I will *never* be able to forgive the fact you purposely set out to split up Natalia and me—and kept lying about it. We're finished."

Kinga's chin lowered to her chest, and hands that hadn't been able to keep still earlier now lay limp in her lap. Eventually, her eyes sought his, and she offered a faint smile.

"I expected the worst but hoped for the best," she said, rising unsteadily to her feet. Cash said nothing. She was almost past him when she stopped. "Working for you these past years has been the best thing that's ever happened to me. I'm sorrier than you'll ever know. Please give Tally my love, and pass on my heartfelt apologies to her too."

She laid a hand on his arm. Cash stepped to the side, the movement making her hand fall away. She winced, but he was beyond caring about her feelings.

He opened the drawing room door. "You can see yourself out. My lawyer will be in touch."

Kinga began to make one final plea then closed her mouth, turned around, and stepped into the hallway.

Cash kicked the door shut and heaved a sigh. First problem sorted. Now he just had to decide what to do about the second.

~

WHEN HE ARRIVED BACK at the house, his mother met him at the front door, arms folded, eyes narrowed, pissed-off attitude coming off her in waves.

He raised his eyebrows. "Something wrong?"

"Seriously?" She shook her head in disbelief. "Follow me." She set off down the hallway.

A bolt of fear shot into his bloodstream. "Is Natalia okay?"

She ignored him, which ratcheted up his worry. He might be furious with Natalia at that moment, but the thought of something happening to her...

When they entered the living room, his mum pointed to a chair. "Sit."

Cash did as he was told. "Where's Natalia?"

His mother stiffened her jaw. "She is upstairs. I asked her to stay out of the way because I think certain things between a mother and a son should be said in private."

"O-kay," Cash said as a sudden sense of unease made him stiffen.

"I realise you grew up without a mother, Cash, and that is something I will spend the rest of my life feeling guilty for—no, don't interrupt me," she said as he opened his mouth to disagree. "But I'm here now, and I plan to make up for lost time, which also means calling you out when you are being a complete and unreasonable idiot."

Cash's head jerked back. "What the hell are you talking about?"

"That girl," she said, flicking her head towards the ceiling, "is extremely upset. She made a decision, and yes, you could argue she should have done it differently, but everything she did was with *you* in mind." Rachael pointed at him. "You. She knew she was taking a risk, but she took it anyway because she loves you and wants you to be happy. And this is how you repay her? Cold shoulder, flat stares, sleeping in separate rooms? I expected better from you."

He winced and stared at the floor. Wow, his mother certainly knew how to deliver a bollocking with impact.

"I understand you feel hurt and betrayed," she said in a softer tone. "And Tally understands too, but behaving like a child and refusing to discuss things is going to get you precisely nowhere."

He scrubbed his face with his hands before wearily getting to his feet. "I'll go and talk to her."

"Good. Oh, and Cash," she said as he reached the door. "Make sure you think before you open your mouth."

His lips twitched, and he was still smiling as he reached the top of the stairs. He'd always thought of himself as a guy who understood women. His mother and Natalia taught him that he didn't have a clue.

When he entered their room, Natalia was sitting on the side of the bed, her legs dangling over the edge. She looked up, and his heart twisted. Her eyes were red-rimmed with dark smudges underneath, and she looked so forlorn that he couldn't stop himself from sitting beside her and tugging her onto his lap. He cradled her in his arms as tremors wracked her body.

"I'm sorry, sweetness." He buried his nose in her hair, the scent of her strawberry shampoo tickling his nostrils.

She sniffed. "I am too. I should have told you, but I thought I was doing the right thing."

He lifted her head, cradling her face between his palms. "I know." He brushed his lips over hers. "I hated being apart from you last night."

When she sniffed again, he reached over to the bedside table and plucked a tissue from a box of Kleenex. After she blew her nose, he kissed her again, a little deeper this time.

"How's Kinga?" Natalia asked.

Cash shook his head. "We're done."

She nodded. "I guessed that's what you'd do. She did want to tell you, but I persuaded her my way was better."

"It wouldn't have made a difference either way. I don't care whether she maintains she was ill or not. The fact is she did a cruel and hurtful thing, and I can't forgive that."

"I still feel bad."

Cash clipped her under the chin. "No more Kinga talk. I don't want her ruining our holiday."

Natalia tilted her head to the side. "I thought you might have changed your mind about us going away."

Cash laughed. "No chance. We had a row, that's all. And you know what the best thing about rows is?"

"What?"

Cash eased her onto her back and gave her a wicked grin. "Make-up sex."

33

Tally jogged up the steps onto the plane. When she got inside, she glanced over her shoulder at Cash. "You're not taking me somewhere in Europe, then?"

He tilted his head. "What makes you say that?"

"Because this is your other plane. When you whisked me off to Paris, you told me you have a plane for short-haul trips and another, larger one for longer journeys."

"Bloody journalists," Cash said. "Never forget a thing."

Tally tossed her handbag onto a nearby chair and wrapped her arms around his neck. "I also remember you telling me this plane had a bedroom." She shimmied against him, and he laughed.

"You're correct. It does. Which is just as well. I'm sure you'll get tired during the flight."

A giggle erupted from her mouth. "Sleep is for wimps."

Cash smiled down at her. "Buckle up," he said, nodding at the chair where she'd thrown her bag. "We'll be taking off soon."

Tally did as he asked, and minutes later, they were airborne. Cash released his murderous grip on her hand as soon as the plane levelled out.

"Still no better, ace?" she asked as he flexed his fingers.

"Doubt it ever will be, but having you here with me makes it a whole lot more bearable."

"How long is the flight?"

Cash raised an eyebrow. "Is that the best you've got?"

Tally scowled. He was making fun of her. "I hardly think asking for the time is giving anything away. It's not like I'm insisting on longitude and latitude."

"It's thirteen hours. Does that temper your curiosity?"

"No," she said with a pronounced pout, which made Cash even more amused. "That's a long way."

"Here," he said, tossing her Kindle across the table. "Perhaps that will keep you occupied."

"The bedroom will keep me occupied," she muttered, drawing a huff of laughter from Cash.

He unfastened his seatbelt and wandered to the back of the plane. When he returned, he was holding a bottle of champagne and two glasses in one hand. He took her Kindle from her.

"What are you doing?" she said, not that she'd been reading anyway.

"Hopefully, providing better entertainment," he said, helping her to her feet. He knitted their fingers together and led her into the bedroom.

The room was decked out in soft cream accents with oak cabinets sitting at either side of a proper double bed. Tally ran her hand over the satin quilt cover and glanced around at Cash as he closed the door behind them.

"Impressive," she said with a smile.

He set the champagne and glasses down beside the bed and slipped his hands around her waist. He tugged her forwards, his head bending to nuzzle her neck. After a few moments, he stepped backwards and folded his arms across his chest. "Take off your clothes. Slowly."

Tally's stomach clenched, and her pulse jolted. Cash had that look, the one that made her knees tremble and her brain forget her own name. She unbuttoned her jeans and slid them down her legs, kicking them to one side. Lifting her T-shirt over her head, she stood in front of him in only her pale-pink underwear, a set she'd purchased a few weeks earlier. The set was delicate and racy, and she felt sexy wearing it, particularly when Cash studied her the way he was right at that moment.

She reached around her back to unhook her bra.

"Stop." He crooked his finger, indicating for her to move closer. She obeyed, taking two steps towards him. Cash traced the top of the lace bra with his finger before slipping his hands inside it. He cupped her breasts. The material bunched underneath, making her boobs sit proud, the way she'd love them to without a bra. She was too large for that to happen naturally. Gravity won out every time.

She exhaled on a shudder as Cash brushed a thumb over the tip of her erect nipple. Tally threw her head back, her mouth falling open as her stomach contracted. Cash stood back to examine his handiwork.

"Beautiful," he whispered, his gaze burning hot as he stared at her breasts. He saw her as no one else ever had. "Lie down on the bed."

She did as he commanded. Her heartbeat shot into overdrive as Cash hovered over her. He was still fully dressed, although Tally could make out his erection straining against his jeans. She reached out, her fingers urgent as she unfastened the buttons. Cash moved her hands, yanked open the remaining buttons, and kicked his jeans off.

"Desperate much, ace?" she said, a broad grin finding its way across her face.

He shrugged off his T-shirt and threw it on top of his jeans. "You have no idea."

Caging her with his body, he bent his head and sucked a hard nipple into his mouth. Tally arched her back, a soft whimper escaping her lips. He cupped the back of her knees and tugged her until her backside was on the edge of the bed.

"What are you going to do?" she asked as she began to pant with excitement.

Cash leaned in close, his warm breath tickling her face. "Fuck you senseless," he whispered, his expression intense as he gazed down at her.

He slipped his hands underneath the lace of her knickers and tugged them off her legs, and they joined his pile of clothes. There was something so sexy about the sight of her knickers on top of his stuff.

He pressed his hands to the inside of her knees, easing them apart. His eyes widened, and a soft groan fell from his lips. "God, you're wet," he murmured as he knelt at the foot of the bed.

He moved between her legs and pressed the tip of his tongue against her clit. Her hands clenched at the satin covers.

"Jesus," she muttered as a tremor ran through her. She raised her hips, and he cupped her backside, using the extra leverage to press closer, harder. The feelings he drew from her were too much, too intense, her pending climax arriving too quickly for her to control it.

Her orgasm hit fast, pulses of pleasure coursing through her as her toes curled and her back arched off the bed. She squeezed her eyes closed as Cash continued to lap at her and suck hard at the tight nub of nerves at the apex of her thighs, his attention such that her clit throbbed.

"Too much," she muttered, barely aware he was crawling up her body until he pushed himself inside, a low groan sounding in his throat as he eased all the way in.

Her muscles involuntarily clenched around him. He placed her legs on top of his shoulders, and with his hands gripping the flesh of her bottom, he thrust hard. He'd said he would fuck her senseless, and he kept his promise.

He called out her name as an orgasm tore through him, and as he tilted his pelvis, she climaxed again.

"Jesus Christ." Tally squeezed her eyes shut and waited for the aftershocks to subside. She wiped sweat from her brow and opened her eyes to find Cash gazing down at her. She giggled. "Never thought I'd be saying I'm a fully paid-up member of the mile-high club."

$\sim$

THE PLANE BANKED to the right, and the colour drained from Cash's face.

"It's okay," Tally said, wrapping her hand around his clenched fist. She brushed her thumb over his knuckles in what she hoped was reassurance. Five minutes later, the plane landed, and as the door opened, bright sunshine poured inside. Cash unclipped his seat belt. Whereas normally he'd relax the minute they were on the ground, today his shoulders remained tense, his back stiff and taut.

"Ready?" He held out his hand.

"I was ready hours ago," Tally said, giving him a questioning look.

Cash ignored her. At the bottom of the steps, a man in a smart suit and a turban greeted them. He shook Cash's hand and smiled warmly at Tally.

"Mr Gallagher, right on time. Welcome to the Maldives, sir."

Maldives? Her excitement ratcheted up. She'd never been this far afield in her life.

Cash dealt with the formalities while Tally fanned herself with a folded-up piece of paper she'd found in her handbag. The oppressive humidity already made sweat drip between her shoulder blades.

"I need your help through the next part," Cash said to her.

Tally frowned. "Why?"

He pointed, and Tally glanced in the direction he'd indicated. About a hundred feet away stood a helicopter, its blades slowly rotating and catching the light from the sun.

"You've got to be kidding me." Her eyebrows shot up. "You're going to get in that?"

"It's the only way to get to where we're going." Cash swallowed hard, and his forehead beaded with sweat. His damp brow probably had more to do with mild panic setting in than with the oppressive heat. Now she understood why he hadn't relaxed as the plane came in to land.

"You can sometimes take a boat," he continued. "But the conditions aren't right today. Believe me, if there was another option, I'd grab it."

The next twenty minutes were amongst the longest of Tally's life. Cash began muttering to himself the minute the helicopter left the ground. He held onto her hand so tightly she wouldn't have been surprised to learn he'd broken a bone. But she did manage to glance out of the window as the helicopter began its descent. The island they were heading for was almost perfectly round, covered in dark-green trees and vegetation, and she spotted several golden sandy beaches with blue-green waves lapping at the shore. When the helicopter finally set down, Cash's whole body sagged with relief.

"Where are we?" Tally said. "And don't say the Maldives."

"A private island. In the Maldives," he added with a laugh. He climbed out and helped her down from the helicopter and into a waiting limousine. The car was cool inside, the air conditioning blasting out. She gazed out of the window as the car set off. They passed several beachfront villas, each one more spectacular than the last.

"When you say 'private,' what do you mean?"

"It's privately owned. You can only stay here by special arrangement."

"I hope the neighbours aren't too nosy."

"I've hired out the whole island."

Tally gaped at him. "You've what? So it's only us?"

He shrugged. "Plus a few staff."

"Jesus, Cash." She rubbed the space between her eyes. "That's a bit extravagant, don't you think?"

He squeezed her hand. "Maybe. But after the stress of the last couple of months, I want a few days on our own. No paps. No fans. No friends or family. Is that so bad?"

"Of course not," she said as relief surged through her once more that they'd been able to put the Kinga debacle behind them.

"Come on," he said as the car slowed to a stop. "Let's go and see where we're staying."

Their villa sat atop a hill and looked to be the largest on the island. As Cash ushered her through the door, she stepped into a large open-plan living area, but her eyes skimmed past the luxurious surroundings. Forgetting her exhaustion, she crossed the room and flung open the doors on the far side.

"Oh, wow," she murmured as she stepped outside and leaned against the wooden railings to take in the view. Far below, the Indian Ocean lapped the shore, the vibrant green waters giving way to deep blue the farther out she looked. She closed her eyes, tasting the ocean on the back of her tongue as she breathed deeply. She'd always loved being by the water, but this was something else entirely. Her own personal slice of paradise.

"Pretty incredible, huh?" Cash said, wrapping his arms around her waist and resting his chin on her shoulder.

"Something of an understatement."

"I did good?"

"You did fantastic, ace." She yawned, and even though she wanted to stay up a little longer, jet lag was catching up with her. "Sorry," she said, clamping a hand over her mouth.

"Let's go to bed. We've got plenty of time to explore tomorrow."

"More surprises."

"Oh, yeah," he said, backing up into the bedroom. "Starting right now."

Tally giggled. They might be going to bed, but sleep wasn't going to be the first thing on the agenda.

34

Cash swung his legs out of bed and tugged on a pair of joggers. Sunlight streamed through the blinds, but the piercing brightness hadn't stirred Natalia. He wandered into the kitchen. As per his request, the butler had left a jar of ground coffee beans and stocked the fridge with milk and juice. Five minutes later, Cash carried a tray precariously loaded with apple juice and freshly brewed coffee into the bedroom. He placed it on Natalia's side of the bed.

Her skin had turned a burnished copper from the last few days of lazing on the beach and going for the occasional stroll. He enjoyed relaxing with her and watching her soak up the sun, but today, he had something a little more active in mind. He poured a cup of coffee and wafted it under her nose. She murmured, and her nose wrinkled, but her eyes remained stubbornly closed. She was clearly knackered, and he wished he could let her sleep a little longer, but they had to be at the harbour by ten. He brushed a finger down her cheek, and she murmured again, louder this time. Eventually, her eyes flickered open, and as they focused, she smiled.

"You've made coffee." She pushed herself upright, taking the cup from him. She took a deep breath. "Mmm, not bad."

"Sorry to wake you."

"No, you're not."

He laughed and held his hands in the air. "Guilty."

She took a sip, peering at him suspiciously over the rim of the cup. "What are you up to?"

"You'll find out, in"—he glanced at his watch—"an hour."

She raised her eyes heavenward. "You love this, don't you?"

"Surprising you? Yes."

"Okay. I won't sulk and spoil it." She finished the coffee and flung back the covers. "At least tell me what I need to wear."

"Swimsuit, shorts, and T-shirt."

"Aha. So we're going in the water."

Cash smacked her behind as she climbed out of bed, making her yelp. "Get ready. I'll order breakfast."

Forty-five minutes later, they wandered hand in hand down the trail that ran in front of the house and led all the way to the marina. Cash spotted Adam, their PADI instructor, and waved, but when Natalia saw the diving gear lying on the wooden dock, she froze, and her hand tightened beneath his.

"Cash," she said, uncertainty tinged with fear coming through clearly in her voice. "I don't think I can do that."

He studied her panicked expression and then dropped her hand and rubbed soothing circles against her back. "It's okay, baby. We'll go at a slow pace. I'll be there the whole time, and we have an expert instructor."

As she glanced at him, her eyes appeared huge in her face, the pupils dilated, eclipsing the navy colour of her irises. "Have you done this before?"

"Yes. I'm PADI qualified. If you don't like it, we don't have to do it. But try to give it a go." He gave her a quick hug. "I'll hold your hand as tight as you do with me every time we fly. How's that?"

She swallowed, and her breathing quickened. He thought she

was going to flat-out refuse, but after a few seconds of staring at the gear, she nodded. "Okay. I'll try."

"Good girl."

They set off walking again, and as they arrived at the wooden dock, Cash shared a look with Adam, who nodded in understanding.

"Welcome," Adam said, shaking both their hands. "I've got a great day planned for us." He fixed his dark-brown eyes on Natalia, his smile warm and comforting. "I understand you're new to this. Don't worry about a thing. We'll start with the basics, and I'll take my cues from you."

She nibbled at the inside of her lip. "I'm a little nervous."

"I'd be concerned if you weren't. Everyone is the first time. But once you see what's beneath the ocean, the sheer beauty and wonder of it takes over. I promise you. Let's get you kitted up, then we can head out."

Natalia's face turned ashen, and she gave Cash a panicked look. "We're not starting in the swimming pool?"

"No," Adam said, answering for him. "In my experience, people find it harder to go under in a swimming pool. Out there, you'll get distracted and forget you're underwater. Trust me."

"It's okay, sweetness," Cash said, trying to make his voice calm and soothing. He rested a hand on her back and gently coaxed her forward. Her feet seemed glued to the floor, but with a little encouragement, she finally moved.

They donned their wetsuits and climbed aboard the boat. Adam had already loaded the oxygen tanks. As Natalia's gaze flickered to where the tanks were stacked against the side of the boat, the speed of her breathing escalated. Her eyes grew wider, and Cash began to have second thoughts. If she was this frightened before they'd even left the bay, was it fair to push her? His instincts had told him she would love diving, but the signals she was sending had him questioning whether he'd made a big mistake.

It took thirty minutes to reach the dive site, and by the time Adam had dropped anchor, Natalia was in full-on panic mode. Her breaths were short and shallow, and her cheeks puffed and deflated at alarming speed. When Cash caught Adam's eye, he stopped prepping the oxygen tanks and knelt down in front of Natalia, taking her hands in his. Under normal circumstances, Cash would have bristled at another man touching his girl, but these weren't normal circumstances.

"Natalia, look at me," Adam said in a firm tone.

Her gaze flickered to his before she stared at the ground. "I can't do it."

"No one is going to push you into anything. How about we get into the water and have a swim around. Then if you feel up to it, we can do a bit of snorkelling. That way, you can get a look at what's down there without having to go underwater. How does that sound?"

She nodded, and her breathing slowed a little. With her hand firmly in Adam's, she climbed down the side of the boat and into the water. Cash breathed a sigh of relief. At least they'd got her that far. For a minute, he'd worried she wouldn't even go for a swim.

After a few minutes of floating on her back, she relaxed and even started playing about, splashing Cash and laughing when he splashed her back.

"How about a little spot of snorkelling?" Adam said, dropping a mask into the water. "Only if you feel ready."

Natalia's eyes brightened. "I think I'd like that."

Cash helped her put on the mask, and after a few aborted attempts, she began to trust the breathing tube. As she seemed happy and occupied, Cash swam over to where Adam was sitting on the boat steps.

"Think we'll get her to do it?"

"I'm certain we will," Adam said. "She's far from the worst I've seen. And I haven't had a failure yet. It's hard for some people to trust the equipment and the experts around them. But look at her. She's taken to snorkelling much quicker than I anticipated. She's going to be fine."

"Hey, ace," Natalia shouted from about twenty feet away. "You've got to see this."

"Looks like you may be right." Cash grabbed the snorkel mask Adam held out. He swam towards where Natalia was bobbing in the water, her face wet from the sea but flushed with excitement.

"It's *amazing*," she said, grabbing onto his arms. "The colours and different species of fish and the rocks and everything."

After they'd snorkelled for about twenty minutes, Natalia tapped Cash on the shoulder. He surfaced and pushed his mask on top of his head. "What's up?"

"I want to do it. The diving. I want to see more."

"You're sure?"

"No," she said. "I'm scared to death. But I trust you. And I trust Adam."

Cash pulled her to him and kissed her wet, salty mouth. "I'm proud of you."

"Don't be too quick with the praise," she said. "I haven't done it yet."

Thirty minutes later, they were suited up and ready to go. Natalia's breathing was still heavy but nowhere near as fast or shallow as earlier. She leaned towards Adam, eagerly listening to every instruction. He talked them through the hand signals they'd use to communicate and assured her he wouldn't leave her side. For that matter, neither would Cash.

"Ready?" Cash said as they sat on the edge of the boat with their backs to the water.

"As I'll ever be," Natalia said.

They inserted their regulators into their mouths. She clutched his hand, and together, they somersaulted into the water.

35

Tally lost her grip on Cash's hand the minute she hit the water. Disoriented, she began to panic. This was a mistake. She couldn't breathe. Bubbles from the oxygen distorted her view, and as her survival instinct kicked in, she swam for the surface.

She hadn't got far when Cash gripped her shoulders. She forced herself to concentrate on his face. He pointed two fingers at his eyes then at hers. Tally focused on him, and gradually, her heartbeat began to slow down. Adam made a hand signal to Cash, who replied by making an O sign with his finger and thumb. Good. Cash thought she was okay. She didn't want to spoil this for him. He was so keen for her to experience diving, and after the brief view of what the ocean had to offer while she'd been snorkelling, she was too.

Flanked by the two men, Tally sank deeper into the ocean, holding tight to Cash's hand. Gazing at what had previously been hidden from view, she forgot she was scared. She forgot she was breathing air from a tank, and she forgot her concerns about not being able to touch the floor. Fear dissipated as the ocean sprang to life, teeming with colour. A shoal of tiny yellow fish with blue flashes on their scales swam past her. They brushed against her body, her hands, her face, and if she could have yelled with pleasure, she would have.

Adam pointed at a coral reef, and they swam towards it. As she got closer and the world opened up around her, adrenaline surged through her body. The coral was the most stunning thing she'd ever seen. Multicoloured, vibrant, and alive, the reef was home to hundreds of species of fish and marine life. Tally's eyes widened as she tried to take it all in, knowing without doubt this was the best thing she'd ever done in her life. Letting go of Cash's hand, she gave him the signal that she was okay. She swam off on her own, suddenly needing the space. Wonderment and awe slammed into her, and tears welled up behind the mask.

She could stay down here forever. It would be easy to forget the world above—a chaotic, difficult, and sometimes cruel world. Underwater, peace and tranquillity reigned, the silence only interrupted by the sound of her breathing.

She held her arms out wide, the only way she could think of to communicate to Cash how overwhelmed she was. Thank God she'd found the courage to do this. He put his thumbs up and swam across to her. Adam must have realised she was doing fine because he gave them the space to explore together, but when he sought them out and pointed to his oxygen tank, Tally knew their time was up. She rammed down disappointment, assuring herself they would do this again. And again. And again.

The three of them surfaced simultaneously, and Tally dragged off her mask and pulled her regulator from her mouth. She couldn't speak. Her mind was overflowing with the things she'd seen, the feelings she'd experienced.

"Well?" Cash said.

"Oh my God." She swatted his arm. "Why didn't you tell me it would be like that? Amazing. I... I can't find the right words. It's another world. When can we do it again?"

Cash gazed at her steadily. His grin, when it came, was slow and wide. "Anytime you want, baby."

On the way back to the island, Tally stared out to sea, trying to organise her feelings. Her legs were weak, and tears pricked behind her eyes at the overwhelming experience of her first dive. Cash and Adam were thoughtful enough to leave her alone and chat amongst themselves.

When they docked, she shook Adam's hand warmly. "Thank you for all of your help. I don't think I would have plucked up the courage if it hadn't been for you."

"That's what I'm here for," he said. "I knew you'd do it."

"Then you knew more than I did."

Adam smiled. "Let me know if you want to go out again. I'd be more than happy to take you."

"I think we'll be making that call," Cash said.

He placed his hand in the small of Tally's back, and they headed back up the trail to the villa. Tally's legs refused to hold her up properly. Exhausted, she sank into the first chair she saw, which happened to be beside the pool.

"Don't be surprised if you're tired," Cash said. "It's the adrenaline. Are you hungry?"

"Starving."

"I'll have a plate of sandwiches brought up, then you can get some sleep."

"How come you're fine?"

"It wasn't my first time."

"I'm not fit enough," she said with a groan, leaning back in the chair. "I need to exercise more."

"You are fit," Cash said, cupping her breasts from behind. "And if you want more exercise, I have just the thing in mind."

She giggled and pushed his hands away. "I need food."

Cash picked up the phone. "You shouldn't exercise on a full stomach."

"Thank you, ace," she said as happiness washed over her.

"What for?"

"The best time of my life."

36

"I can't believe we've been here nine days." Tally folded up the last pair of shorts and put them in the suitcase. "It's flown by."

"We can come back in the close season."

"I'd like that." A wave of melancholy swept over her, and she let out a soft sigh. "I wish we didn't have to go home."

"Who said anything about going home?"

Her head snapped up. "But the holiday's over."

"No. *This* part is over."

She frowned. "What about Montreal?"

"We don't have to leave until the third. That's over a week away."

Excitement unfurled in her belly. "Where are we going?"

Cash tilted his head to one side. "Will you never learn?"

She stuck out her tongue. "You're mean."

He caught her around the waist. "Come on, admit it. You love being surprised."

She pouted. "Sometimes."

"You're a terrible liar."

He called for the butler to collect their luggage then held out his hand. "Ready?"

"Yeah." She took a final glance around, sad to be leaving but excited about what the next leg of their journey could hold. With Cash, anything was possible.

Twelve hours later, their plane landed. Tally had played along with Cash's wishes and hadn't even peeked out of the window as they'd come in to land. As they taxied to their stand, she caught sight of Cash out of the corner of her eye—dangling an airline sleeping mask in the air.

She laughed as she remembered their first date when he'd asked her to wear a mask to hide their destination. "Ah, how I've missed you," she told the mask, snagging it from his outstretched hand.

She slipped it on and held tightly to Cash's arm as he helped her down the steps. His hand rested on top of her head as she climbed into the waiting car.

"Welcome back, sir, Miss McKenzie."

"Isaac," she said, recognising his deep voice anywhere. "How great to see you. Or not."

Isaac chuckled. "Good trip."

"Yes, wasn't it, Cash?"

"The best," he said, gently rubbing the back of her hand. "How are things, Isaac?"

"Everything is fine, sir."

"Mum?"

"She's doing well. I've been keeping an eye on her, as you asked, but there hasn't been anything for me to do."

"No intrusion from the press?"

"None."

"Good," he replied, his tone hard and flat.

They hadn't driven for long when the car eased to a stop. "Are we here?" she said.

"Yep." Cash gently removed the mask, and she blinked a

few times until the blurriness cleared. She gazed out of the window. Directly ahead was a row of arches with green canopies and lanterns hanging beneath each one. She recognised this place.

"Oh, Cash," she whispered. Tiredness and emotion overpowered her as hot tears sprang from her eyes. "You brought me back to Paris."

"I hope they're happy tears," he said, wiping the wetness from her cheeks.

"They are." She flung her arms around his neck.

"Come on, baby. It's been a long day. Let's get inside."

As they crossed the lobby towards the bank of lifts, memories of their first night hit Tally. She thought of how nervous she'd been, how scared that she wouldn't be enough or that Cash would realise he'd made a huge mistake in bringing her. So much had happened between then and now, and yet those first-night nerves were making a comeback. Maybe that was because they were in the place where her life had changed forever. Or she could be overwrought and jetlagged. Regardless of the reason, a serious case of butterflies swamped her abdomen when Cash pressed the button for the top floor.

As the lift doors closed, he steered her to the back, his body flush against hers. He lowered his head and kissed her, and when his tongue played with hers, a groan eased from her throat.

"Make that sound again, and I'll be pressing the emergency stop button," Cash said. Tally grinned as the lift doors opened, and Cash grabbed her hand and almost marched down the hallway.

"Same suite?" she said when Cash stopped outside the third door on the left and inserted the key card.

He nodded. "Same suite."

He opened the door and ushered her inside. He hooked the Do Not Disturb sign on the door before deadlocking it. His slow gaze swept over her before his eyes lifted to meet hers.

"I know you're tired," he said, reaching for her. "But I've always been a selfish bastard."

She touched his face, gently running her hands over his beard. "Funnily enough," she said, drawing his mouth down to hers, "I'm not tired anymore."

37

"here are we going?" Tally said as Cash helped her into the car the following evening after they'd spent the day reliving the sights from their first trip.

"Jules Verne. I know how much you loved it last time."

Tally smiled. "Oh, I did. The view from the top is fabulous."

When Tally stepped out of the elevator into the restaurant, Cash's warm hand in the small of her back, she halted immediately. Her eyes widened as she scanned the area. Three smartly dressed staff waited to greet them, but whereas she'd expected to see tables of hungry diners, the restaurant was completely empty. Vases of flowers adorned every table, the aroma heavily scenting the air. Candles provided the only light, their flickering flames creating a deeply intimate vibe, and music played from hidden speakers.

"I wanted tonight to be special," Cash said, his breath warm on her skin as he whispered in her ear.

Tally twisted around. "You're spoiling me."

"You deserve to be spoilt." He gestured with his hand. "Let's sit down."

Tally followed the waiter over to a table that had been set up next to the window overlooking Champ de Mars. The exact same spot as the last time they'd dined there.

"You never forget a thing, do you, ace?"

"Not where you're concerned."

The pop of a champagne cork made her jump, and she squinted. "Are we celebrating?"

He paused until the waiter retreated, then clinked his glass with hers. "It's our seven-month anniversary. Seven months today since you agreed to go on a date with me."

She touched the base of her neck. "Is it? God, you're right. Christmas Day."

"I sat outside your flat for ages. I watched everyone inside enjoying themselves, and I didn't think you wanted to see me."

"I was desperate to see you."

"You never called. After I threw my contact card on the table like a complete dick, I was certain you'd blink first. But you didn't."

"Ah," Tally said with a smile. "You've got Em to thank for that. If I'd been on my own, I'm sure I would have caved. Em persuaded me to play it cool, convinced if I did you'd come running."

"Smart girl," he said with a half-grin that looked more like a grimace. "I'm going to fucking kill her the next time our paths cross."

Tally chuckled. "Do you think we'd be sitting here now if I had chased after you?"

"Yep."

She raised her eyebrows. "You do?"

"You'd captured my heart, even then. Of course, I was totally in denial because I'd never felt so strongly about a woman before."

"It was a long five weeks."

He grimaced. "Longest of my life."

Tally drummed her fingers on the table, desperate to ask him about that time in Australia but scared of the answer. *Oh, what the hell.* "Did you hook up during those five weeks in Australia?"

Cash frowned. "You mean did I fuck someone?"

Tally winced at his bluntness, wishing she hadn't asked. "Yeah."

Cash's mouth twisted in a half-smile. "You think I'd have been able to get it up for another woman? No, baby. The minute I kissed you at Rupe's place, my screwing-around days were over." He reached across the table and took one of her hands in both of his. "You were the only woman I wanted after that. The only one I'll ever want."

Tally's eyes filled with tears, but she blinked them away. She hadn't realised, until that point, how much it would have hurt if he'd slept with someone in Australia, even though she had no right to demand monogamy. At least, not then.

"How long have you been wanting to ask me that question?"

Her mouth twisted. "Forever."

He chuckled. "Shall we order?"

The food was even better than last time, and when Tally finally pushed her plate away, her stomach felt fit to burst. "I'm stuffed. Couldn't eat another thing."

"They do the best crème brûlée here."

Tally sighed. "What did you have to go and say that for?"

She could take or leave most desserts, but when that particular one appeared on the menu, her good intentions went out of the window.

Cash waved his hand. "Two crème brûlées, please."

Five minutes later, the waiter placed the delicious custard dessert in front of her, and it looked so good she forgot her earlier comments about being full. She stuck her spoon through the crisp top, and the caramelised sugar gave way to a creamy, perfectly made crème pâtissière.

"Oh my God, this is amazing."

She tipped up the shallow bowl to make sure she scooped up every bit of the custard. As she ate the last remnants, she noticed the bottom of the dish had black writing on it. She held it up in the dim light and saw the words, "Will you marry me?"

Her head snapped back so fast she cricked her neck. Ignoring the sharp pain, she stared open-mouthed as Cash got down on one knee beside her. His outstretched palm held a small blue box from Tiffany & Co. Nestled in the satin was a large oval-shaped diamond set in a platinum band.

Tally's hand flew over her mouth, and this time, furious blinking did not stop tears from streaming down her cheeks.

"Natalia McKenzie, I love you more than I ever thought possible. You're my light, my life, my heart and soul. My everything. Will you marry me?"

She dashed away the tears with the back of her hand. "Yes. Oh, God, yes, yes, yes."

In a state of shock, she flung her arms around his neck. She had not seen this coming. Cash hadn't shown even the tiniest bit of nerves. As he slipped the ring on her finger, she suddenly giggled.

"Something funny?" he said.

"What would you have done if I'd refused the crème brûlée? Or if I hadn't finished it?"

He grinned. "I honestly don't know. I hedged my bets on the fact that you haven't refused one yet. Every time they're on the menu, you cave."

"You know me too well."

"I think there's still plenty to learn. And I'm looking forward to you teaching me."

She held her left hand up to the light. The diamond sparkled and glinted as flames from the candles reflected off the polished stone.

"If you don't like it, Tiffany's will happily exchange it for something else."

"Exchange it? I *love* it."

"Thank God," he said, clasping a hand to his chest.

"Did you tell anyone you were going to ask me?"

"Only my mother. If you'd said no, I wanted as little public humiliation as possible. Plus Rupe can't hold water let alone a secret as big as this, and I didn't want to put Emmalee or Pete in a tough spot by asking them not to tell you."

"You thought I might say no?"

"I hoped like hell you wouldn't, but we've never talked about marriage. I didn't know whether you'd think it was too soon."

She skimmed his cheek with her palm. "Not a chance."

His eyes shone as he moved in to kiss her. His lips were warm and soft, and Tally melted into his arms. She forgot everything except the feel of his mouth on hers and the strength of his arms cradling her waist.

And the fact she was going to become Mrs Cash Gallagher.

38

Tally tucked her hand into Cash's arm as they exited at the bottom of the Eiffel Tower.

"If your feet are up to it, shall we take a stroll back to the hotel?" Cash said as they approached the car, where Isaac already had the back door open. "It's warm enough."

"I'd like that."

"You can take off, Isaac," Cash said. "We're going to walk back."

"Yes, sir." Isaac pushed the back door closed and climbed into the car. A few seconds later, it quietly pulled away from the kerb and disappeared down the road.

As they strolled down the busy streets filled with tourists and Parisians alike, Tally couldn't stop staring at the large diamond on her finger, her mind racing. How would she tell Em and Pete? Blurt it out? Wave the ring in their faces but say nothing? The options for fun were endless. Of course, she'd have Em do her hair and makeup, and she'd invite Rachael to go dress shopping with them. Rachael would love that. Wouldn't she?

"You never said whether your mum approved."

Cash grinned. "She told me I'd taken too bloody long and I

was lucky you hadn't got fed up and decided to look elsewhere." His face grew serious. "And that you were already like a daughter to her. All this did was make it official."

Tally's stomach tightened. The fact that Rachael saw her in that way brought tears to her eyes once more. As they splashed down her cheeks, she began to laugh.

"I'm an emotional wreck," she said, dabbing her face with a tissue. "Look what you've done to me. I'm supposed to be a hardened journalist."

"I knew I'd break you in the end," he said, draping an arm around her shoulder and pulling her into his chest. "I may buy shares in Kleenex. At the rate you're going through them, it wouldn't be a bad investment."

Tally giggled. She loved it when Cash teased her. She no longer had any doubts. Cash had finally seen off the last of them. She wasn't a size six. She wasn't a tall, leggy blonde with tresses that gave everyone hair envy. She was a normal girl with boobs and hips and a more-than-generous backside. And she was the girl Cash wanted to spend the rest of his life with.

"Look," Cash said, rousing her from daydreaming. Across the road, a woman was selling flowers out of silver buckets. "Wait here."

He glanced both ways and, dodging a couple of cars, jogged across the road. He pointed to a few buckets. A couple of minutes later, he held up an enormous bunch of flowers. He waved them in the air, grinning like a fool as he stepped into the road.

The next few seconds were like something out of a horror movie—the screech of tyres and the blare of horns as a car, travelling at an impossible speed, careered down the street. Tally's gaze collided with Cash's, and she saw realisation in his eyes—realisation that he was in the wrong place at the wrong time. And there wasn't a damn thing either of them could do about it.

39

The car ploughed into Cash, sweeping his legs from underneath him. His head hit the windscreen with a horrific hollow thud before his body crashed to the ground. The driver didn't even slow down. Tally lost sight of Cash for a second as the car ran over him before speeding away down the road.

A scream ripped from her throat. With her legs barely holding her upright, she staggered across the road and fell to her knees. The flowers Cash had lovingly bought lay scattered around his lifeless body like a bizarre, cruel joke. His right leg was bent at an impossible angle, but it was the pool of thick, gloopy blood growing into a large circle beneath his head that had fear clogging in her throat, blocking her ability to breathe properly.

"Help me," she croaked, glancing around for someone, anyone. "Please, somebody help us."

She placed her ear close to Cash's mouth. A faint puff of air told her he was still breathing. Barely. With trembling hands, she managed to take her phone out of her pocket. She dialled 999, before remembering they were in France. *Oh God, what is the emergency number in France?* She didn't know. Why didn't she know?

Sirens blared in the distance. What was she going to do? He couldn't die. If he didn't make it, she wouldn't want to carry on. Not without him.

When a hand landed on her arm, she screamed.

It was the flower seller.

"It's okay, madame. I have called for help. They are coming."

Tally began to cry, her fear-soaked brain unable to cope with the enormity of the situation. Cash—her strong, handsome, perfect man—lying broken in the middle of a Paris street. He was dying. She knew it. He'd lost too much blood. She bent her head again, but this time, she couldn't tell if he was still breathing. She didn't think he was.

"Cash!" she screamed. "No, no, no. Don't leave me. You can't leave me."

Strong arms wrapped around her, pulling her away—away from Cash.

"No," she yelled, reaching for him, fingers splayed wide as she strained forwards. "Get off me!"

A man wearing an orange high-visibility vest appeared in her sight line, cutting off her view of Cash. He clutched her upper arms. "Madame, we're here to help. Please, let us help him."

Tally staggered backwards as he released her. "I'm sorry. He was buying me flowers." She covered her face with her hands and sobbed. "Please don't let him die."

"We are doing everything we can."

She couldn't see Cash. He was surrounded by paramedics. Her throat constricted, and every breath she took was shallow and painful, her lungs burning with the effort. Fear, longing, and grief surged within her.

"Madame, we're ready to go. Are you coming?"

She hadn't noticed they'd loaded Cash into the ambulance. With a nod, she stumbled inside. The paramedic tending him pointed to a seat, and Tally sank into it. They'd strapped Cash to a backboard, his neck in a brace.

"Is he... is he...?"

The paramedic squeezed her shoulder but made no false promises. The kind gesture brought tears to Tally's eyes again, and she let them silently fall as the vehicle sped away, sirens blaring.

The ambulance slowed to a stop, and the back doors flew open. All around her, people were shouting, pointing, gesticulating, and she didn't have a clue what was going on. They rushed Cash inside, and Tally ran after him, but a nurse barred her way.

"I have to be with him."

"I'm sorry, madame," she said in perfect English. She touched Tally's arm. "Let me show you to the waiting room."

Tally wrenched her arm away as her vision blurred with unshed tears. Screw the waiting room. She wanted to scream. To punch walls. To break glass. To beg to a God she didn't believe in to spare him, to take anything from her except Cash. But apart from clenching her fists, she did none of those things. Instead, she meekly followed the nurse into a sterile waiting room full of blue plastic chairs, with a water cooler and a vending machine serving warm drinks that offered cold comfort.

She sank into a chair and let her head fall into her hands. How could this be happening? There were so many *if only*s running through her head.

If only they hadn't come to Paris.

If only they'd stayed longer at the restaurant. Or left earlier.

If only she'd stopped Cash crossing the street to buy those stupid flowers.

One minute, her life had been perfect. The next, a stranger had ripped it apart. Fear came in waves so high she felt sure she was drowning. She needed to call Rachael but didn't know what to say. She'd wait. For the moment. Until she knew more.

She lost track of time. An administrator visited her, asking questions she didn't know the answers to. Was Cash allergic to anything? Was he on any medication? Any family history of medical issues they should know about? People came and went, a few with hopeful smiles, but most were like her with flat stares and blotched faces.

Still she sat waiting. A couple of times, she wandered into the hallway, but every time she tried to stop someone, they waved her away and rushed off to the next emergency.

The police questioned her, but she couldn't tell them anything other than that the car had been out of control and the driver hadn't stopped. She couldn't even recall the colour or the make of the vehicle.

She rocked backwards and forwards as the police took notes and assured her they were doing everything they could to find the culprit. Tally couldn't have cared less. She only had room to think about Cash. Her fragile mind couldn't cope with anything else.

She didn't know how long she waited, but as she began to drift into a fitful sleep, a warm hand on her shoulder made her start, and her eyes flew open. A young man wearing Harry Potter-style glasses and blue scrubs with streaks of red across the front was standing in front of her.

"Miss McKenzie, I'm Dr Girard." His face had the weary, resigned expression of an accident-and-emergency doctor too used to carnage and death.

A sob caught in her throat. "Is he...?"

"He's alive. His leg is broken in three places, and his right hand was crushed when the car ran over him. But these are minor in comparison to his head injury." He gazed at her solemnly. "When his head hit the windshield, the blood vessels at the front of his brain ruptured, meaning the cavity between the skull and the brain filled with blood. You're lucky the ambulance brought him here, because we have one of the best neurosurgeons in Paris. He's managed to stabilise Mr Gallagher for now, and has removed part of the outer skull to allow the blood to drain away. This will help relieve the pressure, but the next twenty-four hours are critical."

"Oh God." She clapped a hand over her mouth and forced back a scream. *Please, let me wake up from this nightmare.* But she couldn't wake up, because this was real. She wasn't asleep—and this wasn't a nightmare.

"Can I call someone for you?"

Tally shook her head. "I need to see him."

"Of course."

She followed Dr Girard out of the waiting room. They walked in silence. After a couple of minutes, the doctor pushed open a door and waved for her to go in.

When her eyes fell on Cash, a sharp pain in her chest sucked all the air from her lungs. She'd imagined being greeted by a bloodied, broken body. But the reality was much worse. His head was swathed in white gauze, and there were so many tubes sticking out of him that he looked more like a machine than a warm human being who loved her, had proposed to her, and had kissed her.

And bought her flowers.

She shuffled over to the bed, almost falling into a nearby chair. Cash's right hand was in plaster, but his left was free. She covered it with her own. His hand was warm—the warmth of someone very much alive. She lifted it, placing his palm against her cheek the way Cash had, many times, of his own accord.

"Please don't leave me," she begged, rubbing his hand against her face. It didn't feel the same as when Cash did it. "I waited ten years for you. And I'll wait another ten, twenty, if it means you'll come back to me. But we've got too much to do. I haven't had enough time..."

Her voice broke on a sob, and it was only then she realised they weren't alone. In the corner, a nurse was making notes on a chart.

"Will he live?" Tally said as another wave of fear gripped her stomach.

The nurse glanced up and smiled kindly. "He's young, and he's strong."

"But will he live?" she said again, her body trembling, the idea of a life without Cash making her head swim and her heart splinter.

The nurse put the chart to one side. "I wish I could give you a straight answer. We got to him quickly, which is positive, but..." She shrugged. "All we can do is wait."

Tally rubbed her eyes with the heels of her hands. "Will he be the same if he survives?"

"We won't know anything until he wakes up."

She blew out a shaky breath. "But in your experience. Please, I have to know."

The nurse hesitated. It was clear she was struggling with the right thing to say. "He's suffered a severe head trauma. Injuries like this do have side effects, even when the patient survives the initial incident." She rose from her chair, crossed the room, and rested a comforting hand on Tally's shoulder. "But youth is on his side."

Tally nodded. "I need to tell his mum." She began to cry, her shoulders shaking with the effort of desperately trying to hold it all together.

"Can I call her for you?"

"No. I'll do it. I just need to think of the right thing to say." She bent forward, rested her head against his hand, and closed her eyes. Rachael would be devastated. And Rupe. And what about Brad, Jamie, Em, Pete? Oh God, it was all too much. She didn't have the right words.

Her head snapped up. Shit. She'd fallen asleep. How long had she been out? Her eyes sought Cash's face. He was still sleeping. Was *sleeping* the right word when someone was being drugged to stay that way? The whooshing noise from the ventilator providing air to his lungs stole her attention. She was beginning to hate the sound.

"Hey, ace," she said, kissing his cheek.

She glanced across the room. A new nurse sat in the corner, and she smiled warmly at Tally.

"How is he?" Tally said.

"No change. He's stable but still critical. Perhaps you would like to get a drink? Something to eat?"

Tally rubbed sleep from her eyes. "I need to call his mum," she said, digging her phone out of her bag. "I should have done it last night. Why didn't I do it last night?" She covered her face with her hands as more tears began to fall. "I can't handle this."

She found herself enclosed in a warm embrace. "You've had an enormous shock," the nurse said. "It's understandable."

Tally let herself wallow in the moment of comfort before she pulled away. She reached into her bag for a tissue and blew her nose. "Thank you," she said, her voice hoarse from all the crying she'd done.

She slipped into the hallway and frowned at her phone. No signal. She headed for the hospital entrance. As she stepped outside, she shivered despite the heat of the day. Tally spotted a small garden with a couple of wooden benches, each one inscribed with a name and two dates—a memorial to people, like Cash, who'd been brought to hospital but had never left.

Her chest heaved, and she bit down on her lip, the coppery taste of blood spilling onto her tongue. She had no idea how to begin this conversation. What she should say first? It was all moot, of course, because it didn't matter what she said. The news was going to tear Rachael apart.

40

"Tally, my darling. How is the holiday going? Anything to tell me?"

Rachael's voice held a tinge of excitement, clearly signposting the proposal. Despite all the mental preparation, Tally couldn't force the words. No matter what she did, they wouldn't come. A sob broke from her throat.

"Tally." Rachael's voice was harder now, full of concern. "What's the matter?"

"It's Cash," she finally managed to force out. "He's... he's... oh, Rachael, he's in hospital. Please come."

"Hospital?" Rachael said, her voice sharp and shrill. "What hospital? What's happened?"

"In P-Paris." Tally sobbed harder, trying desperately to keep it together yet failing miserably. "He got hit by a car. We're at the American Hospital in Paris."

"I'm on my way."

Without another word, Rachael hung up, and relief hit Tally hard. She'd be able to share the burden and the pain. His mum was on her way, and Tally wouldn't have to manage alone any longer.

She hurried back inside, unable to bear the thought of something happening to Cash while she wasn't there, but when she opened the door to the ICU, nothing had changed. The nurse stood up as she walked inside.

"Are you okay?"

"I'm sorry. I don't even know your name."

"Evelyn," the nurse replied.

Tally nodded. "His mum is coming. She's in Belfast. I don't know how long that will take her. How long do you think it will take her to get here?" She was rambling, but Evelyn didn't react to her incoherence.

"Why don't you go and get something to eat and drink?"

Tally shook her head. "How long have we been here?"

"Since about ten thirty last night."

She glanced at the large clock on the wall. "Eleven hours." She frowned. "Is that all? It feels like longer."

Time seemed meaningless as she sat and stared. She lost track of how long ago she'd made the phone call, but when the door opened and she lifted her head to see Cash's mum standing in the doorway, she swallowed back a sob and threw herself into Rachael's outstretched arms.

"Shush, darling. I'm here." Rachael clutched her hand, and they walked over to Cash's bedside. Tears filled Rachael's eyes. Her face was pale and wan. She took a deep, shuddering breath and gently caressed his face.

"My son is strong. The strongest person I know. He won't let this beat him." She turned to Evelyn. "Can I speak to the doctor?"

"Of course."

Five minutes later, the neurosurgeon arrived, and Rachael stepped outside to speak with him. Tally didn't know whether to follow her or stay put. She decided on the latter. Better to let Rachael handle this side of things. It was easy to see where Cash's strength came from.

"Cash," she said, closing her fingers around his. "Your mum's here. Don't give up. She can't lose you. Not now." Her voice dropped to a whisper. "Neither can I."

When Rachael returned, she pulled up another chair and sat next to Tally.

"What did the doctor say?" Tally asked.

"Not much other than he's stable, but it's a waiting game. There is nothing to be done while he's in the medically induced coma. We have to wait and see."

Tally choked back a sob. "I can't lose him."

Rachael held Tally's hand in a firm grip. "You are *not* going to lose him. *We* are not going to lose him. I refuse to let my son go. I missed thirteen years of his life. I will *not* miss another second."

Rachael's gaze fell on the large diamond on Tally's left hand, and a smile spread across her face. Her expression was out of place yet also fit perfectly. "He did it," she said, her eyes bright with happiness. "And you said yes."

Tally nodded as she twiddled the ring around her finger. It felt heavy and unfamiliar. "It was the most romantic proposal. He was buying flowers when he... when he..."

Natalia McKenzie, I love you more than I ever thought possible. You're my light, my life, my heart and soul. My everything. Will you marry me?

Fresh tears fell, and Tally pushed her chair backwards, the resultant screech zipping through her. "Won't be a minute," she mumbled, stumbling into the hall. She was losing it. Her chest was hollow, her skin numb, and she could barely see through her tears as she staggered into the bathroom. She pressed her hands against the wall and forced herself to take slow, ragged breaths.

Leaning her forehead against the cool mirror, she closed her eyes. *Get a grip.* She'd be no use to Cash if she continued this downward spiral. He'd always been the strong one, and now he needed her to be strong for him. It wasn't fair to put all this on Rachael. She'd barely recovered from a long illness herself, and who knew what stress like this could do to her long-term recovery.

Rupe!

His name slammed into her, and she gulped air through lungs that burned with every breath. She needed Rupe. Oh God, she hadn't even called him. What was wrong with her? Surely, a normal person would want their loved ones around them at a time like this to offer strength and support, to spread the burden, and yet, it had taken her hours before she'd even called Cash's mother. To think he could have died, and Rachael wouldn't have been there.

Tally lurched towards the bathroom door as the room began to spin. She raised a shaky hand to her clammy face as a wave of nausea washed over her. Her legs buckled, and she sank to the floor.

41

Tally came around to find a woman with dark hair and worried eyes crouched over her. She tried to sit up, but the woman placed her hand gently on her shoulder.

"No, chérie. Don't try to get up. Did you hit your head when you fell?"

Tally touched the back of her head. "I don't know. I don't think so. What happened?"

"You fainted. I tried to catch you, but I wasn't quick enough."

Tally tried once again to sit up, and this time, the stranger helped her.

"I have to go. My fiancé needs me."

"Let's get you checked out first."

"No, really," Tally said, struggling to her feet. "I'm okay."

"You don't look okay. Come on. It will only take a minute."

Tally weaved as she came to a full standing position. Reluctantly, she nodded, and leaning her weight on the woman, they walked to the nurses' station. Behind the desk sat the nurse who'd been caring for Cash the night before. She probably worked the evening shift.

"It's you," Tally stupidly said. Jesus, maybe she had taken a blow to the head when she fainted.

"It's me—I'm Marie," the nurse said with a smile. "What's happened to you?"

The kind stranger who'd found Tally briefly explained what had happened.

Marie made Tally sit down and carried out a few tests. After checking her blood pressure and taking her pulse, Marie passed her a glass of water. "When did you last eat something?"

"Last night."

She nodded as though that explained everything. Digging around in her desk drawer, Marie produced a nutty bar. "Eat," she said, handing it over. "And finish all that water."

"I have to get back to Cash. He needs me."

"He needs you to be *well*," Marie said. "You're no use to anyone if you get sick. Now eat. Then you can go."

Tally crammed down the nut bar. It tasted like sawdust, but her stomach settled after she'd finished it.

"Come on," Marie said. "It's time for me to relieve Evelyn anyway. Let's go and see how your man is doing."

When Tally pushed the door to Cash's hospital room open, Rachael jumped to her feet, her face holding so much worry that fresh guilt slammed into Tally.

"Where have you been? What happened?" Rachael said, smoothing dishevelled hair from Tally's face.

"She fainted," Marie explained. "It's likely the stress and shock catching up with her. I've checked her over, and she's fine, but she needs to eat." She gave Tally a hard stare before she and Evelyn began to exchange notes.

Tally sank into the chair by Cash's bed and resumed holding his hand.

"Fainted? Oh, Tally."

"I'm all right." Fresh realisation about Rupe washed over her. "I haven't called Rupe."

"I called him," Rachael said. "Right after you called me. He should be here sometime tonight."

"Oh, thank God," Tally said. Somehow, Rupe would make everything all right.

He arrived a little after ten that evening, bringing with him a life force Tally desperately needed to recharge hers. She barrelled into his chest. Almost immediately, her strength returned, as though he had regenerated her depleted batteries.

"It's okay, Tal," he said, his arms strong and comforting around her. He kissed Rachael on the cheek. "How is he? Any change?"

Rachael shook her head. "No, but the swelling in his brain has stopped growing, which they seem pleased about, and the doctor is going to start withdrawing the coma medication at midnight."

"And then what?"

Rachael shrugged. "We wait. And pray."

Rupe switched his attention to Tally. "What the fuck happened, Tal?"

She met his gaze. Rupe's face was pinched, and dark circles she'd never seen before gave his eyes a sunken look.

"He was crossing the road. The car came out of nowhere. It all happened so fast..."

"Have they found him? The driver?"

"Not that I know of. I don't care about that, Rupe. Right now, I only care about Cash."

"Of course. Sorry."

"I'm glad you're here," she said, folding herself into his arms once more.

"For as long as you need me," Rupe said, rubbing her back with soothing circles. "I expected Em to be here."

Tally shook her head against his chest then pulled away. "I told her not to come. Or Pete. There's nothing they can do, and it's two more people for me to think about."

Rupe gave her an understanding nod as silence descended

over the hospital room, broken only by the noise of the ventilator and the scratch of Marie's pen as she made notes every half an hour on Cash's vital signs. At midnight, when the doctor removed the IV line administering the drugs that kept Cash sedated, Tally didn't even dare to blink in case she missed a twitching eye, a muscle spasm, or the jerk of a finger. But as the hours passed and nothing changed, she began to lose hope.

"I need a minute," she said, scrabbling out of the chair. She almost ran from the room, and when she burst through the hospital doors to the outside, she took huge gulps of air. A sudden dizzy spell hit her, and she shoved her head between her legs.

"Not again," she muttered as wave after wave of nausea flooded her stomach, and she broke out into a cold sweat. Tally breathed slowly in and out, and after a minute, the sickly feeling disappeared. She stood upright.

"He's going to pull through."

Tally glanced over her shoulder. Rupe had joined her, his face more serious than she'd ever seen.

"You don't know that," she said.

"Yes, I do. Cash is the most stubborn fucker I know. In *everything* he does. Why should this be any different?" His gaze dropped to her hand, where she was twisting her engagement ring around her finger. "About time he made an honest woman of you. Do you think after finally plucking up the courage to propose, he'll fuck it all up now?"

"This isn't anything he has control of, Rupe. He can't will himself out of this." Her eyes flickered up to the sky, and she gazed at the stars, the same stars Cash had pointed out to her a few days before during a walk along the beach in the Maldives. Except here, they seemed dull and lifeless. The irony wasn't lost on her.

"The car hit him so hard. I can't get the sound of his head slamming against the windscreen out of my mind." She rammed the heels of her hands into her eyes. "I keep hearing it. Over and over. The dull thud. The sound of his body as he was thrown from the bonnet and hit the ground."

Rupe's arms closed around her, and she sobbed into his chest. He let her cry it out, and only when she was spent did he pull a handkerchief out of his pocket and dab her face. She couldn't help smiling.

"Only you would still use handkerchiefs in the twenty-first century." She spotted the letters *RFW* in blue on the corner, and her smile widened. "And stitched with your initials no less."

"It's part of my charm. Although Cash would call it pretentious shit."

She laughed, even though it didn't feel right when Cash was lying unconscious in a hospital bed. "That sounds like him."

Rupe put his arm around her shoulder and squeezed. "Ready to go back inside?"

She took a deep breath through her nose. "Yes. Let's do this."

THE FOLLOWING MORNING, they removed the ventilator, and Cash began breathing on his own. The doctors assured them this was a good sign. Tally watched carefully for a hint that he was regaining consciousness, but as time passed, she began to realise this was going to be a longer process than she'd first thought. But Rupe was right: this was Cash, a strong and capable man who rarely let anything beat him. She had to hang on to the hope that this particular fight would be no different from his determination to win every tennis match he played.

The police visited again to tell them they had caught the hit-and-run driver. He was a young man, only twenty-two, and had been drinking in a local bar with his girlfriend when they'd had a row and he'd stormed off. After mowing Cash down, he'd driven out of Paris and set fire to the car to try to cover his tracks. But the police had the bar owner's evidence showing the young man had been drinking for several hours. The police told her he was looking at significant jail time. Not that it mattered to Tally. It was immaterial how much time the guy spent in prison. None of it would take away what had happened to Cash and the living nightmare they all had to cope with.

Minutes turned into hours, and hours into days. Despite both Rachael and Rupe urging her to take regular breaks, Tally wouldn't leave Cash for more than a few moments at a time, and only then to grab a bite to eat or to use the bathroom.

She developed a routine of sorts. Each morning, Rupe would fetch the paper, and Tally would look through it, pick out any interesting stories, and read them to Cash. Then she'd choose a novel by one of his favourite authors and read from it, at least four or five chapters at a time, before her throat would become dry and scratchy and she'd have to take a break. Then she'd simply hold his hand and pray.

Dawn broke on the sixth day. Rachael and Rupe were having a well-earned lie-in at the hotel, and Tally couldn't stand the distance from Cash any longer. She needed his body next to hers. They had always used physical contact as a way to connect, and she craved that connection now more than ever.

Carefully lifting the tubes and wires, she managed to make a space for herself, and she crawled onto the bed, curling into his side. She rested her hand over his heart, gaining comfort from the gentle rise and fall of his chest. His beard had grown longer than he normally liked to wear it, and she made a mental note to ask Rupe to bring his trimmer from the hotel.

"Wake up, Cash," she whispered, gently kissing his cheek. "Please, babe. I need you."

He didn't, but even so, being physically close comforted her, and gradually, she drifted off to sleep.

She awoke some time later, not sure whether it was of her own accord or from the gentle touch of Marie's hand.

Marie smiled kindly, although her eyes held a reprimand. "You shouldn't be up there with him, Tally. What if you moved in your sleep and pulled a tube out?"

"Please, Marie. I need to touch him."

Marie nodded and patted her arm. "I know, honey. All right, but only while I'm in the room with you. If I have to leave, even for a moment, you get down. Deal?"

Tally nodded and curved back into Cash's side. She was tired, so tired. She closed her eyes for a second, but when they snapped open the next time, it wasn't Marie who had woken her—it was the slight rumble in Cash's chest beneath her left ear. She half sat up, looking for signs of him regaining consciousness, and when his eyes flickered open, hope surged within her.

"Hi," she said—stupidly inadequate but the first thing that came to mind.

"Hi." His voice rasped, and a flicker of confusion crossed his face, but Tally didn't care about any of that. He'd survived. Against all the odds, Cash had survived and come back to her.

"Marie, he's awake," she said, trying to stay calm for Cash's sake, even though mounting excitement made her want to scream with delight—and relief. The tension she'd carried on her shoulders for days evaporated.

When Marie didn't respond, Tally glanced over her shoulder. *That's odd.* Marie's chair lay empty. What had happened to her rule?

"Stay here, babe," she said, loath to leave him but knowing she needed to get a doctor. She climbed down from the bed as carefully as she could. "I'll get someone."

"Wait." Cash's left hand snapped around her wrist, stronger than she'd expected, given what he'd been through. "What happened? Where am I?"

"You're in Paris. You were hit by a car almost a week ago. You nearly didn't make it."

"Paris?" His brow furrowed in confusion. "What the fuck am I doing in Paris?"

She tried not to worry about what his apparent lack of memory might mean. She held up her left hand. "Proposing to me."

His gaze raked her from head to foot, and given the disdainful look on his face, earlier hope was replaced with fear. Cold, terrifying fear. Something was very wrong.

"This is a joke, right? I mean, look at you. I like my women blond and tall. And *thin*," he added, a sneer marring his handsome face.

Tally's knees buckled. This couldn't be happening. Pain sliced through her chest, and she clutched at her shirt. "But... but you proposed. We're together. We've *been together* for seven months."

Cash snorted. "Dream on, sweetness. As if I'd waste my time on someone like you."

A cry ripped from her throat, and as her knees gave way, she fell to the floor.

"Tally!"

She awoke with a start, gasping for air. Her lungs were burning, and her chest heaved, breath coming in short, sharp bursts.

"Tally." Marie's face swam before her, and she tried to focus. Her head snapped around to Cash. His face was serene, eyes moving behind their lids. *He must be dreaming. And so was I. Fuck, it was only a dream.*

In her haste, she almost fell off the bed, bile burning her throat. It had seemed so real. The way he'd looked at her. The way he'd ridiculed her, hatred spilling from his eyes as he'd pointed out her deepest fears, spoken them aloud.

Except he hadn't.

"I'm going to be sick," she said.

Marie grabbed a surgical kidney tray and shoved under her chin. Her stomach rolled, and she retched, but nothing came up except yellow bile, which she spat into the tray. She shivered violently as Marie wiped the bile from her chin. Her abdomen stopped heaving, but she felt bruised inside. Her mouth tasted gritty, and she reached for a bottle of water. She swilled out her mouth and spat the excess into the tray.

"I'm sorry," she said. Sweat poured off her, and her legs wobbled—for real this time.

Marie grabbed a chair and encouraged her to sit. "What happened? You were sleeping, then all of a sudden, you yelled 'No' at the top of your voice. You were thrashing about, and I was worried you'd pull out a tube. That's why I was a little rough with you."

"I dreamt he woke up. Oh, Marie." She buried her face in the nurse's shoulder, her body heaving with wracking sobs.

"Honey." Marie held her, rocking her back and forth until she calmed.

"He's not going to wake up, is he?"

The skin bunched around Marie's eyes, and she gave Tally a pained stare. "The longer he remains unconscious, the less likely it is he'll make a good recovery. But you more than anyone know miracles happen. Look at his mum. Maybe it's in the genes. We know so little about how the brain operates. There are no hard-and-fast rules."

Tally turned away, her gaze firmly on Cash. She desperately wanted him to wake up, but what if her dream was a prequel to a new world? What if, when Cash woke, he couldn't even remember her?

The horror of that potential reality didn't even bear thinking about.

42

"Now," Tally said, digging a book out of her bag, "I know you won't like this, but I am sick of reading the sports pages, and Saturday's paper is mostly full of whether anyone will catch Chelsea at the top of the league. Therefore, I've decided I'm going to read a novel *I* like. Not one of those crime novels you love so much. Nope, we're going to have a good old-fashioned romance. Suck it up, mister."

Rupe groaned. "Buddy, I'm sorry, but you're on your own. No fucking way I'm sticking around to listen to tripe." He quickly rose from the chair beside Cash's bed, and in five seconds, he'd left the room.

Tally grinned at Rupe's retreating back. "We don't need him anyway, although your mum will be gutted she's missing the first chapter of *True Devotion*."

Tally was trying so hard to keep her spirits up. In her darker moments, she wanted to scream at the unfairness of it all, but that wouldn't help anyone. She *had* to believe Cash would recover, because the alternative was too horrifying.

She climbed onto the bed, even though she shouldn't because Evelyn had popped out for five minutes. She lay on her side. With one hand on the book and one on Cash's chest, she began to read. She wasn't even halfway through the first chapter when her eyelids began to droop. She was so tired these days. Reluctant to move from her comfortable position, she dropped the book on the floor. On the cusp of sleep, the halfway-there state that brought brief moments of peace, she felt a hand brush against her back. She snuggled closer.

Her eyes snapped open. She twisted her head.

Cash was staring, his eyes focused directly on hers, and for the briefest moment, Tally assumed it was one of those times when an involuntary impulse would cause his eyes to open even while he remained unconscious. But then his hand moved again.

She froze. Was she dreaming this time too? She couldn't take another day like the one before. The pain, when reality hit, that she'd been sleeping—regardless of how vile Cash had behaved in her dream—had been awful, and she hadn't built up the strength for round two yet.

Taking great pains not to disturb any of the wires and tubes surrounding him, she sat up.

"Cash," she said, clasping his hand.

His eyes flickered to where her hand clutched his fingers. He opened his mouth, but nothing came out. He briefly closed his eyes again, and Tally feared he'd lost consciousness, but then they reopened once more.

"Don't try to talk, babe," she said, touching a finger to his lips. "You've had an accident."

A hint of a frown creased his brow, but as if the effort was too much, his eyes closed again.

"I'm going to get the nurse." She climbed off the bed and almost tripped over her own feet in her haste to get someone. She spotted Evelyn behind the nurses' station.

"He's awake," she shouted, waving her arms in the air. "He woke up."

Evelyn dropped the file she was holding and ran towards Tally, her shoes squeaking on the tiled floor. "Are you sure?"

"Yes. He touched my back when I was lying next to him. And he looked at me. I mean, right at me."

Evelyn rushed into Cash's room, with Tally directly behind her, and began doing various tests. Tally hovered by the door, unsure what to do. Cash didn't look awake anymore, but she *knew* she was right. It hadn't been a dream. Not this time.

Evelyn finished her checks and rushed off to get the doctor. Tally settled into the familiar chair by the bed and wrapped her fingers around Cash's. "Come back to me, Cash. Please, I'm begging you."

She felt a faint pressure against her hand. The movement was almost imperceptible, but it was enough for Tally to know he'd heard her. Tears streamed down her face.

Everything was going to be okay.

OVER THE NEXT WEEK, Cash drifted in and out of consciousness. The day after he'd first woken up, he'd tried to rip his tubes out, so the nurses had restrained him for his own safety. They assured Tally it was normal for some patients to try to do this, but it had shaken her up, and she'd barely left his side since then, worried out of her mind he'd find a way to harm himself.

On the morning she crossed off two weeks since Cash's accident, Rupe arrived with a cheese croissant wrapped in cellophane. When she began to unwrap it, he stopped her. "Go and sit in the garden and eat."

Tally shook her head. "I'm okay here."

"You have two choices, darling." He pointed at the door. "Either you walk out of that door unaided, or I'm carrying you. One way or the other, you are taking a break. You look like shit."

Tally half-laughed. She raised her eyebrows at Rachael for

support. Rachael put her hands in the air. "I'm with Rupe on this one. You need to get some fresh air. Now go. If Cash so much as twitches, we'll call."

Tally sighed and accepted defeat. She tucked the croissant in her bag and headed outside to the private gardens at the back of the hospital. At least the press couldn't get to her there. She'd only once made the mistake of leaving through the front entrance. The hordes had descended, pushing their microphones and cameras in her face and bombarding her with questions about Cash's progress, or lack thereof. She'd frozen, like a deer in headlights, until Rupe had come to her rescue.

Today was one of the hottest days so far, and Tally began to sweat the minute she sat on one of the wooden benches. She closed her eyes and lifted her face to the sun. Despite her protestations to Rupe and Rachael, it did feel good to be outside, to breathe fresh air instead of the reconditioned stuff in the hospital. She took a deep breath, revelling in the smell of the flowers planted in borders around a small patch of grass. Being surrounded by nature and birds tweeting overhead reminded her life did exist outside the four walls of the hospital.

Her phone rang, and she scrambled to get it, hoping it was Rachael saying Cash had regained consciousness again. When she spotted the caller ID, her excitement waned.

"Hi, Em."

"Hey, babes. How's Cash?"

"The same. He wakes, he sleeps. He freaks out occasionally. The doctors keep telling us he's making progress, but it doesn't feel like it."

"Why don't I come over? Only until tomorrow. I can be on a plane in a couple of hours."

Tally was about to refuse, as she had every other time Em had offered, but suddenly, she needed to see her friend, to be *normal,* if only for a brief time.

"That'd be great."

Em's answering sigh was full of relief. "Good. That's good, Tal. I thought you'd say no again. I'll be there as soon as possible."

Tally hung up, finished her croissant, and headed back inside in case she missed a precious moment of consciousness.

"Any change?" she said as she walked into Cash's hospital room.

"Back already?" Rachael frowned her disapproval. "You need to take better care of yourself, Tally. You'll be no use to him if he gets better and ends up visiting you in hospital."

"Em's on her way over."

Rachael's frown turned into a smile. "Good. Maybe she'll have more luck getting you out of here. Why don't you go back to the hotel tonight?" When Tally vigorously shook her head, Rachael sighed. "I'm not kidding. You look awful. You need the downtime."

"What if he wakes up and needs me?"

"Then I'll call. The hotel is ten minutes from here. If you run, you'll make it in five."

Tally scrubbed her eyes with the heels of her hands. A short break did sound good. With a horrible feeling of guilt swarming through her gut, she nodded. "Okay."

When Em arrived later that day, she and Tally went for dinner in the hotel restaurant. Sitting opposite Em, nursing a large glass of wine and waiting for her rare steak to be delivered, she could almost believe life was normal.

It was anything but.

"You look fucking awful, babes."

Tally glanced at Em over the rim of her wine glass. "Everyone seems to be saying that."

"They're right. Harsh, I know, but you clearly haven't been taking care of yourself. Some use you're going to be when Cash properly wakes up."

Tally's gaze on Em was unwavering. "What if he doesn't?"

"He's making improvements, right?"

Tally shrugged. "Of a sort."

"What does that mean?"

She sighed. "He's in and out all the time, Em. When he looks at me, it doesn't feel as though he sees me, you know? I could be a doctor, a nurse, a cardboard cut-out. His eyes—they're cold. Emotionless." Tears pricked her eyes, and she dashed them away. She was so bloody *sick* of crying.

"He's had a serious injury, babes. Don't expect too much too soon."

"Don't you think I know that?" Tally snapped, ignoring the unwelcome attention from other diners. "I've been living with this for two fucking weeks."

Em's eyes widened, and she grimaced. "I know, babes."

Tally's shoulders sagged. "Sorry," she muttered. "I'm just tired."

Em's hand closed over hers. "You snap at me all you like. That's what best friends are for."

"What if this is as good as it gets?" she said, voicing her deepest, darkest fear.

"I don't believe that," Em said, her tone firm and resolute. "Cash is young, strong, determined. Madly in love with you. That alone will drag him back to the land of the living."

"I hope you're right." Tally leaned back as the waiter put her steak down. She had to admit it smelt great. For the first time in ages, her stomach rumbled. She tucked in, eating it faster than she'd ever eaten anything in her life. When the waiter brought the dessert menu, she couldn't resist choosing a large slice of chocolate cake.

"Let's go for a walk," Em said after they'd settled the bill. "I've never been to Paris."

"Sightseeing may be off the menu," Tally said with a wry grin.

"Doesn't mean we can't visit a bar or two. Take in the Parisian atmosphere."

"Ogle a couple of Frenchmen, you mean," Tally said, feeling the shroud of despair lift a little.

"And what's wrong with that?" Em said, linking her arm through Tally's.

They found a small, artistic bar not too far from the hotel and still within sprinting distance of the hospital. They picked a table by the window where they could watch the world go by, the summer evening providing excellent light for people watching.

Tally sipped at her third glass of wine of the evening, the buzz of alcohol lessening the heavy load she'd been carrying around the last couple of weeks. Even though Rachael and Rupe had been amazingly supportive, nothing could fill the enormous hole caused by Cash's accident. But by spending time with Em, the pain in her chest had eased, although she knew it wouldn't last.

"It's good to see a little colour in your cheeks," Em said, clinking their glasses.

"That's what alcohol does for you."

"I've missed you, babes. I wish you'd let me come earlier."

"It wouldn't have done any good. It's been easier without you here." When a flash of pain crossed Em's face, Tally rubbed the back of her friend's hand. "I don't mean to sound cruel, but it took all my strength to wake up each day and face the reality of what had happened. If you or Pete had been here, it would have been a whole lot harder."

"And yet you let me come this weekend."

Tally shrugged. "I needed to feel normal, if only for a short time." She pressed her fingertips to her temple. "Does that make me sound awful?"

"Not in the slightest." Em let out a long, deep breath. "You've been through a terrible experience. I can't imagine..." Her voice faded, and a single fat tear spilled onto her cheek. "It kills me to know there isn't a fucking thing I can do to help."

Tally moved to sit next to Em and wrapped her arms around her friend, tugging her close. "You're here. That's enough."

It was a while before they broke apart, and when they did, Em's gaze was steadfast. "For as long as you need me."

They staggered back to the hotel with Tally more than a little drunk. She couldn't seem to stop giggling, and she received several weird glances from passers-by. Tally fell up the hotel steps, landing in a heap on the floor.

"You were supposed to save me," she said to Em, who was doubled over with laughter.

"And go down with you? Fuck that," Em said, making Tally laugh even more.

Em grabbed her arm and hauled her to her feet as Tally's phone bleeped with an incoming text. The two of them froze, and then Tally scrambled to get her phone out of her bag. Her heart almost stopped when she saw the sender.

She opened the text—and ran.

There's pain. Everywhere. Lights flicker on and off, and hands are touching him. Strange hands. His arms flail as he tries to get them off. *Don't fucking touch me,* he screams, except no sound comes out.

They're speaking, but he can't understand them. A blurred face appears in front of him, and he blinks furiously, trying to clear the image. He hears a strangled groan. Then another, longer, drawn-out groan. *What is that? Sounds like a wounded animal.* He wishes someone would either help the damn thing or put it out of its misery, because the noise is getting on his fucking nerves.

A bright light shines in his eyes, and he flinches and squeezes them shut. *What the fuck is going on?*

"Cash, stop. Let them help you."

A familiar voice. Worried. Anxious. He strains the far reaches of his mind, but the memory is shrouded in fog. Thick, dense fog. Frustration crashes over him. Why can't he remember?

His eyes snap open. Another face swims in front of him. Clearer this time. A hand touches his cheek, warm, comforting.

"Cash, it's Mum. Can you hear me?"

Mum? *My mum's in a coma. She's been in a coma for thirteen years.* Wait, hang on. That's not right. She woke up. Didn't she? *Shit, why am I so confused?*

"You were in an accident."

What accident? Nothing is making any sense.

"Hurts," he mutters.

Another face. A man wearing a white coat. A chuckle bubbles in his throat. He's finally lost the fucking plot, and they've sent him to the loony bin. *Bet I'm in a padded cell.*

"Cash, I'm Dr Arnaud. You're in hospital, in Paris. You were hit by a car over two weeks ago. If you can hear me and understand what I'm saying, squeeze my hand."

Two weeks? Fuck. He concentrates as hard as he can, reaching into the far corners of his mind. And comes up empty. How can he have been in an accident and not remember? His heart thuds in his chest. *I have to get out of here.*

"Calm down, Cash. You're okay. Nurse!"

Hands on him again, restraining him. He fights, but there are too many. He grows weak, concerned faces fading. He can't keep his eyes open. Blackness.

CASH CRANKED HIS EYES OPEN. Bright sunshine caused a piercing pain in his head, and he squeezed his eyes shut, willing the blazing light to fuck off.

"Close the curtains, Rupe."

Rupe's here?

He forced his eyes open again, blinking furiously. The room wasn't as bright this time. He twisted his head, wincing against the agony such a tiny movement caused. For a minute, he thought he'd died. She was shrouded in light, an angel without wings, and her voice calmed his rapidly beating heart.

"Oh, babe." Tears streamed down her face.

He licked his lips. They were dry and cracked. A straw was pressed to his mouth, and he sucked greedily, the cool water soothing his throat. It dribbled down his chin. Someone wiped it away.

"Cash?" The voice again. Tentative, scared, exquisite. He focused on her face. Still blurred. He squinted. Better. He could see her properly now. Natalia. His heart constricted.

"Hey, sweetness." His voice sounded different. Raw. Throaty. Harsh. He didn't like it.

A sob tore from her throat, and she lifted his hand and pressed it to her cheek. "You came back."

"About fucking time." Rupe's grinning face swam into Cash's sight line.

The longer he kept his eyes open, the clearer the faces became. He tried to smile, but another spasm, which shot through his skull, made him stop. "Fuck you, Witters," he muttered.

"Charming as ever," Rupe said. "Try and stay awake, you useless git. I'm going to get your mum."

"Wait." He grabbed Rupe's wrist, but he was so weak his fingers couldn't hold on, and his hand fell back to the bed. "She's here? She's not in the coma anymore?"

A flash of worry crossed Rupe's face, and he glanced sideways at Natalia. "She recovered. Remember, bud? Months ago."

Cash frowned. "I think so." He sighed. "Foggy."

"That'll be the crack on the head. Maybe it'll have knocked some sense into you. Let me go and get Rachael."

Cash closed his eyes. "Tired," he mumbled.

A soft hand brushed his forehead. He tried to force his eyes open but couldn't. He slept.

When he woke, it was dark outside. How long had he been out? He slowly twisted his head. Natalia was sleeping in a chair next to the bed, her head uncomfortably bent to the side, a pillow supporting her neck. She had dark shadows beneath her eyes, and her face was terribly pale. He turned to the other side, and his heart skipped a beat. It was true. His mother was fast asleep, a flat palm against her cheek, her elbow braced against the arm of the chair. With considerable effort, he managed to touch her hand.

She jerked awake, her eyes wide as they fell on his. "Hey, my beautiful boy." She leaned across the bed and cradled his cheek. "How are you feeling? Any pain?"

He grimaced. "Lots." He reached for her hand as she began to stand. "No, don't go. It's okay. I want to feel the pain. It reminds me I'm alive."

"Do you... do you remember anything?"

He screwed his face up. "Not the accident. And I was confused at first about you. When I woke up, I thought you were still in the coma. But I remember now."

"And Natalia?" Unmistakeable hesitancy and concern laced her tone.

"Don't worry, Mum," he said, weakly squeezing her hand. "I remember her. How could I forget?" He looked over at Natalia, still blissfully unaware of their conversation. His gaze fell to her left hand. "I remember proposing, if that's what you were worrying about. Best day of my life."

His mum sighed, the air leaving her lungs in a whoosh of relief. "She was so worried." Her voice caught. "You're lucky to be alive. It was touch-and-go for a bit."

"What about my hand?" He half-lifted his right hand from the bed before the weight of the plaster, and his significantly weakened state, meant he had no choice but to let it fall back.

"The car rolled over you and crushed your hand. And your right leg is broken in three places."

He grimaced. "What's the prognosis? Don't sugarcoat it. I need to know."

She blinked slowly, her breathing slow and measured. "Your leg should heal fine in a few weeks. The breaks were clean. The doctors don't know whether you'll regain full use of your hand, but you'll need physiotherapy."

He clenched his jaw. "When do we begin?"

Rachael smiled. "Your bones need to heal, Cash, and you've suffered a severe head injury. Give yourself time."

"I *have* to play again," he said firmly.

Rachael leaned over and kissed his cheek. "You will."

44

Tally stood off to the side as the doctor pulled apart the broken cast on Cash's leg. He handed the two halves of the plaster cast to the nurse and gently placed Cash's foot on the floor.

"Any pain?" the doctor said as Cash gingerly rose from the chair.

"No." Cash put weight on his damaged leg. "It feels fine. Looks a mess, though."

The doctor smiled kindly. "All completely normal. I'd advise trying not to scratch if your skin becomes itchy. Better to gently wash with mild soap and water every few hours."

Cash walked up and down the doctor's office. "What about the muscle wastage?"

"Again, completely normal. Your muscles will be atrophied, but with gentle exercise and physio, they will completely recover without any lasting effects."

Cash nodded. "When can I start exercising it?"

"You need to take it easy for a while. At the risk of sounding clichéd, you need to walk before you can run. We'll need to see how you do over the next few days and then complete another X-ray, and then we can look at a longer-term strategy."

Cash met Tally's gaze. "Fancy a stroll around Paris?"

She grinned. "Sounds wonderful."

He looked over at the doctor. "Okay?"

"Yes, but take it easy. No running, no climbing stairs."

Cash took Tally's hand. "Thanks, Doc."

As they walked out of a private entrance to the hospital to avoid the press camped at the front, he took a deep breath. "Freedom."

Tally laughed. "You've hardly been in prison, ace."

"Feels like it," he muttered.

They'd wandered around Paris for an hour or so when Tally noticed Cash beginning to drag his leg.

"You okay, ace?" she said, giving him a concerned look.

He grimaced. "Bit of discomfort. Stop fussing."

She pointed to a bench beside the Seine. "Let's sit for a while."

He sighed heavily, and a flare of irritation crossed his face. "I said stop fussing."

She touched his arm. "It's going to take a while to get back to normal."

He wrenched his shoulder upward. "For fuck's sake, Natalia. I've been lying in that goddamn hospital bed for weeks. I said I'm okay. Now, leave it."

The flashes of anger had been steadily growing over the last few days, a situation the doctors had warned her about, given the severity of his head injury. She thought she'd been prepared to deal with mood swings, but the surge of pain that spread through her chest every time he snapped at her said she was kidding herself. She fiddled with her handbag and stared at the ground, waiting for Cash to make the next move.

"Fine," he finally bit out when the silence had stretched

between them for several minutes. "I suppose a few minutes' rest won't hurt."

Tally didn't reply because she instinctively knew he wouldn't want her to, but she took comfort in the small victory.

"I'm sorry," he muttered as he flopped onto the bench. "I'm so fucking frustrated."

"I know." She crossed her ankle over her other knee and took off her shoe, digging her thumbs into the soles of her feet. "Wrong shoes for walking," she said with a grin.

He held out his hand. "Give it here. I can still give a mean foot massage with one hand."

The rare offer of intimacy made her pulse jump, and she placed her foot in his lap. As his thumb dug into her instep, she groaned.

"You are the foot-massage master."

He smiled then, and hope swelled within her, but then his thumb stilled, and his razor-sharp gaze settled on something behind her.

"What?" she said, glancing over her shoulder.

"Wait here." Her foot fell from his lap as he clambered to his feet and sprinted across the street.

"You're not supposed to run," she yelled as she rammed her foot back into her shoe.

She set off after him, catching up in a narrow alley where he'd cornered a guy who was clutching a camera with a long lens. *Brilliant. A pap.*

"Give me the fucking camera," she heard Cash say as she approached. The guy responded in French but spoke too quickly for her to understand. Cash clearly did, though, because his face reddened. Before she could track his movements, Cash had hold of the camera. He must have caught a glimpse of her hovering at the end of the alleyway because his head spun around, his eyes flashing with utter fury.

"I fucking told you to stay put!" He spun away as the photographer made a lunge for his camera. Unfortunately for the pap, Cash was taller and faster, and the pap retreated empty-handed. Cash removed the memory card, snapped it in two, and dropped the pieces to the ground. He shoved the camera into the photographer's chest and leaned in close.

"If I catch you taking pictures of my girlfriend again, I'll break this camera over your fucking head." He marched to the end of the alleyway and clutched Tally's elbow. "When will you learn to do as you're told?"

"Don't take your bad mood out on me," she replied, yanking her arm out of his grasp. "It's not the first time we've been photographed, and I'm sure it won't be the last."

"I don't want pictures of intimate moments between us in the paper."

"Then you shouldn't have been massaging my foot in the middle of Paris."

He planted his hands on his hips, his chest heaving. He closed his eyes as he took several slow breaths. When he opened them, they were glistening with tears, and Tally's heart cracked.

"Oh, ace," she said, wrapping her arms around his waist. "What can I do? What do you need?"

He buried his face in her neck. "I want to go home."

45

Tally bit down on her lip to stop herself crying out when Cash winced in pain. He screwed his face up as Liam, his physiotherapist, made him push beyond his comfort zone. This was his eighth physio session since they'd returned to Northern Ireland from Paris four weeks before, and though he was making progress with his hand, it came at a cost.

"Again," Liam said.

The physiotherapy was brutal, and it didn't take a genius to work out that Cash was having real difficulty managing his frustration. The reddened face, clenched jaw, and sweat on his brow and upper lip as he tried to grip the tennis ball in his right hand gave it away.

"I can't."

"Yes, you can," Liam said.

No matter how awful Cash was to him, Liam refused to give up. He didn't take anything personally, even when Cash's temper made him say terrible things. The problem was that Cash had recovered quickly from his broken leg, and he'd assumed his hand would do just as well.

It hadn't.

They'd been at the exercises for an hour or so, and Tally could tell Cash's patience was wearing thin. His moods since he'd regained full consciousness were unpredictable at best. Sometimes, he'd be so loving, and by a mere look, he'd send her heart racing, and she could fool herself into thinking everything was the same as before the accident. At other times, his anger and frustration would boil over, and Tally would have to admit that he scared her.

"I said I fucking can't!"

"Are you giving up?"

"Yes! Fuck, yes!"

Tally blanched, but Liam didn't even flinch. For Cash to give up meant he was utterly exhausted, and that brought its own challenges. He hated how weak he'd become, how much his body had been affected during what, in reality, was a fairly short time in a coma. But this wasn't the movies. People didn't wake from a coma one day and compete in a triathlon the next. This was real life. And it was shit.

She tentatively touched his shoulder. "Want to rest for a bit, ace?"

He pulled away, and her hand fell to her side. "Don't fucking call me that."

She glanced at Liam and tilted her head towards the door. Taking her cue, he left.

She knelt in front of Cash, her hands on his thighs, and fixed him with a hard stare. "You'll *always* be my ace. I know you're frustrated, and you can yell and scream at me all you like. But you and I both know all that will do is make you feel like shit in the long run."

He rammed his knuckles into his eyes and rubbed hard. When he faced her again, his eyes were bloodshot. "I can't do this."

"Yes, you can. You're the strongest person I've ever met. You have to do this, Cash. For you and for me. For our future." She grabbed his face and forced him to meet her gaze. "I *believe* in you."

He jerked his head back. "Then you're a fucking fool. What are you still doing here anyway, huh? I mean, you hardly signed up for this. I'll never play again. You know that, right? And what does that leave me with?"

Her hands fell to her sides. "Me," she said quietly.

Silence hung over them both until the lack of sound became almost painful. Cash let out a deep sigh.

"Sorry," he muttered.

His apologies were never expressive, but Tally knew he felt them deeply all the same.

She sat cross-legged on the floor in front of him. "The only person who is saying you'll never play again is you, Cash. I haven't heard Liam say that, or any of your doctors. I can't believe you'd give up this easily."

"Easy?" He glared at her, fury sparking deep in his eyes—eyes that used to look at her with such love and affection. "You think this is fucking *easy*?"

"There you go again," she said, throwing her hands in the air. "Hearing what you want to hear. I didn't say *this* was easy. I said you're giving up too easily. Where's all that determination gone? Where have *you* gone, Cash?"

He launched himself out of the chair. "I guess I disappeared when a car smashed my fucking head in and left me with this useless fucking thing," he yelled, waving his right hand in the air, his left hand balled into a fist.

Tally scrambled to her feet and stood directly in front of him."Let me get this right. You're saying the accident turned you into a quitter? With everything you've had to overcome in your life, you're going to let *this* beat you?"

Cash pressed his lips together in a hard line as though if he didn't clamp them shut, he'd say something he didn't want to. Or something he'd regret.

"Fine," he finally said. "Go and fucking get him."

Tally stood on tiptoes and kissed his cheek. "Thank you," she whispered.

46

On the way home from the physio, Tally pulled over into a lay-by. Cash was staring out of the window, his hands limp in his lap but curled into fists as they so often were these days. She killed the engine and sat in silence. Eventually he seemed to realise they weren't home yet, and he turned to her with a deep frown.

"Why have you stopped?"

"I thought we could go for a walk."

He shook his head. "I want to go home."

Tally removed the keys from the ignition and jumped out of the car. "Two choices, Cash. Either come for a walk with me, or stay here. Up to you."

She closed the car door and, after looking both ways, jogged across the road. *Please follow. Please follow.* As she disappeared into the trees, the slam of the car door reached her, and she breathed a deep sigh. Cash caught up with her, his hands stuffed deep into his pockets and his shoulders hunched—his way of telling her he was there under duress.

She kept to a reasonable pace so he wouldn't put undue pressure on his healed leg and headed for the centre of the woods.

The atmosphere around them crackled, the sound echoed by twigs breaking underfoot. As the trees parted, a large lake came into view, lilies floating on top of water still as a millpond.

"I forgot I'd told you about this place," Cash said, momentarily breaking the tension between them.

Tally smiled. "I've been meaning to come for ages, but…"

She left the sentence hanging and went to sit on a bench that allowed for a perfect view of the surroundings. Cash sat beside her, his legs splayed in a relaxed fashion even as his hands remained clenched.

"Talk to me," Tally said. "I need to know what you're thinking."

"Why?" he said in a petulant tone. "What's the point?"

"Because I want to know what's going on in your head," she said, tapping his temple in an attempt to keep the atmosphere light.

Cash jerked out of her reach. "I'm not sure you do, Natalia."

A jolt of pain made her rub her chest. "I do, Cash. How can I help you if I don't know how you're feeling, what you're thinking?"

He shifted around, his gaze hard and cold. "You can't help. No one can."

She briefly closed her eyes. "How do you know if you don't give me a chance?"

"Oh, sorry," he said, his tone bleeding sarcasm. "I missed the part where you qualified as a miracle worker, because that's the only way you can help me to fix this."

He waved his damaged hand in her face, and she flinched, both from his words and the proximity of his hand.

"Why are you being so hurtful?" she whispered.

Cash launched himself to his feet and began to pace at the edge of the lake. Tally could see him taking several deep breaths, and he kept flexing his fingers before curling them into fists once more. She sat nibbling on her nails without a clue about what her next move should be. The doctors had warned about the effect of head injuries on personalities, and she'd done her own research, but the reality of living with someone with a brain injury was very different from reading about it.

"I'm going back to the car," he announced and stomped off into the woods. Tally waited for a few moments before climbing to her feet and following him. When she reached the road, Cash was standing by the passenger door, his arms folded across his chest, a deep frown on his face. "You took your time."

She ignored him and unlocked the car, but as she went to start the engine, his hand closed over hers.

"You want to know what I'm thinking?"

"Yes."

He laughed, but the sound had a hard edge. "Well, brace yourself, because you may not like what you're about to hear."

Tally sat on her trembling hands because she didn't want Cash to see how much his words hurt, how easily he could affect her.

"Okay," she said in a low voice.

"I'm living in a world of what ifs, and it's driving me crazy. What if we'd taken the car back to the hotel? What if I hadn't bought those stupid flowers? What if we'd stayed in the Maldives or never gone on holiday in the first place?" He took a deep, shuddering breath. "What if I'd never met you?"

Tally gasped as agony tore through her chest. "You don't mean that."

He threw his hands in the air. "Yes, I fucking do. Ever since I met you, my life has been one disaster after another. I may have been living a shallow existence before you lied your way into my event, but at least I had my career, my friends. Now what do I have, huh? Nothing."

Tally resisted the urge to shrink away from him. Instead, she straightened her spine. "You still have your friends, and your career. It's just on hold. And I did not *lie* my way into that event. I had an invitation."

"That's true, but let's face it, you haven't exactly been averse to lying to me, have you?"

She shook her head. "Oh, come on, Cash. This is the best you have, dragging up the past?"

"You said you wanted to know what's in my head."

"I do, but—"

"I cannot forget how you lied to me about Kinga's role in the photographs. I am still furious that you kept it from me and yet you saw fit to tell Emmalee, like she was more worthy or something."

"Jesus, Cash." Tally dragged a hand through her hair. "That was months ago, and we sorted it out."

"No, we didn't. I just buried it because my mother had a go at me, but every time I think back to that time..."

Tally stared out of the window as she found it difficult to breathe, an uncomfortable tingling sensation spreading from her chest to her fingers. She sat in silence as she braced for his next onslaught, but it never came. When she turned around, Cash had his head against the back of the seat, his eyes closed.

Tally started the car and drove home, the heavy atmosphere between them making her want to cry. But she had to ride this out. Cash's behaviour wasn't unusual. Painful, yes, but normal with injuries of his type. As she pulled into the driveway, Brad and Jamie were waiting outside.

"Damn," she muttered. "Forgot they were coming over."

Cash gave her a withering look. "Oh, you'd like that, wouldn't you? Cut me off from my friends."

He almost threw himself out of the car in his haste to get away from her. Tally watched as Cash greeted Brad and Jamie. He shook their hands and smiled brightly, the sort of smile he used to regularly have for her but now rarely did.

She waited until they'd gone inside before trailing after them, but as she heard laughter coming from the living room, she couldn't face the falseness of it all. She wandered into the kitchen and poured herself a large glass of wine.

"Aren't you joining us?"

Her head snapped up to find Brad lounging by the kitchen door. Tally held up her wine glass.

"Want one?"

He shook his head. "Your man's poured me a whiskey."

Tally grimaced. "Not sure he's my man anymore."

Brad crossed the kitchen and pulled her into his arms. "You're getting the brunt of it because he loves you the most."

Tears sprang from her eyes as she clung to him. "Lucky me."

Brad released her so he could grab a tissue and wipe her face. "How did he get on today?"

She shrugged. "Okay, I guess. We had another tantrum when it all became too much. Liam reckons he's making progress, just not fast enough for Cash." She took a large gulp of wine. "I'm sorry we were late, but I completely forgot you were coming. I stopped on the way home from physio because I wanted Cash to get some fresh air." She laughed, the sound hollow even to her ears. "He said some pretty awful things."

Brad put his arm around her. "Come on. I'm not having you hiding in here."

As they walked into the living room, Cash's gaze flickered to where Brad's arm lay across her shoulders, but whereas once Cash would have bristled at another man touching her, he didn't react at all.

After an hour or so, Cash put his whiskey tumbler down and yawned. "Sorry, guys. Hope you don't mind, but I'm heading off to bed. It's surprising how doing fuck all makes you this tired."

"We'll try not to leave it so long next time," Brad said as he and Cash clapped each other on the back.

Cash waved his hand dismissively. "Don't worry about it. I get you're busy." His tone was light, but Tally could discern the underlying hurt. Brad and Jamie had moved on with their lives. Not that they'd had a choice, but she knew it still stung.

"Natalia," Cash said, cocking his head in a signal for her to follow him.

"We'll get off," Brad said, but Tally shook her head.

"If you hang on, I'll see you out," she said. "Give me five minutes."

She followed Cash upstairs. Once they reached their bedroom, he closed the door and sat on the end of the bed. "I'm sorry about before," he said in a sullen tone that didn't exactly scream an apology.

Tally shook her head. "Forget it," she said even though it would take a while before she could, if ever.

He shrugged and began getting undressed. Tally averted her gaze. They didn't exactly have sex very often these days, but it didn't mean she wasn't still attracted to him. Quite the opposite in fact.

"Won't be long. I'll just see the guys out."

He shrugged again. "No rush."

As Tally entered the living room, she gave a wan smile to Brad and Jamie, who were hovering as though they didn't know quite how to behave.

"God, honey, I'm sorry," Brad said, giving her a hug for the second time that night.

"Me too," Jamie added, an expression of sorrow and regret prevalent on his craggy features.

"We'll try to visit more often."

She shook her head. "I wouldn't blame you if you didn't. He's difficult to be around." She sipped her drink and met Brad's gaze over the rim of her glass. "Maybe he always will be."

A flash of pain crossed Brad's face. "And you? What about you?"

She shrugged. "What about me? I'm not leaving him if that's what you mean. I love him, and he loves me, even though he doesn't exactly show it right now. I've read up about this, Brad. I know what I'm in for. Frontal-lobe injuries change personalities, make people frustrated, prone to extreme angry outbursts. But I've also read stories of miracles, where, over time, people almost become the same person they were before the head injury. Cash has the strength of mind to be one of those people. I know it. At the moment, he's depressed. He needs time to come to terms with the work ahead of him. Then he'll be fine."

"Do you think he'll ever play again?"

She didn't hesitate. "Yes."

Brad nodded. "I'm sorry we had to move on, but if he does ever return to tennis, please make sure he calls us. We'll both be back in a shot if the schedules line up."

"First on my list," she said with a smile she wasn't feeling.

After she'd seen them out, Tally locked up and trudged upstairs to bed. Cash was lying on his back, his left arm thrown over his head, his too-long hair unkempt. The strain of the last few weeks showed on his face, even in sleep. And yet, to Tally, he'd never looked more beautiful, because he was *alive*.

She'd thought the worst was over when he regained consciousness. Little had she known that the worst was yet to come.

She quickly undressed and climbed into bed beside him. She snuggled against his side, and his arm automatically closed around her. Even though the movement was involuntary, instinctive, she savoured the intimacy.

"Don't give up, babe," she said. "Because I won't."

47

A month later, Tally awoke with a start, heart pounding and drenched in sweat. She'd had yet another night-mare, although the familiar sense of dread was already fading. A shadow lingered in her mind, almost within reach, but as she grasped to remember, it faded, leaving her with an over-whelming sense of loss.

She reached for Cash. His side of the bed was empty. She glanced at the clock and groaned. Too early. Throwing on a dressing gown, she tiptoed onto the landing, her ears straining. The house was silent, and as she crept downstairs, a flickering light came from the living room.

She peered round the door. Cash was sitting on the edge of the sofa, his forearms resting on his knees. The Shanghai Masters tennis tournament was on TV. Cash was focused on the game and didn't notice her until she sat beside him. She stroked his arm.

"Who's playing?"

He shot her a glare, the agony on his face tearing through Tally. "Not me," he bit out.

She picked up his hand, the damaged one, and kissed it. "It will be. Soon."

He snatched his hand away. "What makes you psychic?"

Tally held back a sharp retort. Arguing didn't help when he got like this. "It's not even three months since the accident. You're being far too hard on yourself."

His mouth twisted into a smile, but it didn't reach his eyes. "Shocker."

She tried to lean against his shoulder, but he shuffled along the sofa, out of reach. The rebuff was like a knife to her gut, and her eyes welled with tears.

"Oh, for God's sake," he said with a huff. "Don't start, Natalia. I can't deal with your shit as well as my own."

"Cash—"

"For fuck's sake!" He launched to his feet and scraped a hand through his hair. "Go back to bed, and leave me alone."

"No. That's not what you need."

"Don't you fucking dare tell me what I need. Right now, I need you to leave me the hell alone."

He slammed his undamaged fist into the wall. Tally flinched, and even though she tried not to, she began to cry. Who said words couldn't hurt? Cash's sure packed a punch. She walked over to him and reached out her hand. "Please don't push me away. I love you."

He stared at her with hard, flinty eyes, nothing like the man she'd fallen in love with. Right at that moment, he looked as though he hated her. "You never know when to leave it alone, do you?"

"I'm trying to help you."

"I don't want your fucking help!"

He moved so quickly Tally barely caught sight of the vase until it went sailing past her head. It smashed against the wall behind her, and she instinctively sank to the floor, covering her head with her hands as shards of ceramic scattered across the carpet. She couldn't speak as her heart nearly punched through her chest. She waited for him to fall at her side, to beg her forgiveness for scaring her. He did neither.

She slowly lifted her head. "What are you doing?" she whispered.

His breath came in short pants, and his nostrils flared as he glowered at her. "Well, you seem incapable of listening to anything I say. Maybe that will get the message home."

This wasn't Cash. He'd be contrite as soon as he'd calmed down. She could handle this. He hadn't aimed the vase at her.

"What message?" she said gently.

He rolled his eyes. "Are you really that fucking dumb? I don't love you anymore. I want you gone. We're finished. Over. Get out of my house. Out of my life."

Tally's throat constricted, and she wrapped her arms around her body. "You don't mean that." She began to sob.

"I mean every fucking word." He looked up and down her body, his gaze disparaging. "The accident has knocked some fucking sense into me. You're not my goddamn type. Never were, never will be."

He wasn't angry now. He was cold. Impassive. Hatred poured from his eyes as he held her gaze. She clutched a hand to her chest, trying to hold together her shattered heart. Her dream had become reality.

"I know you love me. You said you'd never stop loving me."

His top lip turned up in a sneer. "Things change. I don't love you anymore. I don't want you. In fact, the only thing I *do* want is for you to get the fuck out of my house and leave me alone."

Tally choked back a sob. She'd thought the worst was over when Cash survived the crash, but she didn't know this person at all. White dots flashed in front of her eyes, and she steadied herself against the wall, waiting for the light-headedness to pass. She looked down at her engagement ring and slowly tugged it off her finger. Cash watched her the whole time, and she searched for signs of sorrow, regret, but there were none. She put the ring on the mantelpiece and left the room.

Her movements were wooden as she packed a suitcase. She recognised the signs of shock, of course. She'd had enough experience of that these past few months.

It took less than fifteen minutes to pack. She kept expecting Cash to run upstairs, to beg her to stay. But he didn't.

She lugged her suitcase down the two flights of stairs until she found herself standing in the hallway. She called for a taxi and was told one would be there in ten minutes, but she couldn't bear to spend another moment inside the house. When she walked back into the living room, Cash was standing in exactly the same spot. He glanced over his shoulder as she entered.

"I'm leaving now," she said, her eyes pleading with him to reconsider as tears dried on her cheeks.

"Good." He turned his back, one hand resting on the mantelpiece.

Tally choked back a sob. "I'll send someone for the rest of my things. Say goodbye to Rachael for me. I hope you find happiness."

And with that, she walked out. Broken. Shattered. Alone.

CASH WAITED until the sobs faded to whimpers, and eventually, the front door slammed, and silence took over the house. He edged to the window. Natalia was dragging her suitcase behind her, head bowed against the ever-blowing Northern Ireland wind. As he watched her walk down the long driveway to the road, a piece of him died.

His life was in tatters. He'd lost memories, the full use of his right hand, his tennis career. *Why me? Why did I have to lose everything?*

God, he still loved Natalia, but he couldn't deal with her at the moment. He knew her better than she knew herself. She never would have left unless he could convince her he didn't love her anymore. It would be the only thing to make her go. She had too much pride to cling to a relationship she believed to be dead.

He couldn't trust himself. Even he didn't know what he was capable of any longer. Rage burned within him. He'd always had a temper, even before the accident, but then it would be like lighting a match—quick to flame and equally quick to burn out. But the anger he now felt was different, like a bubbling volcano. He didn't know how to control it. One day, he'd explode, and Natalia would be caught in the fallout.

He couldn't allow that to happen. It would kill him if he ever hurt her physically. Better for them to be apart.

He picked up her engagement ring and closed his fist around it. The day he'd given it to her had been the happiest day of his life, and as he sank onto the sofa, he allowed those memories to flow over him, a crumb of comfort in the midst of a bleak future.

ACKNOWLEDGMENTS

My thanks to my writing mentor, Beth Hill, a wonderful lady without whom, I wouldn't be where I am today.

To Incy—thank you from the bottom of my heart. Not only are you amazingly talented, but you are generous with your time, help and advice.

To Louise. You're very special to me. Thank you for everything.

And last but not least, to you, the readers. Thank you for being on this journey with me.

I do hope you enjoyed Losing Game. Cash and Tally will be back very soon in Grand Slam, the final instalment in their tumultuous story

FROM MY HEART

Thank you so much for reading Losing Game. That you've given your time to read my novel means more to me than I'll ever be able to express.

I'd love to hear from you. Please feel free to get in touch via email, Facebook, Twitter or by signing up to my reader group at www.traciedelaneyauthor.com

Would you consider helping other readers decide if this is the right book for them by leaving a short rating on Amazon? They really help readers discover new books.

Cash and Tally will be back very soon in the finale—Grand Slam. They'd love to see you there!

ABOUT THE AUTHOR

Tracie Delaney is the author of the *Winning Ace* trilogy. She loves nothing more than immersing herself in a good romance, although she sometimes, rather cheekily, makes her characters wait for their HEA.

When she isn't writing or sitting around with her head stuck in a book, she can often be found watching The Walking Dead, Game of Thrones or any tennis match involving Roger Federer. Her greatest fear is running out of coffee.

Tracie studied accountancy, gaining her qualification in 2001. Her maths teacher would no doubt be stunned by this revelation considering Tracie could barely add two plus two at high school.

Tracie lives in the North West of England with her amazingly supportive husband. They both share a love of dogs, travel and wine.

Tracie loves to hear from readers. She can be contacted through her website at
www.traciedelaneyauthor.com